The City at Night,

By Charlie Revelle-Smith

Text copyright © 2018 Charlie Revelle-Smith

All Rights Reserved

For Bill. (1916-2018)
The man of a century.

"Green upon the flooded Avon shone the after-storm-wet-sky
Quick the struggling withy branches let the leaves of Autumn fly
And a star shone over Bristol, wonderfully far and high."
　　　　　　　From *"Bristol"* by John Betjeman. (1906-1984)

1.

Rowan sat on the edge of Ruby's bed and sipped from a glass of red wine. Her sister had been getting ready for over an hour but had only just sat down before her mirror to puff blusher onto her cheeks.

"The secret to makeup isn't less is more," she declared, before blowing her own reflection a kiss. "*More* is almost always more. Just try keeping it below drag queen level."

"I'm not sure I really like it - for me, I mean. It looks good on you."

Ruby twirled around on her stool, the impossibly thin drapes of her scarlet dress pirouetted about her. "You do *you* Rowan Kaplan, but trust me, if any guy ever tells you that he prefers you without makeup, that guy is a *liar*."

"What kind of message is that to give to your little sister?" a voice reprimanded from the open doorway. It was the two teenage girls' mother. "Pay no attention to Ruby, she's a bad influence." The woman's smile showed no trace of anger.

Ruby scrunched mousse into her tight ringlets of dark hair and let it bounce playfully in a sexy mess of curls around her head. "I'm just trying to let Rowan in on a few universal truths. She has to learn eventually."

"Your father happens to like it when I wear less makeup," the woman said.

"Sure Mum. I think it's adorable that you believe him." Ruby swung back round to her mirror and began fishing through her vast makeup bag.

"Rowan, I suppose you have your sister to thank for that glass of wine."

Rowan winced. "It's just the one."

"You'd better believe it's just the one," Rolinda Kaplan turned to face Ruby's reflection. "She's sixteen. In the future you should ask me or your father before you pour your sister a drink."

"Sorry Mum. But it's a Saturday. Everyone should be having fun - including you."

"I have fun!" Rolinda exclaimed.

Ruby just smirked and raised an eyebrow. "I suppose Dad's out with his friends already?"

"He's playing dominoes tonight at the Old Caravel," she replied flatly. "And I'll thank you not to use that tone with me."

Ruby stood up from her makeup table and twirled before her sister and mother. "How do I look?"

Rolinda sighed. "Nineteen years old. God I wish I'd had your confidence when I was your age. You look *gorgeous*."

Rowan didn't disagree, for there was simply no other word to describe the breathtaking beauty which stood before her. Radiant, coffee coloured skin which seemed to give off its own light, nearly six foot tall in her ridiculous heels and wearing a dress that managed to show too much leg and too much cleavage whilst somehow still looking effortlessly classy. She wore flashes of red, her signature colour matching her dress; a shock of crimson in a weave she had combed dramatically through her hair and the outrageously cheap, plastic, ruby red ring she had found in a Christmas cracker several years before and had never taken off, her sole concession to jewellery.

"Nineteen," Rolinda sighed again as she drew away from the doorway and out of sight.

Hurriedly Ruby topped up her sister's glass of wine and offered her a sly wink.

"Where're you going after the rehearsal?" Rowan asked her.

She shrugged. "Who knows where the night will take me? That's what's so *thrilling* about living in the city."

"The city," Ruby repeated with a smile. "You talk about it as if we live in London or New York."

"Watch your mouth," Ruby intoned as she checked herself a final time in the mirror. "Never let anyone tell you Bristol isn't good enough. You step out that door and I promise you, there's nowhere in the world more exciting than the city at night."

Rowan offered a single, dismissive nod.

"Rowan," Ruby asked. "Can you keep a secret?"

2.

Snow wasn't falling but Christmas made its approach known by other means. It sparkled in crystalline frosts across the lawn of Gallow & Sons Funeral Home, choking the life from even the hardiest of flowers in its wintry grasp. Ice formed in vast, deep sheets across car windows and slithered treacherously across pavements, hiding in the shadows well into afternoon. Rowan had spent most of the morning de-icing the various vehicles about the property. The collection vans, the hearse, Franklin's Smart car, all the while knowing the futility of this endeavour. Winter had truly set in and she was powerless to hold it at bay for long.

At midday her boss and friend, Franklin Gallow returned to his business and found her idly scrolling through her iPad in his office. "Your podcast has been released."

"Fan-bloody-tastic. It's going to be open season for all the cranks in Bristol still banging on about the Blackbeard murders."

The podcast in question was part of a deal with the hosts of *The Murder Club*. Franklin had hastily promised them an interview about his near-miraculous survival at the hands of one of the most sensational serial killers in recent British history. He had hoped that this promise, offered in exchange for vital information on another murder case, would somehow be possible to keep kicking it down the road until the pair got bored of asking him. The technique had not worked and Franklin, being a man who kept his promises, eventually acquiesced.

"Please don't listen to it," he asked Rowan.

"Trust me, if I never see or hear anything from that pair of ghouls again I'll be very happy."

Franklin nodded his appreciation. "Where's Meredy? She wasn't on the front desk."

"She had to leave. Her son got into another fight at school. This time they're threatening to suspend him."

"Little tearaway," Franklin shook his head. His trusty, blameless receptionist had been totally unprepared for her son to mutate overnight from her little soldier to a near-feral teenage boy.

"So, who's on the menu this morning?" Rowan asked, nodding past the window to the van waiting on the driveway.

"Twenty-four year old man. Suspected suicide."

"Suspected? We don't usually get the bodies until the police know for sure."

Franklin shrugged. "Jumped in front of the Temple Meads to Clevedon train by all accounts. No suicide note but the driver says he saw him all by himself. He'd drunk the best part of a bottle of vodka. Poor chap."

Rowan rolled her eyes. Her lack of sympathy for the suicides they encountered had caused friction between the pair in the past, so they opted to veer from it in their conversation. "So it's a messy one. Wonderful. Can't Peterman handle it?"

"Peterman's dealing with twin babies who were murdered by their father as revenge for his wife filing for divorce. Would you rather we handle that one?"

"Good Lord, no! I'll take the splattered dude, thanks. What an awful world."

"Trust me, when you're in this job for long enough you'll learn that the world has always been terrible."

"What kind of person does that?"

"They're called family annihilators." Franklin said bluntly.

Rowan narrowed her eyes at him. "There's a term for that kind of monster?"

"What can I say, I started listening to *The Murder Club* before my interview with them. They did a whole episode about them."

"And just before Christmas too. That seems to make it even worse somehow."

"I don't think there's ever a right time to do it, but yes, I know what you mean." Franklin took a step closer to Rowan. "Talking of Christmas, I've been meaning to ask something. Do you need extra time off or something, because I might have to make arrangements in advance if you do?"

"Why would I need extra time off?"

"Well, because of what you are now…"

10

"Franklin, you are allowed to say Quaker, it's really not that awful."

"Fine, Quaker. Do you need extra time off?"

Rowan thought for a moment. To many, her flirtations with religious groups seemed to land randomly upon the Quakers, as if when the music stopped in some existential game of pass-the-parcel she had unwrapped the box only to discover Quakerism within. In truth the story had been much more fortuitous - and rewarding. To Franklin, however, all religions were equally absurd but just like her views on suicide, he knew to keep this opinion to himself. "I don't need extra time off, but thank you for asking."

"Christmas is a surprisingly busy time for us. Lock a bunch of people in a house for three days, pour alcohol in them from dawn till dusk and just watch the fatalities clock up. Improperly cooked turkey alone paid for my Nile cruise last February."

Rowan smiled at Franklin's dark humour. "So what are we going to do with this body? It hardly seems necessary on a day like today but we should get him in the freezer."

"You know the drill," he said, and the pair proceeded to their well-worn routine.

As Franklin reversed the collection van into the garage, Rowan typed the 1-7-7-6 code into the keypad, which allowed her entrance to the surgically pristine room where the bodies were held which had become affectionately nicknamed the Death Chamber. Inside she cranked open the metal shutter to reveal the back of Franklin's van from which he was already extending a ramp.

The body was like a grim gift in a fuchsia-pink bag bound in string. No attempt was made to hide the fact that this had once been a living man, his shape unmistakably outlined beneath the plastic. The head bounced unpleasantly as the corpse slid down the ramp onto Rowan's waiting metal trolley. She heaved it aboard.

"What a waste of a life," she huffed, barely concealing her contempt. "People *fight* to squeeze just one more day out of their lives and people like this throw away *years* that someone else could've lived."

11

Franklin watched Rowan wheel the trolley into the death chamber. He didn't need to wonder whose years she'd like to exchange for the ones the man had squandered. He pulled the shutter down and immediately stopped the harsh December wind that had invaded the room.

"Why don't you get yourself a coffee?" he suggested. "The unveiling is always horrible anyway. I can take it from here."

"Ignore me," she said. "I just get livid with these idiots."

"Livid," Franklin repeated, allowing the word to bounce around the inside of his head for a while. One of the things he appreciated most about Rowan, and indeed much of her maligned generation of Millennials, was her insistence on using the kind of old-fashioned words he had not heard in decades.

Franklin began loosening the ties around the body before swiftly unzipping the body bag to reveal the stark form beneath a light, white sheet. There was never a need to draw this process out so he whipped away the sheet to reveal the naked corpse.

Rowan gasped at the sight of it and Franklin found it hard not to do the same. The young man's body was a broken mess of torn skin and alarmingly angled bones. Through the brutal stitching that had been carried out as hurried repairs by the mortician it was clear that the man was almost hollow, with all internal organs crushed beyond recognition and all blood drained from his torso.

"It's a bad one," Franklin eventually declared.

Rowan was frozen. Her hands were drawn to her face as if attempting to hold a scream back. "It's Doug Bennett," she gasped.

"Oh my God. Rowan do you know him?"

"Yeah... well, not really. He was Ruby's boyfriend. He was with her on the night she was murdered." Rowan turned and ran from the death chamber.

3.

Franklin hurriedly slid the body of Doug Bennett into the cold storage unit and then watched the clock for ten minutes, supposing it would give Rowan time to recover from her initial shock. On leaving the death chamber he spied her through the glass door of the reception, sitting blank faced in the passenger seat of the hearse which was parked in the drive.

"Rowan, I'm so sorry you saw that," he said as he slipped beside her in the vehicle. "If I'd have known I never would've taken on this service."

Rowan just shrugged limply. "I feel stupid now. I acted like a little girl."

"You wouldn't be human if this job didn't get to you from time to time but it's a whole lot different seeing the body of someone you know."

"I barely knew him. I hadn't seen him since the funeral anyway, it's not like we were friends or anything. In fact I wasn't even sure he was still living in Bristol. A lot can change in three and a half years."

"Sit this one out, Rowan. I can handle it by myself - and take the rest of the day off too."

Rowan shook her head. "It doesn't make any difference whether I knew him or not. He might've been Ruby's boyfriend but all the bodies that come into the death chamber had *someone* who cared for them. They were someone's boyfriend, or girlfriend, or mum. I can handle this."

"I don't think you should have to. Trust me with this one - the human mind can be very fragile and one too many knocks can send it spiralling out of control."

Rowan did not need to ask what Franklin was referring to. A year ago his older brother Edison had been struck by a debilitating anxiety disorder following a traumatic encounter while working as a police officer. "Maybe you're right. It just feels like I can't run from this forever though. As long as Ruby's murderer is still out there I'm never going to be free from it. D'you know, when I saw Doug's body it wasn't even really the shock of it being him, or even how terrible he looked. I think what got to me was that I hadn't even thought about him since the funeral, not properly anyway. As far as I knew he'd gone on with his life and had found somebody new, maybe even got married and moved to the country, but no. He was just as screwed up as the rest of us and all these years he's been living with her death too, until it got too much for him. Christ, throwing yourself in front of a train isn't exactly a cry for help, is it? You must really want it all to end."

"That's what a person's life can do. Even in a short amount of time one person's life can affect so many others. Ruby sounds like she was one of the special ones."

Rowan blinked back tears. "She was. I know everyone says that about people who die tragically, but she really was. It wasn't just that she died young, or even that she was murdered - it was that she was so *alive*. It was in her like this electricity, this enthusiasm for every minute of every day. That's what died when she was killed, it was *so much* life."

Franklin squeezed her shoulder gently. "There's tissues in the glove box if you want to cry."

Rowan snorted a dismissive chuckle. "Does anybody ever want to cry? You end up looking like a deranged mess and it changes absolutely nothing at all."

"That's not entirely true," said Franklin. "Apparently tears of sadness leach magnesium from your body which is a depressant, so it genuinely helps cheer you up."

Rowan looked pitifully at her friend. "Which bullshit inspirational Facebook meme told you that?"

"It's true, trust me! This job makes me cry far more often than you might expect. Do you know where I go?"

Rowan smiled. "You sit right here and cry."

Franklin's mouth fell open. "How did you know that?"

"I saw you. The first ever service we did together. Ernest Pascoe, remember."

"You saw me crying?"

"Yes. I didn't want to ask you at the time as it seemed a bit too personal, but something must have got to you."

Franklin nodded. "We're not supposed to admit it, but some deaths get to us more than others. It's totally selfish but even more than the kids it's the men who make me think of my mortality. Ernest Pascoe was my age and he just dropped dead, and immediately I start thinking about getting closer to that day and how no matter how much I think I may have a handle on death, and understand it's every bit as vital to life as birth, one day it *will* happen to me and there's nothing I can do to prevent it. Even if I keep myself healthy, get regular check ups, even if I find some miracle cure which doubled my life span, the end will still come…"

"…And it goes on forever." Rowan added.

"So to conclude, that's what makes me cry. The end of my life."

"This job messes with your head."

"I know, but somebody has to do it. It might as well be us."

To Franklin's surprise, Rowan reached into the glove box and tugged a loose tissue from the open box and mopped around her eyes. "Winter hay fever," she said with a smile.

"Yes, I've heard it's very bad this year."

"I've been thinking about Ruby a lot lately, even more than usual. Edison giving us copies of those files just churned everything up again. It's always there, but sometimes it feels more raw, more real."

In the dog days of the previous summer Edison had gathered together several folders of photocopied evidence the police had kept in storage, both at Franklin's request and at great peril to his employment. The contents had been remarkably blunt. Forensic analysis of stab wounds and Ruby's stomach contents, reams of interview transcripts with Rowan's family and friends and grainy CCTV images of Ruby walking to her death along the streets of Stokes Croft. It had been jarring but the cover letter was even worse. Within a couple of paragraphs the open-but-cold case concluded that *"despite a lack of evidence to convict him, the prime suspect in the murder of Ruby Kaplan remains Oscar Kaplan. Her father."*

"It was probably a mistake getting those folders. A load more heartbreak for you and we barely found out anything we didn't already know."

Rowan shrugged. "It was comforting in a way. All this time I kind of assumed that the police were half-arsing the case but to see it all on paper was reassuring. They were doing their job properly, the evidence just wasn't there."

"We'll catch whoever did it. I promise."

"You can't promise that. Nobody can. The police said the same when they interviewed me. Years later and *nothing*. Ruby's dead, her killer's still free and now her boyfriend has killed himself."

"When we catch her killer, what will you do?" Franklin ventured.

"You're asking if I'd kill them, aren't you?"

"I guess I am."

"I really want to. When I'm at my lowest I lie awake in bed imagining stabbing her killer over and over again. Face to face so whoever it is can see me as I take their life, but then what? Would it make me any happier? Anyway, I don't believe in capital punishment and neither did Ruby."

"It's not the same as capital punishment though, is it? It's more primal than that."

"But then what would I do? Her killer drops dead and is gone forever - all I'd want to do is revive them and murder them again and again until the end of time. Because that's what they'd deserve - to be punished forever. I keep on thinking of that final night, when she was home and getting ready and everything felt exciting and safe and she looked glorious, I mean absolutely *stunning*. And I think how through all of history there had never been a Ruby Kaplan before, not *that* one anyway, and there will never be another. It's like the Mona Lisa; there will only ever be one. Completely priceless and irreplaceable. What punishment could anyone inflict that would make up for that?"

Franklin had never heard his friend talk so vividly about Ruby before. For the briefest moment he found himself tumbling through time to the night when she was murdered, when a young woman, full of hope for the future was cut down before her life had even begun. Rowan, as if sensing that her words would elicit such a reaction, handed him a tissue.

"Well this is a great start to Monday isn't it?" He laughed as he dabbed his cheeks. "Not even lunchtime and we're both in tears."

"Maybe you're right about one thing though," said Rowan.

"I find that hard to believe."

"I actually do feel a tiny bit better for crying."

Franklin knocked his shoulder against hers. "You're my best friend. I try to help out when I can."

Rowan laughed. "*Best friend?* Are you a teenage girl?"

"Don't be mean. I thought I was being nice."

Rowan thought for a moment. "Oh crap. You're right - I know hardly *anyone* anymore and now I'm best friends with my boss. That's worse than women who say their mum's their best friend."

"It's creepier when men say it though."

Rowan smiled softly at Franklin. "Just don't go telling anybody else. It's embarrassing."

"Scout's honour," said Franklin, offering her a salute.

"There was one other thing that's been playing on my mind. D'you remember Martin Maybridge?"

"Are you joking? That psychopath who tried to murder you? Yeah, I remember him."

"I think you mean that psychopath who nearly beat me to death with a pair of Doc Martens."

"Why are you thinking about that lowlife?"

"I got a letter at the weekend."

"Another of those anonymous ones?"

"No," Rowan dismissed the mention of the mysterious, typewriter written notes which had plagued her for years. "This was a letter from his prison."

"Why in the world are they contacting you?"

"It's a new initiative they're trying out in a few prisons across the country. They want me to meet an intermediary and discuss the possibility of meeting Maybridge face to face."

Franklin was outraged. "How dare they ask you to do such a thing!"

"Apparently it works. Victims meet their assailants in a safe, mediated space and discuss what happened and why.

The letter said there was no obligation but Maybridge put his name down for it so they contacted me."

"What good can come of talking to that bastard? In fact, you should say no just because he wants to take part."

"Well, it's not up to you, is it? I looked it up online and some people swear it helped them deal with PTSD after an assault."

"PTSD? I thought you said you had no lasting effects from the attack. You said you were surprised how little it damaged you."

"I know, and it's true."

"Then why do it? Let that monster rot in jail. He's probably thinking he can use it as part of an early release deal."

Rowan offered him a sly look. "Trust me, Franklin. I know what I'm doing. I'm hatching a little plan."

"Oh," Franklin nodded. "Care to share it?"

"Not yet," she said. "But soon."

4.

Edison waved at Franklin from across the bar. Since his severe and very public breakdown at the start of the year Franklin had met his brother at the Tobacco Factory on Mondays as well as their regular Friday arrangement. Whilst the brothers rarely discussed the older of the pair's mental health issues, it was an unspoken contract that Franklin would want to check every few days that his brother was still on an even keel.

"Evenin' Frank," Edison beamed a smile which immediately made Franklin feel concerned. It had been a while since he had seen such a broad expression of happiness on his brother's face.

"How's it going?" He asked as he sat across from Edison, a freshly pulled pint of Ashton Press cider waiting in place.

"Magnificent," Edison replied, punctuating the word with a loud belch.

"You seem... spirited. Have you been drinking?"

"First pint since Friday," said Edison. "I am what they call, high on life - that and high on this bloody marvellous cocktail of mood stabilisers they've put me on. I went for a jog this morning. Honest to god, *me!*"

Having spent countless mornings attempting to lure his brother out of bed while in the throes of a depressive collapse, the image of Edison jogging at the break of dawn did seem unlikely - and alarming. "How are you sleeping?"

"Like a baby whose mum spiked his bedtime milk with whisky. It's good sleep too, none of the nightmares or sleep paralysis. Just eight hours of uninterrupted bliss, you won't believe what that does to a man."

"I bet," Franklin agreed, trying to remember the last time he had experienced such a night.

"And guess what else has made a return? My libido! I never thought I'd see that again. I tell you, Frank, I woke this morning with the biggest..."

"...I really don't need to hear that, Ed. But I'm pleased for you, I really am. What happened? On Friday you seemed worried that the drugs weren't working."

Edison just shrugged. "Doctor said they might take a week or so to kick in and look at me now. I'm like a new man!"

Inadvertently Edison had given word to why Franklin felt so concerned by this encounter with his brother. He *was* like a new man. Not the morose and anxious man who could suck down a cigarette in less than two minutes, but neither was he the man he was before his breakdown, the prematurely aged grump who complained about political correctness going mad and how young people had it too easy. Edison seemed to be an entirely new man, one that Franklin had never met before - and the feeling was uncanny.

"I was thinking about starting a YouTube channel," Edison went on. "Nothing too fancy, you can do it just with a phone camera nowadays. Get this, I'm going to call it *The Mental Cop* and it'll be all about my breakdown and how I finally got better. It's brilliant isn't it? I could get some sponsorship, maybe even make some money out of it!"

"Finally got better?" Franklin ventured cautiously. "Edison, are you sure that this isn't just a response to the drugs, or that you might be going through a manic episode. Maybe hold off from the media empire just yet."

Edison took a gulp from his beer, leaving a thick, foam blob on the end of his nose. As he replaced the pint glass to the table Franklin noticed that his brother had a slight tremble in his hand. "Maybe you're right. Maybe tomorrow I'll go back to feeling like shit again and won't see the point in living but I've had three whole days of feeling good. Do you know what that's like? It's like the sun has finally come out from behind a cloud and I feel completely alive. If this is all I get before I shrivel away back inside my head then I'm going to make the most of this time while it lasts."

Franklin couldn't argue with that. Edison truly did seem to be happy. "Just be careful though and if you find yourself slipping then call me, any time."

"Yes sir." Edison smiled. "So how are things at home?"

Franklin had never quite got used to his brother referring to Gallow & Sons - the business their father had run in the house the two boys had grown up in, as *home*. Franklin may have begrudgingly inherited the house and business on his father's retirement, but he knew neither of those things were truly his own. "Not a great day, not for Rowan anyway. A body turned up this morning that turned out to be her dead sister's boyfriend. Suicide by train."

"Nasty!" Said Edison. "I've been to a couple of those before, it's like trying to put bits of jelly back together."

"Rowan's seen a lot of dark stuff before but it wasn't the gore that got to her. She was pretty shaken up about it. I was too."

"Well, we've all got to go some way or another. At least it was quick."

His brother's callousness irritated Franklin but he chose to ignore it, deciding that this too was a side effect of whatever drugs he was on. "So, did you get the pictures for me?"

"I did. It's gonna cost you though. Your round, mine's a red wine."

"Red wine?"

Edison shrugged. "That beer didn't sit well with me. It's time for a change, anything fruity and make it a large one."

More than anything else about his brother's behaviour, his change of beverage disturbed Franklin the most. Nevertheless he returned with a large glass of the second cheapest wine on the menu and his own reassuringly standard pint of cider. Edison swished his wine around the glass and sniffed deeply. "Really good body on this one, a vintage year."

"Right," said Franklin. "So, the pictures?"

Edison reached inside the pocket of the overcoat he had draped on the back of his chair and produced a pair of A5 colour photographs which he slammed face up on the table.

Franklin immediately snatched them away. "For god's sake, Edison!" The bar was only half full and none of the nearby patrons appeared to have seen the graphic images but it was the man's nonchalance that infuriated Franklin. "Not a word of this to Rowan."

Edison drew an invisible zip across his mouth. "They're pretty gruesome."

"Did you have any trouble getting hold of them?"

"Nah. Just the same as the rest of the file. Nobody cares about those cold cases anymore. I barely had to sneak anywhere. They're photocopies so the originals are still in Ruby's file."

"How much trouble could you get in?"

"A heap, but who cares. It's better that you have this stuff than it just gets lost in the evidence locker, besides, all they can do is fire me and what do I care? I'm going to be a YouTube celebrity!"

Franklin turned over the first of the images and immediately choked on his cider. "You weren't lying when you said they were gruesome." The photograph showed the body of Ruby Kaplan, bathed in a pool of cold artificial light at the scene of her murder. She lay on her back with her hair matted into the stone floor of the abandoned warehouse, her eyes were upturned so that only the whites were visible, her mouth was agape in a silent scream of rage and despair. The next photograph was a close up of her chest and neck. When he had heard that Ruby had been stabbed nineteen times he'd imagined the wounds to be clean and precise, but these were savage slashes tearing open her red dress and ripping apart the skin beneath in long, tangled strips of flesh.

"Where's the blood?" Franklin asked.

"That's what I thought too, but did you read the full and final autopsy report?"

Franklin shook his head. "You didn't include it in the file, just the preliminary one. Can you get me a copy?"

"I can try but you won't learn much more than you can from those photos. Except for the twist…"

"The twist? This isn't a game, Edison."

"She wasn't stabbed to death," Edison said, bluntly. "She was strangled. That's why there's hardly any blood. Her heart had stopped beating by the time her killer started slashing at her."

"Why doesn't Rowan know this?"

" There were wounds on her neck that suggested whoever strangled her did it from over her shoulder with his thumbs pressing at her throat. At least it was probably quick. So she was probably attacked from behind, they waited for her to go down and then got out the knife - regular old kitchen knife - and stabbed her almost twenty times. That's one theory, the other is…"

"...Two killers. One strangled her from behind the other had the knife in front of her."

Edison nodded. "That's the kind of crap they keep from the families. Not because it's too upsetting but because somebody could be trying to cover up for somebody else. Most of the police on the case didn't even know about it, including me."

"How do two lunatics like that ever find each other?"

"You tell me," said Edison. "You're the guy who caught half of the Blackbeard murderers. That was two people."

"The Roker's saw themselves as terrorists on a mission. This is something above and beyond a simple crossbow murder."

"Simple? My head's all screwy because I witnessed one of those *simple* murders, remember?"

Franklin patted the scar on his chest. "He got me pretty good too. What I mean is that a crossbow is clean and distant. It might take skill to aim but you don't even have to look your victim in the eye to do it. *This* is up close and frenzied."

"Strangulation from behind is usually a sign of a reluctant killer," Edison added. "You see it a lot in domestic crimes. They may want their victim dead but there's no pleasure in the kill for them. Stabbing, however, is something different, especially mutilation like that. That comes from a pure hatred of the victim, that's someone wanting to punish and brutalise their body."

"Who could hate a teenage girl that much?"

Edison scoffed. "You would not believe the crimes that go on between teenagers. If you ask me though, this is the work of someone who cared about Ruby. Maybe even loved her."

"You're not going on about her dad being responsible again, are you?"

"Oscar Kaplan is still the prime suspect."

"Well, who's the second killer then?"

Edison leaned back in his chair and folded his arms behind his head. His eyes widened, almost gleefully. "I'm just going to sit back while your little grey cells mull this one over."

"Ed, you can't think her mother did that. D'you know what kind of a mess she's been in these past few years."

"I didn't say anything, but you thought it. It has to have crossed your mind. Four hours Rolinda Kaplan was home alone that night. She didn't make any calls or go on the internet, nobody can vouch for her whereabouts save for herself. The first call she made was after Oscar came home and that was well after midnight."

"I'm not going to listen to this, it's beyond depraved to even imagine it." Franklin handed Edison the photographs. "Get rid of them, and do it properly."

"Aye, aye captain. So will you be joining me for a glass of rum for the road?"

"You're drinking rum now?"

"It's a night of limitless possibilities Frank. Why waste it?"

"Ed, d'you want to come home with me? You can spend the night in your old bedroom."

"Don't trust me with a splash of the dark stuff?" Edison drawled in a poor imitation of a pirate accent.

"I think I have some rum and a few bottles of those Christmas spirits Mum used to buy. They're probably about twenty-five years old by now."

"Keepin' an eye on your big brother?"

"It's this or the hospital," Franklin replied.

Edison simply nodded and followed his brother home.

24

5.

A troubled mind prevented Rowan from sleeping so she pulled on her duffel coat and headed out into the frosty city. Her destination was her boyfriend's new business; a frozen yoghurt shop on Park Street he'd named "Ghurt Lush."

"It's half eleven at night," she said to Jude across the formica counter. "In December. Why is this place so busy?"

Jude leaned over and kissed Rowan on the cheek. He was wearing the red and white striped uniform he had selected for the business in a pastiche of American 50's diner culture, complete with a retro, paper soda-jerk hat. "I told you this was a good idea. People want good fro-yo, day or night."

Rowan looked around, bewildered. Jude had designed the interior himself, a celebration of vintage kitsch in garish colours with tables separated into little booths with faux-leather couches. Eighteen types of frozen yoghurt were delivered by chunky, steam-punk looking dispensers that lined a wall and before which a queue of patrons stood, each holding a paper carton.

"The world's gone mad. Who could predict that ice cream was going to be the next big thing?"

"Frozen yoghurt," Jude corrected as he straightened his bowtie. "And *I* predicted it. I think I've a genuine success on my hands!"

Rowan discarded a laminated menu on the counter. "How can people afford ice cream at these prices?"

Jude just smiled. "Look around, Ro. Look at these people's faces, look at their eyes."

It was then that Rowan noticed it. The customers were unusually quiet. Some were attempting to use the dispensers, some were gazing thoughtfully into the back of spoons, one was hypnotically watching the ceiling fan gently rotate. "Wait a minute. Ice cream isn't making a comeback, cannabis is. All these people are stoned!"

"Bingo. But fro-yo really is big at the moment. During the day it's all wholesome families but at night... things get a little weird."

"Jude, please don't tell me that you're dealing to these people. D'you know how much trouble you'll get in?"

"Relax. These people got stoned of their own accord and came in search of sweet munchies and artificial lighting. I am simply fulfilling a social need."

"What a dumb, weird world we live in," Rowan sighed.

"You can help yourself to the machines. On the house for my special girl."

"Pass. I only came out for a walk and to see how you were doing."

"At this rate I could be in the black by July. That's pretty impressive going, who knew I was an entrepreneur?"

"It doesn't work like that though, does it? It's not like you got yourself into debt opening this place up."

Jude's smile slipped from his face. "This again."

" I'm just saying it's a lot easier to succeed in business when you're so wealthy you don't have anything to lose."

"If it makes you feel any better I'm not wealthy anymore. I spent my last penny on this business."

Rowan resisted the urge to point out that his last penny actually belonged to his father. After a tearful confession last summer Jude told how he'd fled the home of his abusive father from a small Yorkshire town along with £42,000 of his money. In doing so he had both severed ties with his family and abandoned his mother to her tyrannical husband.

"Can I have more hundreds and thousands?" Asked a bleary-eyed youth who had appeared beside Rowan like a spectre. He held out his paper carton of half melted ice cream like Oliver Twist. "The machine's empty."

"You certainly can, my son." Jude leaned back and called to his assistant through the open door behind the counter. "Are you busy, Alf? We need a top up on the hundreds and thousands."

"I'll be right up," the familiar voice replied.

"It's so weird that Franklin's son works here," said Rowan.

"He's got tuition fees to pay for and those political t-shirts he's always wearing don't come cheap. Besides, I actually like him." Jude replied.

Rowan nodded. "Try as I might, he's growing on me a bit. He's stopped being a total dick to Franklin which makes him a bit more bearable."

"And he's helping to introduce a range of dairy-free frozen yoghurt. That stuff is so hot right now - so to speak."

Alf emerged from the doorway and offered Rowan a friendly nod. No matter how many times she saw him in the Ghurt Lush uniform he never stopped looking comically mismatched, his studiously dishevelled red hair tamed beneath a paper hat, the radical left slogans across his t-shirts hidden beneath a parody of 50s American consumerism.

"Evening, Rowan," he said as he carried an enormous bag of hundreds and thousands to one of the dispensing machines. The stoned teen trailed him like a hungry puppy.

"I never thought I'd say this but the clean-cut look actually suits Alf," Rowan said to Jude.

"I know what you mean. He's been quite a hit with certain gentlemen who come in here. He scored himself a date earlier this evening, with a trainee vicar!"

"Why did nobody inform me that frozen yoghurt shops are now dens of drugs and vice?"

"The old world was nightclubs and getting pissed," Alf interrupted as he returned to the counter. "We're a new generation who hate hangovers and love free gender expression."

"And fro-yo," Jude added.

"Exactly. The old world is gone. You go out on a Saturday night and the clubs are full of Gen Xers and Boomers trying to hold on to their fading youths, while we're just having a little toke, and sexually experimenting."

Rowan shrugged. "Ice cream on a Monday night doesn't feel like that much of a revolution to me."

"The ice cream's just the start of it. Look at the three of us, you, a black, straight woman, me a red-head gay guy, and Jude... I want to say bi?"

"I think I'm up for a bit of anything to be honest," Jude replied, casually. "But mostly into girls. What does that make me? Bi-curious?"

"If the label feels good, go with it. My point is that in the past our lives would probably never intertwine, but nowadays we're all just… getting along and respecting other people's life choices."

"I'm pansexual" a teenage girl who had joined the counter informed the group.

"That's super," Jude replies. "Now, a medium carton of fro-yo, that's £9.95."

Rowan felt no desire to argue with Alf so she said her goodbyes and left into the cold, blustery night. In her pocket she felt her phone buzz. A text message had appeared.

"Rowan, this is Orlagh. Ruby's friend. You gave me your number at her funeral. Just heard about Doug! How're you doing? Feeling awful right now about so many things. Everything is all my fault. Can you please come round and talk?"

Rowan barely recognised the name. Ruby was such a butterfly that all of her friends were like drab moths around her. *"What do you mean it's all your fault?"* She replied.

"Please just come round whenever you can. I'm going to lose my mind if I don't tell somebody about this."

Rowan checked her watch. It was close to midnight. *"Whereabouts are you?"*

"Park Row. I can meet you on the street, just please come."

"It's late," she said.

"I killed your sister," the text message was followed by a sad-face emoticon.

"I'll be right there." Rowan replied.

6.

"Barack Obama, you are keeping it *tight!*" Ruby giggled as she flashed an image of the President topless on the beach. "Michelle is so lucky."

She and Rowan were sitting on a bench on Brandon Hill, overlooking the city. In less than two months from that spring day the Kaplan family would come here to scatter Ruby's ashes to the wind. She flicked through a magazine between puffs on a hand-rolled cigarette.

"Isn't he like, Dad's age?"

"Don't make it gross!" Ruby laughed. "Anyway, I brought you here to share my news. Two bits really and it's *big* news."

Ruby had to make a scene. It wasn't enough to just share gossip, she had to haul Rowan across the city and up a hill before she divulged her secret information. "What is it?"

"I'm seeing someone," she smiled.

"No way! For how long?"

"A couple of weeks now. He's called Doug."

Rowan laughed. "You're going out with someone called Doug? That's someone's dad's name, or like, a teacher. That's not a sexy name for someone called Ruby to go out with."

"Trust me, he's hot!"

"I can't believe you didn't tell me sooner."

"I'm sorry. I guess it's like… I didn't want to jinx it, you know. Start it off with bad ju-ju all over it before it gets a chance to take off."

Rowan nodded as if she understood. "So tell me about him."

"He's twenty-one, he's white - you know I got a bit of a taste for that. He's a drummer in this band called Morning Shiver and… well, that's the next bit of news."

Rowan loved this intimacy, the sense of being drawn into the secret world Ruby kept all but hidden from her parents. "What else?"

"He's asked me to join his band as the lead singer."

"Oh Ruby, I'm so pleased for you!"

"You should be pleased for *them*. They've got my voice onboard and now they're going places. They're a little bit rock for my range and their previous singer had this husky Stevie Nicks thing going on, but they've said they're going to take the band in a more bluesy direction to suit me."

"I can't wait to hear you with them. I've never heard you with a live band before."

"I know, it's gonna be so wild. I played them that version of Downtown I've been working on, you know, that kind of jazz bar version, and it just blew them away!"

Rowan watched the setting sun sit perfectly on the horizon. "Talk about good timing, just after the last singer left."

Ruby didn't answer and just drew on the last of her cigarette.

"No, they didn't kick the singer out the band for you did they?"

"They didn't kick her out. They wanted to take their music in a different direction and it just wouldn't work with Orlagh's voice. It was going to happen whether or not I showed up, eventually."

"That's so mean. Poor girl."

Ruby sighed. "It happens all the time in music, you just can't take it personally. There's a reason why Ringo took over from Pete Best in the Beatles - and just look at all those Saturday night talent shows, they're all about destroying people's dreams because they don't have the talent, or the right *kind* of talent."

"Destroying people's dreams? So you admit it was a pretty mean thing to do?"

Ruby blinked sadly at her sister. "This is supposed to be good news. I wanted you to be the first to hear it."

"I really am happy for you but I can't help thinking what she must be going through. You start dating the drummer of her band one day and she's out by the next."

"It wasn't like that," Ruby stubbed out the end of her cigarette on the edge of the bench and popped a mint into her mouth.

"Was she upset?"

Rowan shook her head. "No... Not really... she'll be fine. I'm sure she will."

30

7.

To her enormous surprise, Rowan felt no trace of rage on reaching Park Row. The surreal horror of the moment on her phone had crumbled away into a reflective state of inevitability. This is what all these years had been leading up to, this was the conclusion to everything that had haunted her since that summer night. This was the end; Ruby's death was about to be unravelled.

She had run almost the entire way, surging on adrenaline at this wilful provocation. As she ran, flickering memories of the young woman at Ruby's funeral crackled through her mind. She had been a drab, nothingness of a girl with sandstone coloured hair that hung limply from a centre-parting, her features were pleasant, but ordinary. No wonder she'd been replaced, she was a house sparrow standing next to a bird of paradise.

Orlagh's appearance only shocked Rowan because she hadn't seen her since that wretched day. The miserable creature was seated on the steps of a block of flats with a half empty bottle of vodka at her side. Her once dull hair had been hacked away at, as if with primary-school scissors and had been dyed an unflattering boot polish black. Dark mascara ringed her eyes and ran in dark streaks down her cheeks. Her coal coloured lips were studded with rings. Rowan's first instinct was to laugh at this anguished creature, a girl who had tried to replace her humdrum ordinariness with the off-the-shelf uniform favoured by those too creatively bankrupt to find a look for themselves.

"You," was all Rowan could manage.

"Oh Rowan, I'm so sorry. *Please* understand that I've been living with this ever since…"

"I'm not here to feel sorry for you," Rowan said calmly. "But you have to tell me what happened to my sister."

Orlagh howled with despair. "I don't know how it happened. I never meant for it to happen!" She stood up, sending the bottle of vodka tumbling down the steps where it smashed upon the pavement. "Please… It was never meant to happen!"

To Rowan's horror the woman was approaching her with open arms, attempting to trap her in an embrace. Without a moment of hesitation Rowan swung her arm out and slapped Orlagh ferociously across the face. She stumbled backwards and rubbed her cheek where a savage, red handprint was rising to the surface.

"I deserved that!" Orlagh wailed.

Rowan looked at the shattered remnants of the bottle, to where the base had smashed into a hollow tube of glass shards. "You deserve that in the neck if you're telling me the truth!" She began to sob.

"Please come inside," she begged. "I don't know what I'll do if I'm left at home by myself tonight. Please…"

"You can go where you want but I'm not leaving you until the police get here."

"You've called them already?"

"Yes," Rowan lied. In her frenzy of emotion on receiving the call she'd not thought to call anyone. "They're on their way, so anything you want to tell me you'd better just tell me now."

Orlagh turned to a keypad and tapped in a code, unlocking the door to the block of flats. Inside, motion detectors responded to her presence and began fluttering blue lights on throughout the lobby of the cold, stark lobby. The place echoed and smelled of piss. Rowan had heard that blue lights were used in places like this so that heroin users weren't able to find a vein to shoot up in.

"It's not been a good life," Orlagh said, by way of explanation for the dire surroundings. "It's more than I deserve though."

Rowan just shrugged dismissively. She was not going to feel pity for this fiend.

"I don't mind if you kill me, tonight." Orlagh went on as she climbed the staircase. "I don't care if it's fast or you want me to suffer… I would have done it myself years ago if I had the courage, but I'm weak and cowardly…"

"...Shut the hell up and get up the staircase," Rowan prodded at Orlagh's back to encourage the drunken woman to move faster.

Orlagh's flat was on the first floor. It had several locks on the door and a peephole. Orlagh pushed her way inside and was met by the overpowering smell of incense, tobacco smoke and cleaning products. It made her throat and eyes sting.

The flat was little more than a bedsit, with a single bed in the centre of the room and an old-fashioned cathode ray TV on a chair. A wonky table sat in one corner, bearing a half-eaten bowl of cornflakes which was growing a film of mould over the top. What was most striking, however, was the curious display next to her bed. Atop a small cabinet was inscribed a neat pentagram in the wood and at each of the five corners sat a partially melted candle. The space was scattered with the ash of what must have been dozens of joss sticks and a perplexing quantity of salt.

"It's for protection," Orlagh informed her on following her gaze.

"Protection from what?"

"Ghosts," she replied, flatly. "Vengeful spirits."

Rowan almost rolled her eyes at this paranoia. Were her sister truly a ghost she would be spending her time partying with Janis Joplin and Amy Winehouse, not wasting her afterlife on this pathetic wretch.

"Take a seat," Orlagh pointed to the edge of her bed.

"I'd rather not." Rowan replied.

"Can I get you a drink? I have some more vodka. Don't have anything to mix it with but you can water it down if you want."

"I don't want a drink, Orlagh, I want to hear what you did to my sister. Tell me everything... before the police get here."

Orlagh sank onto her bed and fell backwards. "I'm so sorry, Rowan. I never meant to harm anyone, not really. If I'd thought about it for even a moment there's no way I would've done it. I just needed to let off some steam, I was so furious with her."

33

"So you stabbed my sister? You stabbed her nineteen times because you were pissed with her when she replaced you in some band?"

"Stabbed her? No! I would never do such a thing. I *cursed her!*"

Rowan rubbed her forehead, her brain was pounding against her skull. "You cursed her."

"Not just a curse, the darkest, cruelest curse of them all. The most unforgivable spell known to witchcraft. After I heard they'd kicked me out of the band I went home and cast the ultimate hex upon her. I asked the gods to *kill her*! Not only that, I did it six times in six weeks!"

Rowan stood shocked and unblinking for a moment. "You wicked little bitch," was all she could manage.

"You must hate me so much for what I did to her."

"I don't give a shit about your pathetic little Harry Potter games. What's the matter with you? Drunk and bored on a Monday night so you thought you'd get some attention by confessing to a murder?"

Orlagh looked shocked. "You don't understand… It was me!"

"You did nothing. You *are* nothing. You did some angsty teen spell because you felt upset and now you're pretending that *you* were responsible for killing *her*. How dare you even think like that?"

"But I really did the spell. I looked it up online. I even used her hair and a photograph of Ruby. I put my own blood into the candle and I cursed her with ancient words."

Rowan laughed coldly. "Don't you dare even use my sister's name. She was everything and you… you're nothing."

"She usurped my position. How else was I supposed to respond? The rules of witchcraft say you can ask the universe for curses if you've been genuinely wronged but I never should have used that one. Look what happened! The curse came back on me and now I live like this."

"Don't blame the universe for your terrible life choices. You've got a tiny flat and a drinking problem, my sister's *dead.*"

"And it's all my fault!"

"Jesus Christ, I really hope that slap in your face hurts even more than your hangover tomorrow. You've wasted my time and told me some bullshit about my sister. I need to go home."

"She wasn't all that," Orlagh said, quite unexpectedly. She sat up on her bed, her face became the petulant snarl of a child.

"You'd better not be thinking of bad-mouthing my sister. These hands have got a whole night of slaps left in them if you are."

Orlagh folded her arms across her chest and spoke with a disarming clarity. "She knew what she was doing, even though she tried acting innocent about it. Girls see through all that flirty crap better than boys do. Doug lapped it all up. Boring, boring Doug got the attention of a girl like Ruby and didn't think twice what she might be trying to get out of it. I used to watch her in the bar when we were rehearsing. She'd show up all the time and move around like she owned the place. She'd be all, "*Oh Doug, can I get you another drink? Oh your arms feel so big. Have you been working out? Dougie, your shoulders feel so tense, let me give you a massage*" and that stupid boy didn't see through any of it. I knew exactly what she was after, she was after me and my place at the centre of the stage. That's where *I* belonged."

Rowan shook her head. "Three and a half years later and you're still jealous. I've never heard you sing but I can tell you now, Ruby was better. She was better than everyone."

"Better at getting whatever she wanted. She slept her way into the band, like a whore!"

Rowan balled her fists. "You take that back. Don't say that about my sister."

"She was a *whore*! She used men for all she could squeeze out of them and acted like she didn't know why they were always falling in love with her. Poor, stupid Doug was besotted with her - I may be a witch but Ruby had some weird magic and she knew it. That idiot boy has spent all these years thinking he lost the love of his life when all she did was use him and now the poor guy's killed himself because he thought she was the real thing. And it's not just me, ask Lily."

"Who the hell's Lily?" Rowan snarled.

"Lily Angelo. She was the bass player for Morning Shiver and Doug's girlfriend until *she* showed up. She didn't just mess the band up, she broke a couple up too. That's how selfish she was. I didn't want her to die but somebody had to do something to stop her."

Rowan wiped sweat from her brow. Rage was boiling inside her. "I know that whatever drugs you've dropped this evening are starting to work, but she'd never do something like that. This is that evil crap girls like you use to tear other girls down. Call them sluts and whores just because they're ambitious."

"Ambitious," Orlagh laughed maniacally. Rowan wondered just what the woman had imbibed that night. "Go and ask Lily. She runs the vintage shop on Redland High Street where all the mannequins have their tits out in the window. You go and ask her and she'll tell you what kind of girl your *amazing* sister was. Ruby tore her relationship apart and she had to carry on playing because Morning Shiver were about to make it big. Go and meet her and *ask* her yourself!"

Orlagh snorted with wild laughter and collapsed back on her bed. Resisting the urge to throttle the deranged woman, Rowan marched across the bedsit and kicked the bedside cabinet so it crashed into the wall before spilling itself forward, sending the candles scattering about the room and cracking the wooden pentacle in half.

"My protection!" Orlagh screamed. "What have you done!"

Rowan stormed from the room just as the wall of grief became too much and she stumbled to the floor of the filthy block of flats with an anguished, silent howl.

8.

When Rowan awoke to the sound of her alarm clock she blinked wearily and was confronted by shattered, half recalled memories of the night before. Her eyes felt huge and swollen and her mouth was parched. From across Jude's studio flat she heard the ping of a microwave. She focused in on the pair of handcuffs she and her boyfriend used to play with in bed, handcuffs which had been neglected for so long that they'd gathered a layer of dust.

"Weetabix with warm milk," said Jude, standing in the kitchen area wearing a dressing gown. "How have I only just discovered you?" he said to his breakfast.

"Morning," she croaked at him. "Where were you last night? I came home and the place was empty, that was at almost 2 in the morning."

Jude shrugged. "It took a while to close up."

"A while? You're supposed to shut at midnight. I thought that was part of your license."

"Behind the scenes stuff. It's not easy running a business. Anyway, why were you out so late?"

"Same. Work stuff," she lied as she wiped her eyes on the bedsheets.

"Right." She was certain she detected a note of doubt in his voice, she wondered if he noticed the same in hers. Rowan didn't have much experience with relationships but she was certain it wasn't a good sign that both halves of a couple were lying to each other about their whereabouts the night before.

"I'm getting in the shower," Rowan declared, pulling the bedclothes around her like royal robes as she made her way to the bathroom. Jude had seen her naked countless times before but since opening Ghurt Lush the pair had drifted apart so far that some days they seemed like virtual strangers with lives only occasionally intertwined.

At work she found Franklin in his office, drinking coffee from a mug which read "*World's #1 Funeral Directo*r" and eating a cream cheese bagel. "Bloody hell, Rowan. You look even worse than I do this morning," were his words of greeting.

"You had a bad night too?"

"You could say that. Edison's staying with me for a while, his new drugs are doing something screwy to him."

"Is he still here?'

Franklin shook his head. "He still wants to go to work. I'd just rather he stayed here where I can keep an eye on him. So what's up with you? You look like you could use some more sleep."

"That's for damn sure. My eyes are so puffy I look like I've had an allergic reaction and my hair's all…" she had no idea where it came from but Rowan found herself bursting into tears. Franklin immediately bolted across the room to her, throwing his arms around her shoulders.

"I'm sorry, I didn't mean to be insulting…"

"I'm fine, I'm just tired," Rowan sobbed.

"This is more than just tiredness. I've seen you get through a whole week on next to no sleep. What happened last night?"

Rowan did not hesitate in telling him every detail of the events in the flat on Park Row.

"You *stupid* girl," was his first reaction. His tone was soft enough to cushion the words. "What about our deal? We're supposed to do all of this stuff together."

"I know, but when I saw her message it was close to midnight and she was only at the top of the hill. I just had to do it by myself."

Franklin patted the back of Rowan's head as she hiccuped the last of her sobs onto the lapel of his jacket. "I understand. So this Orlagh woman believed she was responsible for killing Ruby all these years?"

"You should've seen the state of that place. I could almost feel sorry for her but she said such nasty things about Ruby."

"You don't know how true any of those things are… and even if Ruby did split up a couple just to get into a band, people have done far worse things, especially when they're teenagers."

"Ruby wouldn't though, I know she wouldn't. Orlagh was just saying it because I was making fun of her and her stupid little spells, plus she was on something weird. You should've seen what happened to her. She just transformed." Rowan broke away from Franklin and helped herself to a box of tissues on his desk. "Honestly though, I'm fine."

"Well, if it helps at all, I've scheduled a meeting with Douglas' mum this afternoon by myself. I don't think it'd be good for you to be dealing with this service and I doubt his family would be all that keen on your involvement either."

"Thanks. I wonder if Peterman still needs some help with those dead babies."

"Of course, it does mean that we have a free morning, if you were in the mood for a little snooping…"

Rowan sat down at Franklin's desk and woke his computer from sleep. "D' you mean visit Lily's junk shop in Redland?"

"Only if you thought you were up to it," said Franklin. "I think I've been past her place before, I think it's what's referred to as a *Vintage Boutique* rather than a junk shop."

"It's called Wandering Lily," Rowan read from the computer screen. "It's open now. What are we waiting for?"

After stopping for takeaway coffee at the Crepe and Coffee Cabin on Prince Street, Franklin and Rowan wove through city traffic in his little Smart car. It was then Rowan thought to address the other problem she had marinading in her head.

"I think Jude might be cheating on me… With Alf."

"Alf?" Franklin snorted. "*My* Alf?'

"Don't laugh, I'm being serious. You should see the pair of them together, all cosy with private jokes and he keeps on coming home late from Ghurt Lush. I don't know when he got home last night but it was gone 2am."

Franklin tutted irritably as he overtook a man on a unicycle obnoxiously demanding attention as he rode up Park Street with his arms folded. "So Jude's a little AC/DC, it doesn't mean he's cheating on you. Alf's just a lot more friendly with everyone nowadays. All it took was his dad to almost get murdered a few times for him to decide he likes me. Besides, isn't he seeing that guy from that punk band?"

"Ozric Testicles? That was like, three boyfriends ago. Keep up."

"I obviously didn't receive the latest newsletter. Anyway, the point is that they're allowed to just be friends without anything going on. Jude's a good kid who's already punching well above his weight with you, he wouldn't do that."

Rowan sighed. "I'm being paranoid again, aren't I?"

"A bit. Remember when you first started working with me and people assumed I was into you? People have minds like sewers. But then again, you've never been that trusting of him have you?"

Rowan couldn't deny this, and had told Franklin many times. "Ever since he told me about the stolen money I've had these doubts creep back in. At first I was like *of course* that explains everything, like his shaky origin story and his fear of policemen, but then I got to thinking, and no, it doesn't explain it. Not properly anyway, something isn't quite right but I can't place what it is yet."

"One mystery at a time, Rowan," said Franklin, as he parked in a vacant space on Redland High Street opposite Wandering Lily.

The window display of the vintage boutique was sparsely decorated with old books displayed in picture frames and a row of mannequins painted in non-human hues, lilac, taupe, tangerine and neon yellow. Across the bare chests of the figures had been spray-painted the word "FEMINISM" with each letter covering one of the breasts.

"That's a striking tableau. What does it mean?" asked Franklin.

"It means that feminism now means women should be getting their boobs out in public," Rowan sighed. "Isn't it funny how new-wave feminism means dressing how men wanted us to dress all along? Like total hookers."

"I forget that you have such a puritanical streak in you," said Franklin as he pushed the door to the boutique open.

A little bell rang to announce their arrival and the pair found themselves surrounded by a strange new world of curios and oddments. The shop space was rendered stiflingly narrow by shelves upon shelves laden with artefacts from bygone days. 1920s costume jewellery spilled out of little wooden boxes, framed black and white images of long-dead strangers lined the walls. On railings dotted about wherever they could fit hung garish mini skirts alongside art deco cocktail dresses. The entire back portion of the shop was a maze of ancient sewing machines, cameras and steam-punk looking contraptions whose purpose had been lost to time.

Lily Angelo was seated behind a venerable looking counter which could have tumbled through time from the Victorian era. She wore an enormous woollen jumper with a chunky weave and balanced a pair of outsized glasses on her face. Her hair was up and held in place by a pair of pencils skewering the bun on top of her head. Franklin felt her eyes pass over him, assessing his style.

"I love your look," were her first words. "It's classic."

Franklin was about to say thank you but he saw her eyes fall on Rowan. Immediately her mouth fell open.

"Rowan Kaplan? Is that you?" She rose to her feet. "It *is* you!"

"Hi," Rowan replied, uncomfortably.

Lily skipped from behind the counter with tears in her eyes and threw her arms around Rowan who froze on the spot as if ice water had been thrown over her. "Oh you sweet, sweet baby angel. I have *worried* about you! You must've heard about Doug by now?"

Rowan nodded. "Yeah, I know. That's actually why I'm here."

Lily loosened her grip and looked at Franklin again. "I know you! You're that undertaker who caught Blackbeard, and that psycho kid who lived in the sewers."

"That's not quite what happened but…"

"…You clever girl!" she said to Rowan. "You've got him to look into Ruby's murder, haven't you? Dear God, I hope this works out for you. I hope it works out for me too - there's not a day when I don't think about her and what happened that night… maybe if I'd done something differently then everything would've played out in another way. What do you need to know? You can come back later when the shop's closed or… actually, no." Lily brushed between Rowan and Franklin and flipped the sign on the door to read "*Closed*." "What do you need to know?"

"I spoke to Orlagh last night. Do you remember her?"

"Sort of, I think. Can you jog my memory?"

41

"She was the lead singer of Morning Shiver until Ruby replaced her."

Orlagh snapped her fingers. "Got it. Yeah, she was *good* - but man, Ruby wasn't good, she was like an extraterrestrial, like that sound didn't belong on earth, like it was too powerful for us to even fully comprehend."

A soft smile spread across Rowan's lips. "That's for sure. She also said something a bit... well, she said you and Doug were going out together and Ruby kind of split you up when she started hanging out with the band. Is that true?"

"Split us up?" Lily's far away expression suggested she genuinely couldn't remember what had happened. "I think Doug and I were together for like a hot minute. It wasn't anything serious at all. It was just casual as far as I can remember and it was only a couple of weeks. I think when the pair of them met they just had a kind of spark where you knew something was going to happen there. I'm not one of those chicks who hates other women just because they get with one of their exes."

"Orlagh seems to think Ruby came between the pair of you, like the other woman or something."

"Wait, is Orlagh that crazy woman who chopped all her hair off and turned into a witch? A friend of a friend posted a pic of her on Facebook a few months back."

"That's the one. She seems to have a bit of a substance abuse problem too."

"Sounds like we made the right decision kicking her out of the band then. In case you're worried about any of us having gripes or broken hearts, that never happened. Before Ruby joined we were this big mess. I mean, we had talent, but it was Ruby who took us to the threshold of greatness. We didn't just become better musicians, the four of us gelled as friends. Those few months after she joined us were the happiest of my life because I felt we were going somewhere, no, not even going somewhere but that all of our dreams were going to be recognised and it was just a matter of time. It was inevitable. Doug and I might have fooled around a bit for a while but I'm not a jealous gal. Ruby made us a family. She made us transcendent..."

"There were four of you in Morning Shiver?" Franklin asked.

Lily nodded. "Ruby was vocals, I was on bass, Doug was on drums and then there's Kay. She played guitar."

"I don't remember a Kay," said Rowan. "I thought there was another guy in the band. Kevin Casey."

Lily winced uncomfortably. "This is the minefield of pronouns I get stuck in when I talk about the past. Kay is a transgendered woman who used to identify as Kevin."

"That makes sense. I tried looking for a Kevin Casey online and couldn't find anyone."

"I have her email if you want to get in touch with her. She'd want to help."

"That would be very useful," said Franklin.

Lily jotted the address down on the torn edge of a ledger's notepad and handed it to Franklin. "She was the only properly sober one among us at the pub that night, her memories are a lot sharper than mine."

"What do you remember of that night though?" Franklin asked.

"I got pretty wasted, to tell the truth. We'd all had a bit to drink at the rehearsal, except for Kay, and I carried it on at home. I was living in a bit of a dive at the time with two other housemates who were kind of burnouts. It's weird how quickly you can pick up bad habits. It was probably three in the morning when I passed out on the sofa, loaded with vodka. I remember waking up to a bunch of missed calls and then Douglas on the phone just... completely devastated. I'll never forget that call and his voice on the line. It was like he couldn't comprehend it but he knew it was shattering news."

"And there's nothing else about the night you can remember?" Franklin pressed.

"Bits and pieces. It feels so long ago, and far away too, like it happened in a different universe that sometimes I'm unsure of what are my real memories and what are just constructions of my imagination or things I've pieced together from reading about the case. But I remember it was quite a tense night. The rehearsal wasn't going as well as previous ones and we had this cameraman in, this videographer who was recording us, just for a little bit and we couldn't get it right. It was meant to be our promo bit online but it just kept going off the boil. I was too fast, or Doug was too slow. Ruby was always just Ruby, which means she was flawless but we got it together for the video. I left with Doug soon after the rehearsal and he drove me back to my place near Millennium Square and I think Kevin, that's Kay, got a taxi home earlier in the evening. Ruby was alone for a bit and she locked up if I recall it right. That's what the police said anyway."

Franklin nodded. Her account matched all of the statements from the surviving band members of their movements that evening.

"I wish I could remember more, but then this selfish part of me is kind of glad I don't. It's hard enough getting to sleep sometimes even now if I think about it too hard."

Franklin looked at the note in his hand bearing Kay's mobile phone number and slipped it into the inner pocket of his suit jacket. "If you don't mind me asking, what happened to Morning Shiver after that night?"

"What else could happen? We split up. Even if a recording contract miraculously appeared I don't think any of us would've gone for it. Ruby's death was like a nail bomb detonating in our little family, it just tore everything to pieces. I don't think I picked up my guitar again after that evening. Doug, well, he was never the same again. He had this quietness about him and this darkness, like all of the shutters were closed and nobody could reach him again. Kay has been on her own journey of course, she still plays music but it took a long time for her to get back into it." Lily sighed and appeared to blink back tears. "Maybe if I'd tried harder with Doug things would've been different, maybe I could've saved him. I gave him a job here, just a couple of days a week in the hope that might bring him out of himself but he was too far gone. When that black dog settles in with someone there's nothing that can be done to make it go away."

Franklin and Rowan offered their thanks and Rowan received an affectionate hug from Lily before the pair left. They did not speak until the car was on the move.

"How're you doing?" Franklin asked Rowan.

"A bit better, I think," she replied. "I liked hearing what she said about Ruby. She seems sincere, don't you think."

"She does. At least, she doesn't seem to have anything to hide. I'll look through the interview she gave to the police and see if there're any inconsistencies but I don't think there will be. She was too forthcoming, she didn't seem to be hiding anything."

"That's what I thought too. At least we know where we're heading next. Kay Casey. Have you ever met a transgender person before?" asked Rowan.

Franklin caught her eye in the rearview mirror. "I hope you're not suggesting that I'd be uncomfortable meeting a trans person."

"Not at all, I know what you're like, it's just..." Rowan exhaled deeply. "I think I might be awkward, just a little bit."

Franklin shook his head. "I'm kind of surprised at you, Rowan. Have you seen the rates of assaults that happen to transgender people? They are far more scared of cisgender people than we are of them.

"I know, but Jude and Alf were talking last night about how fluid everything is right now and how nobody has to be any one thing and I just thought... things used to be so much simpler in the past."

"It wasn't as if you were a bit gay or a bit gender fluid. It was a rough time and plenty of people didn't make it out alive. Trust me, times are better now when everyone can just be honest - and themselves."

"You think I'm a terrible person, don't you?"

"I'm a tiny bit disappointed but I know you're not a bad person. You should probably try working on some of your more... intolerant views. Maybe educate yourself if there are things you don't understand. You're allowed to ask questions of people - or of Google."

The pair sat in silence for the rest of the journey while Rowan pondered if she really did have intolerant views. Franklin dropped her off at Gallow & Sons before driving off to meet the mother of Douglas Bennett. As the car sped out of sight, Rowan unlocked her phone and typed a sentence into Google. *"What does cisgender mean?"* she asked.

9.

The woman across the coffee table from Franklin was of an indeterminate age. Her smooth skin hinted at some contact with a surgeon's knife but was too obscured beneath layers of makeup to give many secrets away. Only her bloodshot eyes gave any indication that a trauma had struck this home, as both Mrs Beverley Bennett and her house were pristinely kept, with the former buttoned up in a silk blouse and with immaculate, pink fingernails and the latter an ultra-modern expanse of white and beige without a trace of the unconsidered chaos and junk of Franklin's own abode.

"Thank you for agreeing to meet me this afternoon," said Beverley as she whipped a handkerchief over a dining chair before sitting upon it. "I know it was late notice but I've heard that organising the funeral service is a merciful distraction during these ghastly times."

"Many do find some solace," Franklin agreed. "May I start by saying how terribly sorry for your loss I am. I will do everything I can in the coming days to ensure that any burdens of the ceremony will be passed onto me and that I and my assistant will endeavour to do everything we can to make the service exactly as you wish it to be."

Beverley nodded and sipped at a mug of mint tea. Franklin mirrored her and did the same. "We haven't fully decided on the music yet but I have some ideas. Last night my husband and I were looking through old photos and we found a couple that we'd like to be part of the service. The first one was taken when he was at college. He thought he was too grown up for photos but I told him he'd want a record of himself when he was that age - so that one day when he was old he could look back and think…" she cut herself off and reached under her chair to produce a shoebox filled with assorted articles from her son's life. "Here. This one."

Franklin took the photograph from her and studied it, allowing the woman to wipe her tears on a tissue she held in her sleeve. The image showed a teenage boy, probably not much older than sixteen, wearing a shirt and tie and an expression of *"this is so goofy, why are you making me do this?"*

46

Franklin smiled. "Handsome chap, I was a mess of spots and greasy hair at that age."

"I was hoping we could have that print enlarged so we could display it beside the coffin during the... during the service."

"Certainly. I will have this copy back to you in no time." Franklin slipped the photograph into his briefcase.

"This is the other one we hoped we could use. My husband and I wanted it featured in the back of the service notes. I think it's what Doug would've wanted."

The sight of the next photograph made Franklin's heart spasm in his chest, causing him to stifle a gasp. It showed the same youth, now a young man posing beside Ruby Kaplan in a restaurant, his arm tightly held across her shoulder.

"I don't know if you knew but Doug had a girlfriend many moons ago who was murdered."

Franklin bit his lip and pretended to inspect the photo closer.

"They never caught who did it - and Doug never recovered from that night. It haunted him, or he haunted it, I suppose. He was like a ghost after that poor girl was killed. He had been so happy but afterwards, I can't recall ever seeing him smile again."

Franklin felt guilt pressing down on him hard. What was he supposed to do? Did he need to mention that his assistant was the sister of Ruby Kaplan? In that instant he decided to keep it to himself. Rowan was going to be kept as far away from this emotionally turbulent service as possible. "I'm sure I could get copies of it made for the service notes."

Looking up at Beverley he discovered that she was applying blusher to her cheeks with a pocket-sized makeup kit. Her hands were trembling and the brush moved at a pace close to a frenzy. He had seen this behaviour before, the repetition of daily tasks consuming a grief stricken person. The everyday fixes used to plaster over the cracks had now gone into overdrive. Manic floor scrubbing, endless showers, anything to bring a sense of normality back to a world which no longer made any sense.

"You said you have some ideas for music?"

Beverley snapped her makeup case shut and nodded. "Doug used to be in a band so we thought maybe a recording from those days... but he was a drummer so it didn't seem right to have anything too raucous. My husband and I don't practice our faith that often but we *do* believe and I'm certain that deep down in Doug's heart, even at the end, he believed too. I think we'd quite like some hymns to be involved. Something classic. Music was in his heart."

"I have a list of suggestions I can send if you'd like."

"Yes please." Beverley stared into the distance, her face became an unreadable, blank mask. "I hope he's at peace now."

"I am certain he is," the soft fib of an atheist had served Franklin well over these years in his profession.

"For some people life is so easy, but not for Doug. Every morning was a new struggle after Ruby died. He went through phases but he was never truly himself again. We knew he was slipping badly this time and we knew what all the telltale signs were, you see, this wasn't the first time he'd attempted it. Twice before he'd tried to kill himself and twice we swore we would do what we could to fix him. We did everything we could, we got him to the finest doctors in the country and walked him step by step along his path, but everything we did still wasn't enough."

Confessions such as these were not uncommon, particularly in the wake of suicides. Voluntary death scorched the earth of those closest to the victim, dismantling everything that was good about that person's life. It was not just that a life had come to an unnatural end, but that living had been too great a torture to bear. "My brother has been dealing with depression for quite some time. I know how difficult it can be."

Beverley nodded but did not seem to care much for Franklin's anecdote. He did not expect her to. When her world and everything in it was crumbling away to dust, why should she feign concern for a stranger who was still very much alive.

"If you don't mind me asking," Franklin ventured cautiously. "You said that the killer of his girlfriend was never found, did he ever offer a theory for who it could be?"

After another sip of her mint tea, Beverley replied. "For a while it consumed him trying to find out what happened, just having somebody who he could blame or hate. The police took him in for questioning a few times, which was terrible for all of us. I know they always suspect those closest to the victim but when they're questioning your son, who you know better than you know yourself', you just want to scream and beat the chests of the policemen, to tell them that you've seen his *soul* and you know he could never, ever be responsible for it. You try but you're helpless to prevent anything. He used to go out late at night, retracing the steps they said she took in the hope he might find some clue or understanding of what happened, and every night I'd wait by the window and pray for him to return with the answers he needed."

"And did he ever find those answers?"

"Nothing. It was as if her killer had evaporated into the night, never to be seen again. I think a lot of people suspected the father. I've nothing against the man and have never had so much as a conversation with him but when all you have is loose ends you just need to find somebody you can tie them to, so in the end he tried finding solace that the dad did it. Does that make any sense?"

"Of course it does," it was times such as these that Franklin was very aware that his job was as much counsellor as it was funeral director. "We all need answers when something like that happens. It must have been devastating."

"I thought it would be the most significant and tragic event of his life. Sometimes I tried reassuring myself by thinking, well, at least they were only together for a couple of months, even longer and it could be worse, or that maybe if there *had* to be some great tragedy in his life it was almost good that he got it out of the way when he was still young and able to recover, that maybe because something so terrible had happened to him God would clear a path for him for the rest of his life, so everything would be simple from then on." Once again Beverley retrieved her makeup kit a swiftly brushed foundation into her face.

"I wish there was more I could do for you, but I can put you in touch with grief professionals. It may not seem like it but I assure you that this is the absolute worst it can possibly ever be. Nothing this terrible can ever happen again and with time you will come to live with what happened, even if right now it seems as if you could never recover."

"I don't know if I want to recover." As her voice cracked, Franklin heard the faintest trace of a Bristolian accent break through and imagined what lengths the woman may have gone through to erase her regional twang. The small, trifling worries such as one's elocution seemed so pointless in the wake of a tragedy. "This is all I can feel right now and even to be thinking about moving on seems disrespectful. But yes, one day I will need some help."

Franklin handed her the printout of grief specialists and charities he kept with him. Ordinarily he would use the final stage of their meeting to discuss flowers, burial clothes and casket options but he had been doing this job long enough to know when the time to wrap things up had come.

"I shall be in touch with you very soon, Ms Bennett. In the meantime, feel free to contact me anytime, day or night. My door is always open if for any reason you need to come to the funeral home. Your son is in very good hands and we will take care of him. I can tell that... he was very loved."

Both he and Beverley rose to their feet at the same time, coughing discretely to quell the surge of emotions that had consumed to room.

"Thank you," she said.

As Franklin left he thought of Douglas Bennett and that lonely death on a train track and of how Ruby's murder had not just claimed her as a victim, but also Rowan, her family and a sweet seeming boy who once had music in his heart.

10.

After she had been working at Gallow & Sons Funeral Home for almost eighteen months, Rowan and Peterman, the disagreeable, drunk and yet somehow very capable other funeral director, had come to a mutual truce. The urge to fling insults at each other had given way first to an icy silence and finally to a casual nod. It was the closest they were ever likely to come to friendship.

Stepping onto his foot as the pair unexpectedly collided while coming out of adjoining offices forced from Rowan a begrudging, "Sorry."

"Watch where you're going," was his gruff dismissal.

Still contemplative after her encounter with Lily, Rowan elected to step into Peterman's path once more.

"Do you mind? I'm trying to get somewhere!"

"Peterman. Why do you hate me?"

To this the old man just scoffed. "Hate you? Whatever gave you that impression?"

"You've never exactly tried to hide it have you? I've been here for ages and I don't think you've ever said so much as hello to me."

"I don't hate you, little girl. I have no passion left to hate anyone. Now if you'd let me pass I…"

"Well you at least dislike me."

Peterman's face drew suspicious as he inspected Rowan's eyes. "Have you been smoking hashish?"

"No. I mean… I don't know what that is but I haven't smoked any. I just thought, why are we like this to each other?"

"I know it may be fashionable for young people to have everything out in the open, to go to therapists and tell everyone about it, or on reality TV where you shower in front of the cameras, but I still remember a time when people were able to keep things to themselves. However, if you *insist,* I never believed that you should have been hired in the first place. Franklin has, for many years managed perfectly well by himself, as have I. One day, quite out of the blue, he takes on a relative infant who is… the colour that you are."

Rowan's smirked. "The colour?"

"Now don't you dare try putting words into my mouth. Do you have any idea what allegations of racialism can do against a man in this day and age. Apparently we're all supposed to pretend that we don't even notice it anymore. My point is not that your colour should prevent you from working anywhere, but that it's the pressure from the *liberals* and the *feminists* and the *Germaine Greer's* of this world that have given white men no option than to hire those from what are known as *minority groups*."

"Are you calling women a minority group?"

"You know damned well what I mean. It's the emasculation of the 21st century man. He can no longer be proud of what he is or has achieved, he's being taught to be ashamed of it all. To tear down statues and insist on women being on our currency because otherwise it's unfair. All the art which is sublime, science, medicine, mathematics, these were all achievements by men who are now taught to be ashamed of themselves. We put men on the moon and yet we are to regard these achievements as inferior as they weren't done by some Hindu lesbian in a wheelchair!"

It was not that long ago that a confrontation such as this would have enraged or upset Rowan, but the man's retrograde thinking was now so comically outdated all she could manage was a pitiful laugh. "Well, it's very good to know where I stand. I'm sorry to have interrupted you in your busy schedule of putting men on the moon, I shall slip on my scold's bridle for the rest of the day."

The look of confusion on the old man's face was enough of a victory for Rowan. She turned on her heels and entered the reception where the receptionist Meredy was absent-mindedly filling in an adult colouring book.

"That man is a joke," Rowan spat. "There must be a way of getting rid of him."

"Another run in with the old drunk?" she smiled. "Trust me, if he could kick him out Franklin would've done it years ago but the business is still his father's."

"It just drives me nuts that attitudes like that still exist. If a woman makes it in anything it must be because they fixed the game to make it easier for her to succeed. When a man triumphs it's because he earned it."

"Amen sister," Meredy offered the air a defiant punch. "Try going a bit easier on him though, he's attending the Christmas meal this year so we're going to have to sit at the table with him for a couple of hours."

"Damn. I thought you said he never went to those things. I was really looking forward to the three of us getting drunk on business-expense cocktails."

"That makes two of us," Meredy agreed.

Rowan felt her phone vibrate in her pocket and stepped through the glass doorway to the gravel driveway outside to answer it. "Hi, Jude."

"You're supposed to say Hey Jude," he replied.

"I forgot," she hadn't. The cosy closeness they once shared had frosted over so much she couldn't bring herself to use terms that came close to endearment. It crossed her mind in that instant that aside from the gorgeous rooftop garden he had planted, despite their electric performances on the dance floor together and even despite the fact that Jude had finally committed himself to a project which was proving successful, she might actually despise him.

"Just wanted to let you know that I'm going out after work tonight. Alf and some of his buddies wanted some drinks so I was going to introduce them to somewhere new."

"Oh yes? Where're you going?"

"I haven't decided yet."

"Could I come?" Rowan didn't want to, but she was testing him.

"You'll only be bored. Too much shop talk, you know. Anyway, you have to be up early again for work tomorrow. It's best that you don't."

The instant she hung up the phone
Rowan made a choice. That night she would follow Jude and find out what he was up to.

11.

Franklin turned the picture of the teenage Douglas Bennett face down on the coffee table of his living room above Gallow & Sons. The boy's eyes revealed a glimpse of embarrassment but shimmered with that irrepressible glow of youth. He would have been firmly devoted to music at that age Franklin thought to himself. Perhaps he looked into his future, imagining record contracts and experimental albums, touring across Europe in a coach filled with hedonists and groupies. Everything that was doomed to never happen, a life that would never materialise because of one tragic night he would forever relive in his mind, until he could take it no more.

All the deaths Franklin dealt with found a way under his skin, but some held their grip for longer than others. The young deaths, the violent ones, the accidents caused by sheer stupidity or dumb luck but it was always the suicides that haunted him the most. He patted the back of the photograph and found his mind lurching through Doug's final moments - the fear and the hopelessness, the sound of the train approaching, the apprehension and that little voice of self preservation that tried to beg him not to jump and then the instant of collision beneath unstoppable, grinding wheels and relentless metal.

The sound of his phone whirring to life made Franklin jump. After a dinner of beans on toast and a mug of hot chocolate he'd found himself laying back on the sofa dozily contemplating the events of the day, as his cat, Felicity, slept fitfully on his chest in a tight coil. The display on the screen informed him that it was an unknown caller using a Bristol landline. He cleared his throat and answered. "Good evening. Gallow & Sons Funeral Home. How may I help?"

It was a woman's voice that answered. "Hey, handsome."

"Verity!" He gasped, sitting bolt upright, sending his cat tumbling onto an adjacent cushion. "You're the last person I was expecting to hear from tonight... and the one I most wanted to."

"You're too sweet. You know how I like to surprise you so I used the phone in Alf's flat. Are you in for the night?"

Franklin had lost track of the time and consulted his watch, it had just gone ten. "I don't have any plans at all. Are you in Bristol?"

He heard an excited little squeal on the line. "You're not going to believe this, but I live here now."

Franklin slapped his cheek, certain that he must have fallen asleep in front of the TV and was having a dream. "What are you talking about?"

"Well don't get too excited just yet. It's a tiny little hovel on Welsh Back that I got a short lease on. I know it sounds rash and ridiculous but with term coming to an end it just felt right to pack it in at the school and once I'd handed in my notice it was just like… why am I still hanging around here? What's keeping me in Cheltenham? So I put the house on the market and found this little den and I just got here this evening and I'm just… So excited!"

"Why didn't you tell me any of this before?" He asked eagerly.

"I hadn't even told Alf the whole story. I think if I actually said it out loud I'd end up hearing my mother's voice in my head telling me to do the sensible thing, to stay the course and not be hasty. I may have just wrecked any security I have at a time in my life when I should be being practical but this just feels *right* to me."

"Of course. Can I come over?"

A man's voice replied, "Get your arse over here Dad."

Franklin was on his feet and unbuttoning his pyjamas. "Alf's there? I thought he was at the ice cream shop tonight."

"Last minute night off to celebrate," he confirmed.

"You're on speaker phone, by the way," said Verity. "We'd love for you to come over."

Franklin was still buttoning up his jacket as he ran from his home. He wasn't the only one heading out into the cold night as across the city Rowan, dressed all in black, slipped from her block of flats and headed off in pursuit of her mysterious, infuriating boyfriend.

55

It was not the first time she had tracked a person. Soon after being employed by Franklin she had found herself stalking the suspicious man who lived above the home of a murdered woman. Her attempts had led to him kidnapping and trying to murder her but she was quite certain she was in no such peril with her boyfriend. On the surface Jude was a buffoon, a sweet and kind-hearted one, but a buffoon nonetheless, a man for whom life was a daily pursuit of whimsy or some trifling project that would never amount to much, but there was something about him, a mystery which she'd always acknowledged but had never let trouble her, but as they grew closer, the questions began to plague her mind. Who was Jude Tindale? The pieces of his life seemed to all be there on display, like a finished jigsaw puzzle, but the closer she looked the pieces seemed to be out of place, or missing, or stolen from an entirely different puzzle.

Anonymity would be of no use to her that night. If Jude saw her and knew he was being followed there would be no going back. She would have to stay hidden in the shadows of the night. She must simply watch and not be seen.

Leaving her bike behind, she wrapped her duffel coat around her and pulled the enormous hood over her hair. The brisk night and howling wind quickened her pace and she found herself reaching the foot of Park Street far sooner than she had anticipated. The steep climb was almost deserted, save for a few drunken thirty-something women who were tottering about in short skirts and high heels and looking thoroughly miserable. Ghurt Lush was half way up the hill and illuminated from within with fluorescent light which pooled out onto the street. Once again it was busy with teens and students cheerfully spooning frozen yoghurt among the retro surroundings. Jude was merrily taking money at the till, his tangled mane of blond hair tied back and tamed beneath a paper hat. He looked happy Rowan thought, and felt a twang of guilt. She felt sadness too. For all the plastic kitsch interior and intoxicated patrons, at least the people inside seemed to be having fun, laughing at nothing and flirtatiously sharing ice creams like 1950s sweethearts enjoying that long forgotten togetherness of being with friends, whilst she stood on the street in the howling wind, completely alone.

On Welsh Back, the waterside stretch of old converted factory buildings and cobbled streets, Franklin was feeling far from alone. Verity had moved into an innocuous looking block of beige stone with little blue Juliet balconies bolted to the sides all the way up. Her flat was on the third floor and on stepping out of the lift he was thrilled to see her standing in the lobby. She threw her arms open to greet him.

"Do you think I'm mad?" She whispered into his ear.

"Not at all. I think you're brave," he replied.

Alf greeted him with his customary one-armed hug and a kiss on the cheek. It was a signature move which reflected both the fondness and frostiness he reserved for his father. Verity beckoned them both inside to a snug little flat she had packed with whatever furniture would fit from her previous home. The lighting was soft with little candles in jars closing the space in, while strings of Christmas lights dangled down the walls.

"I'm going to sort the furniture out when I can," Verity explained. "Most of it will probably end up going into storage but other bits I couldn't bear to be without. It wasn't easy getting the sofa up here."

Franklin looked at the sofa. A worn and threadbare piece of furniture which he immediately envisioned himself seated upon, with Verity stretched out beside him her long legs across his lap. "I love it," he declared.

"I was going to get a tree," said Verity as she uncorked a bottle of red wine. "No idea where I'd put it though. Can I tempt you?"

"Just the one," he smiled. "I'm driving."

"I'm sure there'll be plenty more nights when we'll finish the bottle," said Verity with a wink.

An exasperated sigh came from Alf. "Will the pair of you teens stop being so stomach churning?"

"What are you talking about?" Verity looked shocked but was still smiling.

"We all know where this is going - we all know where it's gone before, otherwise I wouldn't be alive. You two are so infuriating sometimes."

"I don't know what you mean," said Franklin, offering a sly grin to Verity.

"Yes, your father and I are just good friends," Verity seemed to twinkle at him in response.

Alf laughed. "I'll leave you two in peace for the night, but honestly, we all know what's gonna happen. Why hold off the inevitable? Just get it together both of you! I'm off to see if Jude needs any help."

As he left Franklin noticed that Verity had flushed red. "Our son's not the most discreet of men," she said.

Franklin hid a smirk behind his glass of wine.

"You could always have another glass after that one if you want," Verity bit her lower lip.

"But then I'd have to stay the night. It's too cold to walk home." Franklin knew it was a bold move.

"Well then, Franklin," she raised an eyebrow coquettishly. "I suppose you will."

As Alf left the block of flats Rowan had no way of knowing that soon he would be making his way up Park Street towards her. She had waited and watched as the last of the customers ebbed away and Jude was left alone. After turning the sign on the door to Closed he removed his hat and went briskly about wiping the floor and cashing up the till. As the lights inside began to flicker out, Rowan retreated into the dark of a doorway, its shadows obscuring her from the twinkling Christmas lights which hung above Park Street. Her boyfriend locked up the building and pulled down the metal shutter. Weaving through the dark on the opposite side of the street, Rowan found herself ducking behind parked cars and bins as she stalked him. He pulled his phone from his pocket and made a call, suddenly seized by the terror that he would be calling her and that the ringtone would give her away, she grasped for her phone, only to realise that Jude was already talking to someone.

He crossed the road towards College Green and Rowan crouched behind an abandoned phone box until he was some way ahead of her. There was no way of approaching without being fully exposed but she was confident the darkness would be enough to mask her passage. Jude was strolling confidently towards the massive hotel that stood beside the cathedral. Where was he going?

Jogging silently across the grass, Rowan ducked behind the statue of Queen Victoria and saw Jude climb the steps to the hotel entrance, where he was met by a distinguished looking man with a balding head and greying beard. The man held a cane at his side and wore a mustard, tweed jacket. The two men embraced and Jude walked into the hotel behind him.

After the initial confusion Rowan whispered, "Damn," to herself. Jude may have been seeing a man on the side but it was not the man she'd expected him to be with, nor was it the *kind* of man she could imagine him with. The initial sense of closure she felt was replaced by a strange sense of disappointment. Things hadn't fallen into place as she had hoped and nothing had been conclusively proven, except that Jude had been lying to her. What was she to do with this information? Had she learned anything at all?

Shivering in the cold she stood up and turned, only to see the outline of a figure standing behind her.

"Rowan?" The man took a step closer so that the light of a streetlamp fell on his face. It was Alf. "What are you up to?"

"Oh, hi." Was all she could manage.

"What were you doing just then? It looked like you were hiding."

She tried to lose herself as she drew close to him. "I was just going for a walk and I sprained my ankle. These old streets, right?"

"Sure."

"I just needed a little sit down, that's all."

"Cold night for a walk," he said suspiciously.

"I find it bracing. Anyway, what are you doing?"

"I thought I'd see if Jude needed a hand. Is Ghurt Lush open?"

"I think he closed up early."

"Right. Well, I best get going then. Good to see you again Rowan."

Rowan just nodded at him. As he turned to approach the bus stop she felt a sudden and overwhelming urge to cover her tracks. "Please don't tell Jude I was out," she called after him. As soon as the words left her mouth she knew it was a mistake. Alf did not respond and simply walked away.

12.

Rowan lay awake in her bed contemplating what her next course of action should be. She'd spent the night alone in her flat beneath Jude's and felt no compulsion to visit him that morning despite hearing him pace across her ceiling. She'd at first told herself that she was upset, that Jude had betrayed her and that it was with another man - an older man, and that was the second slap to make the first sting harder. She wasn't upset, she was angry. Anger came to her whenever she thought of Jude and from an origin she couldn't define, he just made her angry and the fact that the rest of the world saw him as a lovable dreamer infuriated her even more.

She had received a text message from Franklin while she was still sleeping. *"I'll pick you up at 08.30, we have an appointment with Kay Casey."* Rowan looked at the time and hauled herself out of bed before skipping across her freezing flat to the shower. Within 15 minutes she was ready and Franklin was waiting in the street below in his Smart car.

After checking that Jude was not in the hallway, she tiptoed down the staircase, out the front door and into the passenger side of the car.

"Good morning," Franklin beamed.

"Is it?" she huffed. "It's bloody freezing, is what it is."

"Well, this might help cheer you up," he handed her a paper cup of coffee. Just the smell of it was enough to invigorate her somewhat.

"Thanks. It was just another weird night. I'm getting paranoid about Jude again."

Franklin started the engine. "You can't let yourself get caught in your head like that. Remember when you thought he had a secret room in his flat? It was driving you mad."

"Trust me, sometimes there's reason to be paranoid. I ended up spying on him last night. I followed him from Ghurt Lush and he met somebody at the hotel on College Green. *A man.*"

"Oh no. It wasn't Alf was it?"

"Alf would've made more sense. This was some old dude with grey hair and a cane who dressed like a rural Tory voter."

"That's not the first person I'd imagine Jude having a fling with."

Rowan took a swig of the still too hot coffee and winced as it burned on the way down. "That old man looked like the kind of guy with a wife and kids who lives in the countryside and comes into the city to hire rent boys where nobody will recognise him."

"I see you've been doing a spot of creative writing in your head. You don't know anything yet and I imagine you haven't spoken to Jude about it."

"I don't think I want to. Lately I haven't been able to be in the same room as him without wanting to punch him."

"Listen to yourself. This isn't a healthy relationship."

"No offence, Franklin but I don't think you're an expert when it comes to relationships."

"That is a *little* bit offensive, Rowan..." Franklin replied. "But seeing as you brought it up, I had quite an interesting night last night." He raised his eyebrows to Rowan.

"Franklin!" she gasped, suddenly and quite genuinely joyful. "Is your fancy lady back in town?"

"She's not just back, she lives here now and I think she might be my girlfriend."

"Girlfriend?" Rowan grinned. "So you're finally dating - twenty years after having a son together. You're doing this relationship thing backwards."

"I wasn't going to mention anything when you started talking about Jude but, I kind of had to tell someone and you're my..."

"...Stop it."

"Best friend."

Rowan wiped the windscreen in front of her where the coffee had steamed up the glass. "My relationship may be falling apart around me but that's no reason why I can't be happy for you. I really am pleased and Verity seems nice. Alf is still a little shit but you didn't raise him so your hands are clean."

"It's early days and I think she wants to keep it sort of undefined and take things slowly but the point is that she *lives* here now…"

"…Wait? Did you say she's moved to Bristol? When did this happen?"

"Yesterday. It was kind of on a whim."

"She moves house to a whole new city on a whim but wants to be cautious with a new relationship? The pair of you don't do things conventionally, do you?"

Franklin finished the last, gritty dregs of his now cold coffee. "We may have taken a strange route to get there but the destination was the same. I ended up staying the night with her."

"I don't need to hear that, Franklin… but good for you."

The little car was leaving the city boundary, speeding out into the countryside beyond, bouncing down winding country lanes and past wide open fields that had been brushed silver in the morning frost.

"Where exactly are we going?" Rowan asked, as she watched their progress on Franklin's phone.

"It's a little farm near the Welsh border, specialising in organic produce apparently."

"That's quite a leap from playing guitar in a blues band. Then again, a lot seems to have changed for Kevin Casey since then."

Franklin sighed. "I hope you're not going to say things like that when we meet her, are you?"

"I do have some decorum, Franklin."

"And I'd rather you didn't say things like that to me either, jokes like that make me feel very uncomfortable. Keep your opinions to yourself, or better yet, have different opinions."

"I know and I'm sorry. Yesterday after we got talking I went and did a little reading about it and I feel kind of clued up - or *woke* as you cool kids are saying."

Franklin laughed. "The point is that you should trust other people to know themselves better than you do. If someone tells you they're different in some way, it all just adds to the rich tapestry that is the human experience."

"Wow, thanks Oprah. Trust me, I'm learning this stuff. I've just never met a transgender person before and I've just a spot of trepidation, not judgement or disgust, about meeting her."

"At least you're keeping your pronouns in check."

"So how about Edison?" Rowan ventured.

"Do you mean how is he?"

"Sort of."

"He's back at his place and seems to have calmed down a bit. His drugs are strong and he seems to have responded by having a bit of a manic episode. According to him he's on more of an even keel but I hope it's not a precursor to him getting depressed. It's like a roller coaster with him."

"I bet, but I kind of meant... has Edison ever had a girlfriend?"

"Oh," Franklin glanced at Rowan knowingly. "I hear you. He's had girlfriends, nothing that's lasted, and he's never really struck me as someone who's felt wholly driven to find one. Sort of like only being with women because that's what you're supposed to do. Even when we were teens he was never eager - like me."

"So you think he's gay?"

"No, and don't let him catch you throwing around accusations like that. I sort of get the feeling that he might be... nothing."

"Nothing? Like asexual?"

"That's my conclusion anyway. I think he'd like to be with someone but he just doesn't have that animal drive."

"Right now that sounds like a blissful way to live," Rowan sighed. "No relationship drama, no longer being at the tyranny of hormones. In bed alone at half nine every night with a cup of cocoa and Netflix on the TV. Heaven."

Franklin shook his head. "It's more frustrating to live like that than you think, trust me."

"Only because you have a libido. It's like how dogs are happier after you've chopped their nuts off - they're free from their urges."

The word *libido* never sat well with Franklin, conjuring images of untamed animals hiding barely below the skin of even the most innocuous people, but it also triggered a memory of Edison on Monday night, claiming that such a beast had returned to him - and in overdrive. How well did he truly know his brother?

"You have now reached your destination," the electronic voice on Franklin's phone declared. Franklin parked his car on a muddy driveway which had frozen solid in the cold. Before them stood a crooked little farmhouse with an undulating roof of ancient tiles and tiny little sash windows that seemed to hang awkwardly in oversized frames. In summer the farm probably looked bountiful, with a stocked front garden and vines creeping up the cob walls but in this harshest of winters the garden was a barren strip of twigs and brown decay. Approaching the front door they spied a tastefully decorated tree through the window, decked in gold ornaments and holding an art deco star. Franklin rapped on the pane in the door before he saw the little note Kay had left them.

"Hi Franklin and Rowan. If I'm not in I'll be round the back in the turkey barn."

"Terrific," Rowan grumbled. "We're visiting turkey death row."

"She could just be talking about an empty barn…"

"Christmas is three days away, I think she'd be missing a trick if she wasn't farming turkeys in her turkey barn."

Franklin shrugged, "Well, we're neither of us vegetarian, it seems a bit hypocritical to shy away from how meat is actually farmed."

Franklin led the way around the building to where a huge half-cylinder barn of corrugated metal stood halfway across a small field. "Are you ready?" he asked Rowan.

"I'm ready," she replied.

13.

Bessie Banks' voice haunted the record player in the corner of Ruby Kaplan's bedroom. She had drawn the curtains and turned the lights on around her makeup mirror. She faced her reflection while Kevin Casey sat beside her. Rowan hovered behind them, wary of being a nuisance and getting herself thrown out.

"If my dad knew I had a strange man in my room he'd just about hit the ceiling," said Ruby.

"I'm definitely strange," Kevin replied. "It's the man part I'm not so sure of."

Ruby laughed and kissed her friend on the cheek, her tight curls tumbling over his face. "So what d'you want to know?"

"I just want to know what it's like, you know? Just for a night."

"What it's like being a girl?"

Kevin nodded, gingerly. "That's not too weird is it?"

"Not at all. Rowan, you don't think Kevin's weird do you?"

"No," Rowan replied at once, though she did think the situation was a little strange. An invitation to spend time with her sister was too enchanting a thing to ruin by asking what on earth was going on.

"I'll teach you the basics," said Ruby. "Then you can experiment with getting your look right. My makeup's for dark skin so it will look a bit harsh if I apply too much. I can write down some brands for you to look into afterwards if you want."

"Are you sure your parents won't be home any time soon?"

"They're down in Devon for the weekend. Don't worry, your secret's safe with me - and Rowan."

Rowan nodded at them in the mirror. "I think it's cool," she ventured, knowing at once how childish it made her sound.

"You have very fine features, almost feminine really. I'm going to make you look fabulous."

Kevin smiled shyly. "I'm still a bit nervous, but let's do it."

"I'll start with your eyes and build from there." Fishing through her makeup bag she retrieved a stick of mascara and began apply the wand with a feathery touch. "Close your eyes," she said when she was finished and began to blow gently across the boy's lashes.

"Can I look?"

"Go for it."

Kevin blinked at his reflection and daintily brushed a strand of hair from his forehead. "I can feel it happening already, it's like I'm changing."

"And I'm just getting started." Ruby began dusting smoky shadows around Kevin's eyes and delicately rouging peach into his cheeks. "So tell me more about this band you've joined, what were they called again?"

"We're called Morning Shiver. We're pretty good but we could use a little extra polish or something. Maybe you could watch us rehearse sometime and give us some tips. I heard people at college say you can sing."

"She's the best," Rowan interrupted, partly breaking the spell Ruby had been weaving between Kevin and her.

"Bessie is the best," Ruby pointed a long finger to the record player. "But I'm pretty close behind her."

"So is this why you want makeup? For your band? Like in the 80s?" The questions tumbled naively from Rowan.

"Kevin's also a magician," said Ruby.

Rowan nodded, as if this explained everything. "Can you show me a trick?"

"Sure," Kevin leaned in closer to her. "Give me your hand."

Rowan did as she was asked and offered him her hand, which he held in his own.

"Look into my eyes and think of a number between one and one hundred."

Rowan smiled as she gazed into the young man's eyes. His lashes were dark with mascara and he stared back at her unblinking. "Got it," she said. "Should I tell you?"

"Fifty-one," he declared.

Rowan dropped her hand from his, disappointed. "No."

"Thirty-seven?"

Rowan shook her head.

"Damn, oh well. At least I got your watch!" with a sly smile, Kevin presented Rowan her watch, which he'd miraculously taken from her wrist and palmed away out of sight.

She was astonished. "How did you do that?"

"I'll never tell, but I'm not your regular kind of magician. I'm more about sleight of hand and distractions."

"That was incredible!" she giggled. "So that's why you want the makeup, it's part of the act... like Chris Angel?"

"It's a bit more complicated than that," Kevin replied. His voice already sounded more confident and sultry as he swept an imaginary lock of hair over his shoulder. "I'm just experimenting with how I look and how I feel about how I look."

"Don't you like being a boy?"

"Rowan!" Ruby chastised, sharply. "That's a really rude question. Kevin's just working a few things through and I'm helping him out."

"I'm sorry," she replied instantly.

"It's OK, Ruby. She's allowed to ask questions. It's not that I don't like being a boy it's more like, it doesn't feel like who I am. Not completely anyway, not all the time. I've never felt like I am who I should be, in a way. I wish I could explain it better but..."

"...I understand it." Ruby uncapped a lipstick and began drawing across the boy's mouth, fashioning crimson lips upon his face before handing him a tissue to mop the excess makeup. "Don't look at yourself yet," she placed her hand over his eyes, sliding her plastic ruby ring down his nose to close his lids. "Tell me who you'd like to be. If you were a woman. Who do you feel like when you think of the woman inside you?"

Kevin did not think for long. "She's not beautiful, but she's pretty. She's smart, but in a way that isn't snooty - she's intuitive, that's what it is. She understands things. She can take care of herself and probably owns her own business... maybe something to do with nature. She plays music like me but probably not guitar, perhaps piano. I think she's called Kay."

Rowan watched, transfixed but a little frightened, as if the young man were becoming possessed by a woman who had been hiding away inside him for years, perhaps since birth.

Ruby brushed her hand away. "Well, would you like to see Kay for the first time?"

Kevin nodded and slowly swivelled the chair to face the mirror. He gasped at the woman he saw staring back at him. For all of Ruby's declarations that more-is-more with makeup, she had fashioned a soft refined lady of impeccable elegance. Kevin slowly formed a gentle smile and began turning his head, inspecting the stranger's face, but suddenly Rowan saw the corner's of his mouth began to twitch and his eyes flood with tears. "I need to take it off… It's too real."

Kevin collapsed into a fit of sobs and Ruby flung her arms about his shoulders. "Shhh, shh, sh, it's OK, it doesn't matter. It was just an experiment and it didn't feel right."

But Kevin was shaking his head as he choked on his words. "No, it doesn't feel wrong. It feels *right* and that's what's so scary. What am I Ruby?"

As Ruby reached for her makeup removal kit Rowan found the weight of the room unbearable and backed through the doorframe before darting to her bedroom, terrified of the world of grownups she had just witnessed.

14.

Kay approached them from across the barn, moving among a sea of fat clucking turkeys that waddled out of her path. She wore a long woollen overcoat and mud encrusted wellies. Her hair was long, dyed chestnut red and tied sensibly at the back, and though her face was almost without a trace of makeup, Rowan gasped at the strikingly beautiful woman who stood before her, familiar as the boy who had once been in a band with her sister, yet utterly female. This was no illusion of femininity or garish drag queen, Kay Casey, in her features, voice and gait, was a whole woman.

"Don't look so scared," she said to Rowan. "I'm not going to start chopping heads off. These guys have got one more day left."

Rowan looked guiltily over the barn full of condemned birds, uncomfortable with even the mention of their fate.

"Do you slaughter them yourself?" Franklin asked, bluntly.

"Oh god no. I couldn't bear it. We have a man who comes from the city to do that." Kay's attention was caught by Rowan's stare. "How did this happen?" The woman approached her and cupped Rowan's face in her hands.

"How did what happen?" she winced.

"Last time I saw you, you were a little girl, now look - you're a *woman!*" As if sensing the unspoken words hanging heavy over the barn Kay added, "It's magnificent, isn't it?"

"I guess it is," Rowan laughed and felt herself relax.

"Now, let's get out of the cold and get some hot tea inside us." As she led the way she spoke proudly of her farm. "There's over six hundred of them, all free range, but you couldn't tell on a cold day like today when they all huddle together for warmth. They're fed a completely organic, plant-based diet and are free of antibiotics. Come Friday they'll be feeding six hundred families across the Bristol region, feeding them *well* I should add."

"I don't think I could do it," Rowan commented. "No judgements though."

"It's certainly not for everyone, but I think of it like this. Those six hundred families will have Christmas turkey whether I farm them or not, so I'd much rather they all feast on turkeys which had the best possible lives before they met their end. Far better that they lived good lives than were imprisoned in near darkness and fed until they all but keel over beneath their own weight."

Rowan could not argue with that. Kay reached into her pocket and unlocked the door with a huge, ancient looking key and let them into her kitchen. On the stove something was gently bubbling away. It smelt hearty and healthy and permeated throughout the little cottage. The cosy living room sat beneath low timber beams where a three piece suite was built around a roaring fire and an upright piano stood against a bare stone wall. As Rowan took a seat in an armchair she felt the warmth of the blaze flush her cheeks. At once she fell in love with Kay's life.

Franklin sat beside Kay on the sofa. "Earlier you said *we* have a man who comes from the city," he began. "Does that mean you live with a partner."

"Wife, actually. Ruth and I got married last year."

"Congratulations," said Franklin.

"I know it can get a bit confusing to come into the life of someone like me, but trust me, we're far more ordinary than you might imagine."

"I've no doubt about that. First of all, may I say thank you for allowing us into your home. I know talking about your time with Morning Shiver must be very hard, but Rowan and I have been looking into everything again following... I trust you heard about Douglas Bennett?"

Kay nodded. "What an absolute tragedy. After we all went our separate ways I sort of fell out of touch with him but I heard from Lily that he had a rather terrible time with it all. He was one of those people that you never quite knew was very sensitive or very dumb - I know not to speak ill of the dead but I said the same when he was alive. He was quiet and probably a bit troubled even before that night." She turned to face Rowan. "I'm so sorry about what happened to Ruby. She was one of the rare ones, a gem, which made her name all the more fitting. I'm sorry that I just sort of vanished afterwards too. It was a blight on the whole city when they couldn't catch her killer, and once the investigation went cold I think I sort of ran away from it all. I was running away from a lot, as I'm sure you can imagine."

"I can," said Rowan. "And thank you."

"I owe her a lot. She was so kind to me when we were at college. She saw something in me that was difficult or vulnerable or *lost* and she took me under her wing. When somebody like Ruby sees something in you, you can't help but feel special, because otherwise why would she waste her time? Even if you felt worthless, she saw something of value in you and a little of her magic rubbed off. She started it all in motion, the process, and then one night she was gone."

"Talking of magic," said Rowan. "I remember you doing a trick for me, years ago."

"I got your watch right?" she smiled.

"You should've seen it, Franklin. It was amazing, do you still do it?"

Kay shook her head. "It's just party tricks now. Performing in general didn't sit well with me after what happened. I just let it slide and moved onto new things."

The kettle began whistling in the kitchen and a hurried step on the staircase dashed to silence it. Within minutes a handsome looking woman on the verge of forty appeared with a tray laden with cups, saucers and a steaming porcelain teapot beneath a woollen tea cosy.

"Ruth, I presume?" Franklin asked.

"I see my reputation precedes me," Ruth responded with a smile and squeezed Kay's shoulder warmly. "Are you going to be alright?"

"I'm fine," Kay reassured her. "It's probably good for me to talk about it after all these years."

Rowan watched Ruth leave the room, intrigued and touched by the couple's unconventional relationship. She leaned forward and helped herself to a cup of tea. "What d'you remember about that night?"

"Everything," Kay replied. "Absolutely everything. It's as clear as if it happened yesterday, I suppose that's what happens when you relive a moment over and over again in your head. Memories solidify, like concrete. I remember arriving just after seven. Ruby was already there with Doug and the bar was closed for redecoration, so it was just going to be the band there that night and a guy recording some of the performance for a promo clip on YouTube. We were going to be the first band to perform when it reopened, so we were allowed plenty of rehearsal time. Ruby had kind of pulled us all together and with her there everything went up a notch in quality, it was kind of like she was so good, she made me a better guitarist, she made us all better."

"What time did the cameraman get there? And Lily?" Asked Franklin.

"Lily was always late, it was kind of her thing. It was annoying but I suppose it made her feel important, she's much better nowadays. I could never have imagined her managing to hold down a regular job, or her own business but like I said, that night changed all of us. When I got there Doug was setting up the drum kit and Ruby was singing *Down Town* and it just kind of warmed the whole room, you know. The bar was kind of grungy and dark, one of those places that even after decoration it still smelled of spilt drinks and sweat but her voice transformed the space. It was like everything just melted away in the room and all that was left was her, on the stage, singing into your soul. I just stood there, mesmerised by it all. Lily showed up at about quarter past seven just as Ruby was finishing and the camera operator got there on time at eight. I think he was a wedding photographer by trade, sort of middle aged I guess. He was probably a bit over equipped for the kind of job he was doing but he made a good video. Have you seen it?" Kay asked Rowan.

"I have," Rowan answered. "It took me a while to get the courage to watch it, but I do it all the time now. It's quite comforting."

"I watch it too," Kay smiled. "So the rehearsal was going really well. Ruby, Doug and Lily had all had a few drinks. The bar was empty but they'd brought some cans of cider with them - I've never been much of a drinker myself. They weren't even close to drunk, but it doesn't take much for mistakes to start happening - never from Ruby, she was always flawless - but after a few drinks it's always the timing that goes out of whack. Doug was getting stressed with Lily, and Ruby was annoyed with both of them. I just sat it out at the edge of the stage. A bit later the three of them went outside for a smoke and when they came back in they'd sobered up enough for us to get a decent take for the camera."

"Can you remember the name of the man recording this?" Asked Rowan.

Kay shrugged. "Not a clue. He sort of kept to himself all evening. He must have filmed hours of us, but he instinctively knew that was the take to use as it's the one he sent to us after the funeral. We uploaded it as kind of a memorial to her. It was the only thing we could think to do."

"So there's more footage of the evening?" Franklin pressed.

"There must be. I'd imagine the police have it somewhere. I can't imagine it would reveal a great deal - unless of course, well, unless you suspect that someone in the band was responsible."

"We don't suspect anybody as yet," said Franklin, firmly. "We're just trying to piece together what might've happened on the night."

"Of course. So I think we wrapped things up at about eleven o'clock and the camera guy was the first to leave. We had a discussion about maybe going out or doing something afterwards but I don't think anybody was up for it. I left by myself, I think Doug gave Lily a lift home, she was living in that building complex near Millennium Square, but I was still with my parents in Westbury so I got a taxi from outside the bar. I remember the police showing me CCTV images of me leaving and some more of Lily and Doug leaving with his drum kit soon after. A friend of his had a van to help transport it. Ruby locked up a while after him. I don't know why it took her so long to leave but she left around midnight. The police showed me images of that too so I could confirm it really was her. And that was us for the night. That's all that happened and should've been the end of a decent enough night of rehearsals."

"And there was nothing else out of place that evening?" asked Ruby.

Kay thought for a moment. "There was one thing, the kind of thing you notice at the time but don't really take in until afterwards. Just as I was leaving, I noticed that on the stairs leading up from the bar, there was this... white powder scattered all over the steps."

"Cocaine?" said Franklin.

"No. It was more crystalline, like sugar. It's probably nothing but it was only recently that I started thinking about it and how odd it was."

"I see," Franklin scrawled a few notes on a pad he held on his lap.

"The police said they had me on camera from inside the taxi all the way home," Kay went on, unprompted. "The taxi driver confirmed everything too. My parents vouched for my whereabouts for the rest of the evening but obviously they aren't the greatest alibis."

"We honestly aren't suspecting anybody," Franklin reassured her. "As far as I can tell there's pretty good evidence putting the whole band far away from the crime scene when it happened."

"Except Ruby," Rowan added.

"Except Ruby," he echoed.

"I can't tell you how sorry I am, Rowan." Kay said. "In my head I go back over that night again and again looking for some clue or imagining that I could've changed something, but that's the thing about revisiting the past - you go there with all the knowledge you have from the present but all you can do is watch it, like a TV show, or a crime scene reenactment." Kay stared sadly into the fire before adding, "I hope you catch whoever did it - and I hope you make them pay."

"We will, trust me." Franklin stood up and gestured for Rowan to do the same. "Thank you very much for your time, I know you must be very busy at the moment."

"You have a beautiful home," Rowan added before the pair left.

They did not speak until Franklin had driven the car from the farm.

"How're you doing?" Franklin asked.

"Better than I should, to be honest."

"What did you make of Kay?"

"The bucolic life seems to suit her - and being a woman. What did you think?"

"It's the same with Lily, she was so open and seemed to be hiding nothing, or at least seemed not to be trying to hide anything."

Rowan nodded. "We've always said that it's usually the last person to see a victim, or the first to find a body who's usually the killer, so somebody in the band would make sense as she was with them all evening but they just seem so clean."

"It's been three and a half years, though. That's a long time to get your story straight - and we do know that Kay and Lily have stayed in touch. Of course, there is the fourth member of the band."

"I don't even want to think about that." Rowan said flatly. "For her killer to have got away with it, or bailed out because he was feeling guilty about what he did just doesn't bear thinking about."

"It is a possibility though, just not a good one."

"There aren't really any good outcomes though, are there? When you said we were going to catch the killer all I thought was, *what then*? All these years I've imagined what it would be like to see her murderer and have him brought to justice but I never thought about what it would be like afterwards."

"It'll get better, I'm sure."

Rowan simply shrugged. "Talking of which, d'you mind if I'm a little late tomorrow?"

"Of course not. Why?"

"I have a meeting with a certain psychopath in prison."

Franklin tutted and shook his head. "No good will come of this, Rowan."

"Maybe not, but I just need to do it."

The car sped on through the countryside until the Bristol skyline appeared on the horizon. Rowan began thinking about the strange white powder and what it could mean.

15.

Stepping through the kitchen door in her family home, Rowan was met by a scruffy, three-legged dog which bounded up to her and tore excitedly around in circles.

"Rodney! What are you doing here?" she exclaimed.

Her mother greeted her from the doorway. "Ro! You're early. No Jude again tonight?"

Jude had been absent from these weekly family meals for more than a month now and Rowan was worried that her parents might be beginning to suspect the truth about their dwindling relationship."

"He had to work. Late night Christmas shopping on Park Street," Rowan said. It was truthful enough but she omitted the fact that she'd not bothered to ask him. "What's Rodney doing here?"

"Gordon Hooper's here," Rolinda answered. The former Bristol City councillor for the Liberal Democrats, who had been inadvertently drawn into Rowan and Franklin's world earlier that year, had made fast friends with Rowan's parents after he joined a weekly alcoholics meeting and he and Rolinda were paired up as sponsors. They had both been four months sober.

"Evening, Rowan," Gordon Hooper called from the living room and on entering she was surprised to find the burly, balding man seated on the sofa beside her father, both with Playstation controllers in their hands.

Rowan kissed her father on the cheek but his eyes were fiercely focused on the TV in front of him. "What's going on here?"

"Your father's bought himself a new toy," Rolinda said, leaning against the doorframe and folding her arms. "It appears Gordon's quite the fan." A gesture of her mother's head led Rowan from the room and into the kitchen.

"Dad's playing video games?"

Rolinda opened a bag of potatoes and tumbled half a dozen onto a chopping board. "I'm thinking it's a mid-life crisis. I'm choosing not to worry about it." From the living room the two men burst into rapturous, rude laughter. It filled Rowan with a joy she hadn't experienced in her home for a long time.

"Whatever it is, it seems to be working. I can't remember the last time I heard Dad laugh like that." Rowan joined her mother and began peeling potatoes with her.

"It's a terrible thing to think but your father's misery these past years hasn't just been caused by Ruby's murder, I've been to blame, my alcoholism has made his life here almost unbearable."

Part of Rolinda's counselling programme included these disarmingly frank discussions. It wasn't long ago that Ruby's name was barely mentioned in the house and even then she would say *"since Ruby left"* or *"now that Ruby's gone."* Her rampant and destructive alcoholism was, if mentioned at all, simply her vice. She liked to drink, it helped her relax, it wasn't a problem. This, Rowan thought, had to be progress.

"How's it going with you? And how's Mr Hooper doing?"

Rolinda dropped the potatoes into a bowl of water. "Every day is a struggle, but every day is a bit less of a struggle, if you know what I mean. Gordon has been a god send, I don't think I would be able to do it without him. A few weeks ago we even went to a bar together."

"You went to a bar with another man?" Rowan chuckled. "What did Dad make of that?"

"Don't make it sound so sordid, Ro. It's an important step to take, for both of us. The whole world isn't going to stop drinking just because Gordon and I have, so we've got to get used to being around alcohol."

"How did it got?"

"I've had more enjoyable evenings but it wasn't as terrible as it would have been a few weeks ago. We went nice and early so it wasn't too busy and nobody was drunk. We both had a Diet Coke and went home. Afterwards I felt kind of triumphant. You wouldn't believe how good these little victories feel."

"I can imagine, though. Well done, Mum. I'm proud of you."

Rolinda smiled and began grating a carrot, the nub of which she dropped before Rodney who wolfed it down with barely a bite. "It seems Gordon has had quite an effect on you, too."

Rowan shook her head. "He had nothing to do with me becoming a Quaker, that happened to be kind of by accident. I'm glad it did though, I think it's helped me too."

"Everybody needs some kind of crutch after a murder in a family. Yours certainly seems healthier than mine."

Another roar of glee bounded from the living room. "So what's Dad's crutch?"

"Maybe he's found it," Rolinda offered.

Rowan had missed these chats. Growing up both she and Ruby had been close to their mother, confiding in her, joking with her. The woman responded with sage advice and the kindly understanding of what being a girl meant and the troubles the sisters would encounter. When the bomb had detonated in their house three and a half years ago, all of that had been blown to pieces. Buoyed by this renewed intimacy, Rowan ventured a question she had wanted answered for years.

"Dad was out for a long time that night. Dominoes at the social club only lasts a couple of hours. What did he do afterwards?"

Rolinda froze in place. "What's that got to do with anything?"

"Nothing, it's just that I was so young I think you held a lot of stuff back from me because you thought I couldn't handle it. I want to know all of it now."

"You *couldn't* handle it. None of us should have been made to handle that night but at least your father and I could save you from the worst details that would've been no use to you, except to fuel your nightmares." Rolinda turned to face her daughter. "Please tell me that you aren't rooting around in your sister's murder, no good will come of it, I promise you."

"No, of course I'm not. I just wanted to know what Dad had been up to. It's been so long and we never talk about it."

"Three and a half years. How has it been that long? It could've been yesterday," she said, distantly. "If you really do want to tear open old wounds, your father said that after he played dominoes - and there are *plenty* of people who witnessed him at the social club that night... he went for a drive."

"He went for a drive?"

"Don't take that tone, Rowan. Your father used to do it all the time. He hasn't for years though. It's so hard doing anything we did that night, it's like a curse was put on everything. The police thought it was suspicious that he could provide no alibi for a couple of hours but your dad's just like that. He likes time alone and he always has. He lived in a house with three women and he liked to escape, relished the quietness."

Rowan nodded slowly. None of this was truly news to her as she'd read it all in her father's statement to the police, but she needed to listen to her mother recount it, to hear if she could detect a note of doubt in her voice. "No wonder the police kept on taking him in for interviews."

"Well every time they did not a word of his story changed. They all but dissected his car looking for evidence, but found none, and his phone was recorded switching to different masts as he left the city. He was all the way over on Dundry Hill that evening. It was a clear night before the rain set in, and your father likes looking at the stars."

Rowan could not recall her father ever showing interest in the night sky before. "He was lucky that the police believed his story."

Rolinda held Rowan's gaze in an icy stare which bordered on ferocious. "Nothing lucky happened that night. It was the worst night of our lives - and the reason why the police believed his story is because it's the truth and there's nothing more to it than that. Ok?"

Rowan nodded sheepishly and her mother broke the stare. "Sorry, I know that. I really do, it's just that I want everything in place, to know what happened and it's so hard finding answers."

"It's no good digging through the rubbish of the past, you'll not find any good answers there."

The two men in the living room broke into a round of applause which descended into a fit of laughter. Rolinda slid her casserole into the oven and began gently rapping her long fingernails against the kitchen counter. Rowan followed her eyes to where they were fixed on an upturned and empty glass on a shelf above where once stood a wine rack.

Walking into the living room to join her father, Rowan slyly typed into her phone. "*I need to see you tonight. It's urgent.*" She sent the message to Franklin and waited for his response.

16.

With the promptness she had come to expect from her friend, Franklin was waiting in his Smart car outside the Kaplan's house at 10pm when Rowan bid her farewells and stepped out into the night.

"What's this about?" Franklin asked, urgently.

"Murder," Rowan replied.

"It's always about murder."

"It's just a hunch. Something my mum said earlier I wanted to check out. It's about Ruby."

"OK. Where're we going?"

Rowan tapped "*Dundry Hill*" into Franklin's SatNav. "We're retracing my dad's steps. It's where he went on the night. I want to know what he was doing there."

Franklin nodded, recalling her father's police statement. "I have to admit I've wondered the same thing. Provided that's where he was, of course."

"Well, it's all we have to go on at the moment."

Franklin started the engine and the car sped through the empty streets into the countryside south of Bristol. The city lights gave way to cats' eyes as they trundled up the steep incline which marked the northern edge of the Mendips.

"Did I disturb your evening?" Rowan asked.

"Not really. I was going to watch a film with Verity but it was my night to be on call at work so it was hardly going to be a crazy evening. How far have we got left to go?"

"About half a mile to the top of the hill. If he was really stargazing that's where you'd go, right? As high as you could?"

"It's certainly what I'd do." Franklin hit the brakes as a rabbit darted in front of the car and into a hedgerow. "I hate country lanes," he complained.

At the top of the hill a breathtaking panorama unveiled itself: beneath a blanket of twinkling stars the city of Bristol glowed warm and bright across the horizon and beyond, a seemingly endless tapestry of streetlamps and tower block lights and minuscule cars whizzing through the bafflingly complex system of roads. The black jugular running through the city marked the majestic curve of the river, with little tributaries turning off it like veins. It was breathtaking.

"The city at night," said Rowan.

"It's beautiful," Franklin added.

Turning from the road into a hedgerow lined lay-by, Franklin stopped the car and the pair sat in silence for a while staring up at the stars.

"Good grief," said Franklin. "It's a long time since I remember seeing a sky like that. The light pollution really does a number on us in the city."

Just then, the headlights of an approaching vehicle illuminated the interior of the car. The crunch of gravel indicated that the vehicle was drawing up behind them. Franklin turned on the hazard lights but the car simply pulled into the lay-by. A man stepped out from the driver's side and flicked on a torch which he shone brazenly into Franklin's car.

"What the hell's going on here?" asked Rowan.

"I think I've got an idea," Franklin replied. "Let me handle this."

"You're here for the party?" The man called out to them in a thick, Bristolian accent as he approached.

Franklin wound down his window. "Are we early?"

"A bit. Doesn't properly kick off until after the pubs shut most nights. My wife and I always like to get here early though. Don't wanna miss any of the action. Am I right?"

"Right," Franklin forced a nervous chuckle.

The man was now standing beside Franklin, shining the torchlight directly into Rowan's face. "I don't remember your faces, is this your first time doggin'?"

Rowan attempted to hide her shock. "Yes, first time."

"Well, you won't have much luck partying in that little Noddy car. Are you here for some fun or just to watch?"

"Ah. Well, we were wondering about that," said Franklin. "We've just heard stories about it and thought we'd give it a try but we're not sure what the... etiquette is."

"Didn't you read the guide online?" the strange man asked.

"I must've missed it. My... girlfriend and I just thought we'd try it on a whim more than anything."

82

"Nice," the man purred. "I like an adventurous girl. Don't get many young ones these days, especially not this... exotic looking."

Rowan forced a smile but felt it turn into a snarl as it spread across her face. "How long has this been going on here?"

The man's silhouette shrugged. "I've been coming here for at least five years. Most nights, truth be told. It's pretty addictive once you get into in. Just some good, clean, dirty fun!" The man laughed and lit a cigarette. As he puffed on it the orange glow revealed a face Rowan did not expect. He wasn't an ancient or hideous man, but a strikingly handsome one in his early forties.

"Do most people just watch?" Rowan asked.

"Depends on the night, really. When it's cold like this it's usually just me and the missus with everyone looking through the window. That's probably all it'll be tonight, but in summer we do a bit of car-hopping or take it right out onto the bonnet so everyone can get a good look."

"Nice," Rowan felt her stomach lurch.

"You're a game girl. Tell you what, why don't you join me and the wife in my car. The seats go right back and we'll put on a show for your old man here."

"That might be a bit much for us tonight," Franklin said quickly. "But if you and your wife want to get started then we'll join you in a bit to watch."

"I get it. *Voyeurs*. Works nice as we're both exhibitionists. No cameras though, it's against the rules, but you can take my torch if you want to see better."

"No need, we have our own." Franklin replied.

"Fair enough, I'll just go and get her warmed up for you." The man departed from the open window which Franklin immediately rolled up. He started the engine and with a screech of tyres the little car fled from the scene.

"Oh god," Rowan gasped. "I feel like I need a shower."

"It was a pretty grim encounter," Franklin agreed.

"Who'd want to do that? In December?"

A line of headlights passed the car in the opposite direction. "Quite a few, it would seem we just missed the start of the party."

83

"I thought I was gonna be sick when he said he was going to *warm her up*."

"Now, now. Don't be too judgmental. It may not be your thing and that guy was a complete lech but I'm sure it's harmless."

"Franklin, you're not trying to tell me that's your bag? Dogging?"

"No! I get self conscious just peeing next to other guys at the urinal, but I'm just saying that maybe some people enjoy a bit of voyeurism and it's not necessarily a bad thing."

"Just really pervy."

"Well, perverts are people too, sometimes completely normal seeming people with jobs and families." Franklin caught her eye in the beam of an approaching headlight.

Rowan tossed Franklin's words about in her head, as if testing their weight, fully aware that they were loaded somehow. "Wait a minute. You don't think my dad was… Franklin, don't put that idea in my head."

"Well, you were going to come to that conclusion eventually, weren't you? If you ask me it's a lot better than what he could've been up to."

Rowan shuddered. "There's just something completely gross about your parents even being sexual people, let alone… deviants."

"To be fair your mother doesn't seem to be involved. It's entirely plausible and it would explain a fair bit about what he was up to. If I'd been out dogging I'd probably omit that detail and say I was doing a spot of stargazing instead."

"I know, but still."

"How're you doing?"

Rowan mulled this question for a while. "You're right, you know. It is good news. After I've had a shower and washed the grossness away I'm sure I'll come to appreciate the fact that my dad's a pervert and not a murderer. Does it prove anything though? I'm sure even if I asked him directly he'd deny he was here for dogging - even if he really was. If he didn't tell the police he won't tell me."

"D'you think he'd tell me?"

84

"His daughter's boss he's never had a single conversation with? Yes, I'm sure he'll pour his heart out to you."

Franklin shook his head. The country lane fed into a road in the suburbs of the city, soon the lights in the distance had embraced them and they were back in their welcoming home of Bristol. "Never let it be said that worst things happen in the city. The countryside is full of sordid people, they just hide it better than we do."

Franklin pulled the car up outside Rowan's faceless block of flats and she offered him thanks and a sweet kiss on the cheek.

"Are you going to be alright?" He asked her.

"I think so. I'm just exhausted."

"I know. I was thinking about tomorrow and meeting that... bastard."

"He doesn't scare me, not one bit."

"If you need any help, just call and I'll be there."

Franklin drove off into the night and Rowan climbed the staircase to her flat. Taped to her door in Jude's precise boarding school handwriting was a note. *"I've missed you. Please can we talk. You seem like a stranger. I'm upstairs."*

Rowan tore the note from the door and scrunched it into a ball in her hand. Pushing through into her flat she spied a bottle of Jude's homemade cider on the table. She knew she should be annoyed that he had let himself in. The once shared space had been reclaimed as her private sanctuary in recent weeks and Jude had picked up on the unspoken notion that he was no longer welcome there without an invitation, but she did not feel annoyed. She felt touched.

She lifted the bottle. It was still cold from the fridge. The label upon it read *"Cider with Cinnamon (Special Christmas Blend for Rowan.)"* She unscrewed the top and gulped down a mouthful. It was delicious. She looked at the note she had screwed up in her hand and decided on the spot to visit her boyfriend.

Jude answered the door after her first knock. "Hey girl," he smiled. He was wearing his dressing gown over sweatpants and a t-shirt bearing the Ghurt Lush logo. "I thought I heard you come in. What kept you?"

Looking at the clock Rowan was alarmed to discover it was close to midnight. "Just another night at work. Late shift."

Jude nodded. "It's nice to see you again. I left Alf to shut up tonight, I wanted to get home and be with you."

"Well, that's nice."

"I know I've been kind of distant and distracted by work and I know I've been getting home late. There's a proper explanation, I promise you... Alf said he saw you last night... he said that you'd been following me."

Rowan thought of the doggers of Dundry Hill and her father, "I don't care what you've been up to. Not tonight anyway. I just want things to be normal, just for one night. It doesn't matter that you have secrets, I just want to sleep... with you."

Rowan stepped inside the flat and Jude smiled. As the pair kissed deeper and more truthfully than they had in months, the door swung shut behind her.

17.

Rowan's mediator was a handsome young man with round, wire rimmed spectacles and a fashionably tidy side parting. She warmed to him at once.

"Ms Kaplan?" He asked as he appeared at 9am exactly from a door within the gargantuan steel gate in the prison wall.

She had only spoken to this man on the phone and had imagined him haughty and middle-aged with thinning hair. She told herself not to flirt, this was a serious matter.

"Come on in. Don't worry, this is a secure unit and all the residents are far away and behind many locked doors."

"Residents?"

A smile crept upon the man's face. "It's the latest strategy to make the prisoners feel engaged with their new way of life."

"Is it working?"

"About as well as you'd imagine it would." He held out his hand, "Excuse my manners. I'm Gavin Bradbury, we've been talking for a while."

"Of course, I recognise the voice."

"It's nice to meet you in person," Gavin smiled and appeared to blush slightly. Something was happening here.

Rowan squeezed past him and entered a breeze-block lined and joyless corridor that stretched out for an eternity before her. There was not a hint of decoration or frivolity, just the cold, austere functionality of a grey walkway with characterless doors on either side which were marked by numbers.

"It's not the most welcoming place, and this is just the office block. You should see what the actual prison looks like."

"Will I be going into the prison at any time?"

"Oh no, don't worry about that, I'm not authorised to go in myself. I'm a counsellor, helping people who've been through traumatic experiences, so I'm more experienced with the victims than the perpetrators."

"So has this strategy yielded good results?" Rowan asked.

"It's been a mixed bag. To be honest we haven't studied the inmates' reactions to it as yet but the programme was always going to be primarily about how the victims react to meeting their assailants and… like I said, it's a mixed bag, definitely room for improvement."

Gavin consulted a sheet on his clipboard as Rowan walked alongside him, eventually locating one of the anonymous doors and opening it. Inside the bare and gloomy room held only a single table with a pair of chairs and a water cooler in the corner. A lightbulb dangled from a chord above them and on an opposite wall was a large mirror.

"Two way glas?" asked Rowan. "I've never seen it before in real life."

"Very smart of you to notice."

"I didn't think it would serve much purpose otherwise."

Gavin flicked a switch on the wall and the light in the room immediately went out. In front of her the mirror miraculously became a window, revealing a room on the opposite side almost identical to the one in which she was standing, only this one featured two policemen flanking the table and chairs. Gavin flicked the switch again and returned their room to light.

"Now the first part of this session doesn't require you being in the same room as Mr Maybridge. In fact, it's just a test, to see if you feel able to meet him face to face. Some people have had such a primal reaction to seeing their attacker for the first time since the crime they've not been able to go through with it, so this is our solution."

Rowan nodded. "Honestly though, I'll be fine."

Gavin reversed the lighting between the rooms and pressed a button on the table before he spoke into the air before him. "Officer Collins, could you come forward please?"

One of the policemen stepped towards the window pane and held a hand mirror out to the glass. Within it Rowan saw the man in a tunnel of reflections.

"As you can see, the glass on that side is a mirror. When Martin Maybridge comes into the room he will not be able to see you but you can observe him, for as long as you choose. There's no time constraint and you're under no pressure to go ahead with this if you have even the slightest reservation about your safety. When you meet Martin he'll be handcuffed by one wrist to his chair but will have a free hand. The police officers you see here are both armed with tasers. They're here to protect you from Martin but also to protect him from you - they *can* restrain you if you react violently towards the prisoner, but under no circumstances will they use the tasers on you. That is a guarantee."

Rowan had been feeling surprisingly nonchalant about this encounter but the slow buildup and the gravity of the situation was starting to make her feel anxious. "Thank you. I understand it all."

"Good." Gavin pressed the microphone button. "Thank you Officer Collins. Can you now return to your position."

The policeman gave a smile and a wry salute into the mirror before turning away and strolling to the wall opposite the other officer.

Next Gavin held out what looked to Rowan like a TV remote control which bore only a single, green button. "When you're ready, just push the button and it will alert the prison guards that the resident is ready to be…"

Rowan pressed the button. Immediately the sound of a heavy bolt shifting echoed through the room on the other side of the glass. A metal door opened and Martin Maybridge appeared, held by the shoulder by two bald and stocky prison guards. Perhaps it was the effect of these two giants but Martin looked shorter and certainly thinner. Mostly she had known him as Art, the sleazy neighbour of a murdered woman who had disguised himself with long, plaited hair and a sinister outsized moustache. Her memory had expelled the true man, Martin Maybridge, the psychopathic police constable who'd committed three murders in order to conceal a terrible crime he had committed against his wife.

Rowan shuddered and felt herself drawing back from the glass.

"It's ok, he can't see you," Gavin reassured her.

"I know that, it's just… I didn't expect it to feel this *real*."

"Just take your time."

"I *want* to speak to him."

"You have as long as you want."

"I want to speak to him *right now*."

Gavin needed no further prompting. "Alright guys, we have confirmation here. Please restrain the resident."

With the pliability of a man used to more than a year of being led, shoved and handcuffed by prison guards Martin Maybridge showed no sign of resistance as the two burly men seated him at the table before securing his wrist in place. A sound of an electronic buzz preceded the clunk of a lock being released on the door which separated the two rooms. As Rowan stiffened and drew taller in the darkness, she couldn't help but revel at the sight of Martin shifting nervously in his chair.

"I'm right behind you," Gavin said warmly.

Rowan turned the cold, steel handle and the door swung open. She blinked into the light of the room beyond where her would-be murderer seemed to tremble at her gaze.

"I'm sorry, Rowan!" he blurted. "I never meant for it to happen, it just spiralled out of control and I went too far. I was being blackmailed!"

Rowan refused to turn from the man as she slid into the chair across from him. "I'm not here for excuses," she began. "I want some answers."

Martin gave an obliging nod and seemed to sigh with relief when he heard Rowan's measured tone. "Anything I can do to help. I want answers for my behaviour as much as you do. I've been working with a therapist who believes I had an undiagnosed personality disorder, probably narcissism as well as an acute need for control that…"

Rowan did not meet his gaze, instead her eyes fell on his prisoner ID number. "Did you agree to this meeting in the hope that it might help reduce your sentence?" asked Rowan. She felt Gavin turn to face her in the seat beside her.

"No…no. Of course not. My actions were entirely altruistic, I can assure you."

"The local paper said you got engaged. Is that true?"

Martin slid his free, left hand below the table before thinking better of it and returning it in place. "Yes, it's true. But we can't marry while I'm in high security."

"Fascinating," she said.

"At this point I think it's wise to discuss only the impact the crime has had on both parties." Gavin attempted to steer the conversation to the pre-agreed topics.

"Please, I want to hear about the blushing bride. What a lucky woman."

Her facetious tone did not go unnoticed by Martin. "You wanted answers. We've been engaged for over a month and before that she was writing to me as part of a letter exchange programme. It's quite common, isn't it?" He asked Gavin.

"I'm not allowed to answer questions on your behalf," Gavin replied.

"I suppose she gave you that, instead of a wedding ring?" Rowan nodded at the loose bracelet made of red and green rubber bands around the man's wrist.

"It's a loom band," said Martin. "They won't let you wear an engagement ring unless you were engaged before prison. It's made out of elastic bands so I can't hang myself with it."

"Or strangle anyone else, of course."

Martin's eyes fixed on hers and Rowan saw the barely concealed menace within them. "I've been a model resident in the prison and have been detained at Her Majesty's pleasure without incident."

Rowan leaned forward, holding Martin's stare to let him know that she was not afraid of him. One of the police officers inched nervously closer to her. "Well, I wish you both the best of luck. I assume she knows what happened to your former wife."

"That wasn't me. I mean... that wasn't the man I am today, I've changed."

"Anyway, I'm not here to discuss the details of your love life. But I do have a question about your ex-wife."

"Oh?" Martin seemed to grit his jaws against each other.

"Please stick to the agreed topics," Gavin whispered into her ear.

"I would like to know how murder changes a man. You began your killing spree by murdering two people in a single night, but I'm sure even if it'd just been the one, somebody would've noticed some change in your behaviour. Those murders had to have stayed with you."

"They haunt me every day. Donna, Hendricks, Ben."

"Henrik," Rowan corrected him.

"Yes, Henrik. That's what I said."

"But at the time, did anyone suspect you? You must have had friends. You had a wife. Maybe even co-workers noticed some change in you."

"You'd have to ask them."

"I asked Edison Gallow. He worked alongside you throughout the investigation and didn't notice anything."

"Then ask somebody else."

"Do *you* think it changed you?"

"I was very good at lying."

"It sounds like you still are. How did it change you?"

"I don't know. I couldn't sleep."

"You were very active and conniving for a man who wasn't sleeping. D'you think it's possible that a man could commit murder and live the rest of his life as if nothing had happened."

Gavin touched her shoulder gently. "I'm sorry but I'm going to have to ask Mr Maybridge if he wants to continue with this interview."

Martin smiled with the corners of his mouth and offered her the same nauseating wink he had on the doorstep of Donna's house eighteen months ago. "I'm willing to go on."

"Me too," said Rowan.

"If you really want an answer, Miss Kaplan, then yes, I do believe it's possible for a man to be a murderer and for him not to arouse even a trace of suspicion from those nearest to him. Over the course of those weeks I was no different to how I'd been throughout my life, these were simply deeds that had to be done in order to ensure my ongoing freedom. I knew, of course, that what I was doing was wrong but there was a higher goal to achieve."

"And if you hadn't been caught, you would've lived the rest of your life with nobody being any the wiser that you'd killed... what was the final goal meant to be - four people? I was the one who got in the way."

"It would've been four and yes, I probably would never've been remorseful for my actions. The human mind is incredibly good at self justification."

"I feel it's very important to stick to the facts," Gavin interrupted again. "Let's move onto the kidnap."

"Yes, let's." Rowan leaned in even closer, until the man's rancid breath was close enough to be felt on her face. "D'you know you would never have been able to kill me. If the police hadn't shown up I would've kept pummelling you with that car door until you died. You made a mistake coming after me - and I'm the reason why you're here and your desperate fiancée will never get to marry you."

Martin's face froze like a startled mask. Rowan watched as his contorted features began to twitch before suddenly he exploded. With a roar he threw himself to his feet, swinging the weighted chair from beneath him with the handcuff. "Oh you fucking *bitch!* You think you're so clever, I would've smashed that grin clean off your filthy black face!"

The two prison guards were on him in a second. One had twisted his free arm behind his shoulder while the other restrained him across the chest.

"I'm not finished with you!" he screamed as the guards hauled him backwards through the door. "As soon as I get out of here I'm gonna cut your fucking head off!"

The metal door swung shut as Martin was wrestled away. Beyond it she could hear his muffled, animal screams of rage. She turned to face Gavin. "Sorry about that."

"Are you alright?"

Rowan shrugged. "It wasn't the most enjoyable meeting of my life, but I might've put pay to any future parole hearings."

Gavin crossed his arms and shook his head. "You shouldn't have antagonised him like that. It'll put this whole mediation idea in jeopardy. Was this the only reason you wanted to meet Martin?"

Rowan shook her head. "I wasn't lying. I really want to know how a man can be a killer and yet nobody close to him had a clue. No one suspected a thing."

"I read his case file. *You* suspected him. You're a very smart woman."

"Gavin. Are you flirting with me after a man just threatened to kill me?"

"If you think that's an incredibly unprofessional thing that you should report me for, then of course not."

Rowan smiled. "I think I was just a touch unprofessional too."

Gavin anxiously tapped his palms on the table before asking, "This could get me fired, but to do be honest, this whole thing should be scrapped. At least, how they're trialling it now. But… are you seeing anyone?"

"No, I'm not." The words came so easily from her mouth that Rowan was shocked by herself.

"Would you feel like maybe getting a pint sometime?"

"Sure."

Gavin wrote his number on the edge of a sheet of paper on his clipboard before tearing it off and handing it to her.

As she left the police station Rowan was unsurprised to see Franklin waiting outside, leaning against his car. "You didn't think I'd let you go through this by yourself, did you?"

"Get in the car," she said. "We've got a lot to discuss."

18.

"What were you thinking?" Franklin chastised Rowan as the car pulled out of its parking spot. "I know he was handcuffed to a chair but he could still hurt you."

"I'm not scared of him."

"Well, you should be. That man killed three people and doesn't seem to have got all of that murderous rage out of his system."

" Can you believe he's engaged?"

Franklin nodded. "Sadly, I can. There're a lot of weird women out there, you should've read some of the messages I got when I was on that dating website - freaks who think I represent something dark to liven up their humdrum lives."

"This is a step beyond goths finding a funeral director sexy."

"Trust me, it's the same kind of woman - someone who thinks *bad boys* are sexy. What does bad boy even mean other than a criminal?"

Rowan briefly scrolled through her inconsequential relationship history. If she could draw any conclusion from the handful of men she'd shared any kind of romantic dalliance with the conclusion was that she was into nice but stupid boys.

"What did you think would come out of this meeting?" Franklin asked.

"Something, anything really… a clue?"

"To what?"

"It's the same reason I listen to *The Murder Club* podcast. You can't have experienced murder in your own family without at least wondering what kind of person could do something like that. I'm starting to think that there isn't an answer, at least, not any single answer. Maybe there isn't really a *type* of person who kills - maybe we all have the capability buried inside, it's just closer to the surface in some."

"Not me," Franklin huffed.

"I've seen you when you're enraged, Franklin. I didn't think that was in you either. I guess my point is that... I wanted to know what happens to someone afterwards. Can you just go back to an ordinary life again as if nothing happened, or is it like damage to the soul?"

"You'd have to ask a murderer that question. Oh, wait, I see what you're thinking now."

"Exactly. To catch a killer you have to think like a killer. The brutal murder of a teenage girl has got to have some lasting impact on the murderer, unless they're a total psychopath."

"That *is* a distinct possibility," Franklin cautioned. "It's hard to find reason why anyone would hate a young woman enough to kill her - there's no motive strong enough to make sense. Ruby didn't sound like the kind of person to have enemies, maybe grudges but that's about it. Maybe it really was just some random stranger and Ruby was one of those impossibly unlucky victims."

"I know," Rowan nodded.

"So are you going to see Maybridge again?"

"Not very likely. Gavin said he doesn't think the rehabilitation programme is going to be around for much longer anyway."

"Gavin?"

"The mediation worker. He gave me his mobile number before I left." Rowan ventured.

"So you can set up another meeting?"

"No. For personal reasons."

"Rowan Kaplan!" Franklin gasped. "Nope, I'm not going to be judgmental, but I am a bit surprised."

"It's a mess, I know, but things are winding up with Jude anyway... there's no harm in a little overlap with relationship timelines, is there?"

Franklin didn't answer and simply turned up the radio as he steered through morning traffic on route to Gallow & Sons. On pulling into the drive Rowan noticed the hearse had been moved from the garage and that a casket within was being laden with flowers by the day labourers.

"Barbara Fulton," she said. "I forgot."

"It's just a quick toast and roast, we'll be out of there in no time," Franklin reminded her.

Barbara Fulton had been a sixty-something former primary school teacher until an undiagnosed blood clot in her brain had caused an instantaneous end to her retirement years. Rowan had been charged with organising most of the service but had found it occupying less of her time as the ghost of Ruby and her unsolved murder ate away at more and more of her waking thoughts.

"I can't believe I almost forgot it was today."

"It's understandable that you'd be distracted."

Rowan shook her head. "Not good enough, Kaplan. Get your head in the game."

"You got everything sorted in time - and it looks beautiful," Franklin offered, charitably. "Let's do her proud."

After changing into her service-uniform of black blazer over a cream blouse and a dark pair of trousers, Rowan met Franklin in the hearse and the procession led from Gallow & Sons to the home of Zach Fulton, the only child of the deceased, who, along with his wife and two teenage daughters, bowed their heads from the street outside their terraced house in Southville as the foreboding vehicle drew closer.

"Shall I be on duty?" Rowan asked Franklin. "I think they know me better."

"Go for it. Good luck."

Rowan stepped out of the vehicle and offered a sympathetic smile to Zach, a pleasant, though distraught looking man in his early forties whose only suit jacket could no longer fasten across his belly.

"Good morning, Zach." The pair shook hands and Rowan kept hold of his as she spoke. "We're going to be leading the way with Mum, ok? You can follow directly behind us, or if you'd rather we can slip one of our drivers behind the hearse. Some people find it easier not to look at the casket on the journey."

Zach nodded. "I think I'd prefer that. Thank you."

"We have plenty of time to spare, so there's no rush. Whenever you're ready."

"I think I'd just like to get on with it now if we could," he turned to his wife who gave him a loving squeeze on the shoulder. "Yes. I'm ready."

Rowan was about to return to the hearse when Zach spoke again.

"Thank you, Rowan. You've put so much thought and care into this day and... I just wanted you to know how much we appreciate everything you've done."

"That means a lot," Rowan gulped before returning to the hearse. "My heart feels like it's full of concrete," she told Franklin.

"What's up? Aside from the fact we're going to a funeral."

"It's the worst day of that man's life and I almost forgot all about him and his mum, and he thinks I've done everything right."

"You have. He doesn't need to know that you got a bit distracted - he certainly doesn't need to know why."

In the rearview mirror Franklin and Rowan watched as a trail of mourners left the Victorian house and bundled into cars. She sent a text message to one of the day labourers, telling him to immediately follow the hearse before the procession was on the move, retracing the familiar passage to the hilltop crematorium that almost felt like home.

The numbers in attendance were expected to be slender so Zach had asked in advance if Rowan and Franklin could help fill out the seats for the service, so the pair did their best to mingle with the assembled crowd outside the massive oak doors of the crematorium, before the cold and huddled mass parted to allow the casket to be carried by six of the labourers and the huge doors swung inwards to the opening refrain of "I Got You Babe" by Sonny & Cher.

"That's a new one," Franklin whispered into Rowan's ear as they began filing behind the coffin.

"It was her and her husband's song," Rowan replied, her voice on edge of cracking upon suddenly realising the significance of the music in that moment.

Franklin and Rowan found seats at the end of a pew and were met with the familiar, yet always breathtaking, vista of the cityscape through the Avon Gorge, framed in the enormous window which took up the entire rear wall of the crematorium.

The music faded away and was followed by a single prayer. The mourners were silent until Zach got to his feet to deliver his eulogy and one of his daughters released a single, desperate sob for him. The man, no older than Franklin, stood trembling before the audience.

"I was going to talk to you today about my mum," Zach began, his voice quivering under the weight of the moment. "But all of you knew Barbara, and my dad too - and loved them, so what more could I add to that? You all have your own memories of her and I can't wait to hear some of them later tonight - and have a drink!"

There was a ripple of kindly laughter across the crematorium. Somewhat emboldened, Zach straightened his back and went on. "I wanted to share with you a memory - it's a happy memory, but it's also a regret that I'll have to bear for the rest of my life. We were always very close - the three of us, me, Mum and Dad growing up. For as long as I can remember, Friday night was always special. It was cinema night. The three of us would go out without fail to watch... any kind of nonsense that was opening that weekend and we'd sit in the dark cinema and laugh, or cry or be scared and afterwards we'd go out to McDonalds and talk about what we'd seen, and it was precious. I knew at the time how precious it was. Then one day when I was about fourteen, I went to school and this kid... this horrid little kid called Josh Roache and his horrid little friends started laughing at me, and telling everyone I still went to the cinema with my parents. Someone must've seen me there, and I didn't know this at the time, but when you're fourteen you're supposed to hate your parents and hate spending time with them, and I was so embarrassed because I didn't know the rules. That afternoon I went home and told my mum and dad that I was too old for cinema night and that boys my age don't spend time with their parents. They just nodded and said it was fine, but I knew it wasn't. I knew I'd hurt them - and the really stupid thing was that I really enjoyed cinema night and spending time with them. So instead ,we all stayed in on Friday, like any other night, and I never went to see another film with them again. That afternoon was almost thirty years ago now, and I haven't seen Josh Roache or any of his horrid little friends in almost as long, I imagine they've all grown into equally horrid adults. I don't care what he's up to now, or what he thinks about me, but I would give absolutely *anything* to have just one more night at the cinema with my mum and dad."

A shiver of hushed weeping spread across the mourners. Franklin took Rowan's hand and squeezed it tight as tears rolled down their cheeks.

Zach Fulton turned to his mother's casket and said, "I love you Mum, and I'm sorry. Please tell Dad I miss him."

In lieu of applause, the audience responded with a joint exhalation of breath, deflating the tension in the room until only sobs remained. After the service, as the mourners filed past the casket and out the exit, Franklin and Rowan ghosted themselves away into the hearse.

"Bloody hell," Franklin mopped his eyes on a tissue. "Twenty years of services and you think you've seen everything and then something new comes along to break your heart."

"Not a dry eye in the house," Rowan added. "That poor guy - and his poor parents."

The pair sat in contemplative silence for some time before Franklin asked Rowan, "What are you thinking about?"

"Regrets," she answered.

19.

"Can you keep a secret?" Once she was certain her mother wouldn't be returning, Ruby topped up Rowan's glass of red wine. "Not a word," she said with a smile.

At the age of sixteen Rowan had never really liked alcohol, least of all wine, but there was something irresistible about those nights where she was invited to sit and chat with her glamorous older sister as she prepared for a night out that Rowan found impossible to refuse.

"You know I can keep a secret."

"Turn up Bessie for me," Ruby requested. "I can barely hear her."

Rowan aimed the remote control at Ruby's iPod dock and Bessie Banks' dark, mysterious voice drifted through the room.

"I love this one. *Try to leave me if you can.* Listen to that *voice,* it's like something from another world."

Rowan's phone pinged with the arrival of a text message. It was her friend Lucy.

"Anything important?" Ruby asked, as she gazed at her reflection in the mirror.

"Just Lucy. There's a kind of party over at hers tonight and she asked me if I was going."

"Is Lucy that chubby blonde girl with the lisp?"

"She's not that big anymore. She lost a lot of weight."

"She looks like someone put a blonde wig on the moon," Ruby replied.

Rowan spat wine into a crimson mist, laughing at the sheer cruelty of the comment. "I don't think I'm going. I don't really know anyone there."

"All the more reason to go - you can dazzle strangers for the first time. I love that feeling of being in a crowded room, knowing that all eyes are on me, it's like... a power rush."

This was no exaggeration on Ruby's part. Whenever she entered a room it was as if she was accompanied by the sound of a gasp. Her beauty, her body, her composure, suddenly everyone else handed over to her a little of what made them special and she grew more radiant in their transfixed gaze. Rowan had never been that kind of girl but had often wondered what it must feel like.

"We're making a promo tonight," Ruby said, "at the bar, there's a videographer coming round and he's going to film me doing *Down Town.*"

"Film you?"

"Film us, you know what I mean. It's one thing trying to get attention on YouTube by singing in front of a webcam but this guy's a professional. This could be the thing that breaks us into the big time. All it takes is for the right person to see it and it can happen overnight. It's *going* to happen, I always said it would."

"I'm sure it will. You just need people to hear your voice. Is that your secret? That you're making a video?"

Ruby twirled in her chair to face her sister, the hem of her red dress billowed about her thighs. "If I tell you, promise not to tell Mum or Dad. Especially Dad."

"What have you done now?"

"Promise me?" Ruby leaned forward, holding out her little finger, with its dagger-blade scarlet nail.

Rowan hooked her own finger around hers. "Promise." Both girls let their hands drop, the secret was now sealed.

"I'm not going to University," said Ruby.

Rowan laughed. Her sister had spoken of little else since she had been offered a conditional acceptance at UCL. "Seriously. What is it?"

"A girl's allowed to change her mind. I mean, look at me. I'm not exactly the academic type; oversized glasses and hand-me-down chic. I'm a rock chick, I'm a soul diva. That kind of place stifles creativity. I want to stay here until my big break comes."

"You don't know that's going to happen though. Nobody can guarantee it."

"Morning Shiver's going places. I've never felt so sure of anything before in my life. If I blew my one chance because I was too busy reading about art history, I think I'd rather be dead."

Rowan rolled her eyes at her sister. "Don't throw your future away on a whim. There's time to do it all. At least have a backup - a degree's useful."

"It's expensive and I don't even a want a job that has anything to do with the history of art. University will shave off all my sharp corners and before you know it the system will've pummelled me down into one of those beige squares on University Challenge pretending to laugh at Jeremy Paxman's jokes."

"At least talk to Mum and Dad first."

"I thought you believed in me Ro, why are you being like this?"

The brief silence in the room was punctuated by the sorrowful voice from the iPod. "D'you know what happened to Bessie Banks?"

Ruby spun away from Rowan on her chair. Her face in the mirror was sour and hurt. "I don't care."

"Bessie Banks was all set to be the next big thing. She recorded *Go Now* with her ex-husband as they knew it would be the song that would make her, and it was big for a few months, all across America. Everything was lined up for her to be as big as Aretha or Diana Ross and then the Moody Blues released a cover of *Go Now* and everyone forgot that song was ever hers, because the States were all about the British Invasion in the mid 60s. Everything was in place but it all fell apart at the last hurdle because of something nobody could've predicted. You're amazing, Ruby, but talent has never been enough in the music business. All Bessie Banks sings now is gospel in her local church."

Rowan watched her sister's lower jaw tremble and then a tear fall from her eye. "You're such a jealous little bitch," she hissed through the mirror. "Just because you have nothing going on in your life you want to tear mine down. We're supposed to be sisters, not rivals."

"I'm sorry, Ruby."

Ruby stood up and flounced out the room in a wild flurry of red ribbons. She stomped off down the stairs and slammed the door behind her.

Rowan picked up her phone and was about to text *"I'm sorry"* to her sister but instead answered Lucy Welch's message with *"I'll be there later."*

She would never see Ruby again.

103

20.

For many years the German Christmas Market had become a fixture of Broadmead in December. It had expanded in size to incorporate almost all the shopping district and when it could swell no further, spilled out into late November instead. Franklin and Verity strolled arm in arm past the little wooden chalets selling overpriced baubles and undercooked meats, catching snippets of yuletide songs on the air from a choir assembled in the centre of the thoroughfare as wafts of roasting chestnuts and cinnamon spiced wine caught on the air.

In the middle of the sixties built open air shopping district stood an enormous tree sheathed in bands of orbiting lights. Beneath it were a couple of dozen members of the Bristol Gay Men's Chorus, ostentatiously dressed in garish Christmas jumpers, singing "Silent Night." Franklin and Verity paused to listen.

"When did we hand Christmas over to the Germans?" Verity pondered aloud.

"Sorry?"

Verity was wrapped in scarves which hung loosely over her vintage, knee-length plaid coat. The cold night had flushed her pale cheeks pink. Franklin could not help but gaze longingly at her, still not entirely certain how this extraordinary turns of event had led her to be on his arm.

"It wasn't long ago that Christmas was all about Tiny Tim and Scrooge, figgy puddings and wassailing. It's like we got bored of that and went all Teutonic. I kind of miss British Christmas."

"From the experience of my family I can assure you that the British tradition of getting drunk before the Queen's Speech and having an almighty row is alive and well."

"Sounds fun," Verity smiled. "In my house we always had countless other people around who I'd never met before. We all had to dress very sensibly and my sister and I weren't even allowed to play with our toys until the last guest had left. We weren't even allowed to watch TV."

"Some years we didn't even get out of our pyjamas," Franklin added.

"Posh Christmas isn't like that at all. Having any fun is seen as a bit low class so everyone has to stand around talking about finance and the weather with a single glass of sherry that's meant to last all afternoon."

"I hope you're not trying to make me feel sorry for you for coming from a wealthy family are you?"

Verity laughed. "I know, but trust me, you do miss out on things sometimes. I remember Christmas Eve and seeing the people out my window coming back from the pub or mass, blind drunk and singing in the streets and my father threatening to call the police. He didn't even like it when carol singers sang modern music - he only wanted traditional hymns and would slam the door if even a note of "Jingle Bells" was heard."

Franklin checked his watched. They had reservations at a swanky Middle-Eastern restaurant called Dalida at 8 o'clock. The pair slid through the crowds to the edge of Broadmead where the basement level eatery had marked the arrival of Christmas with a single paper snowflake in the door's window pane.

The jubilation of the street was immediately dimmed by the subterranean surroundings. The only light came from tea-lights in jars, scattered about long, low tables. He took Verity's coat and scarves from her, immediately appreciating their weight and quality. Franklin knew little of women's fashion but knew what expensive clothing felt like.

"Gallow?" A tiny man with a neat moustache and a thick Middle-Eastern accent asked of Franklin.

"Yes, table for two."

Despite the establishment being almost entirely empty, the man put on a show of pretending to look for a suitable table before gathering two menus from the counter and leading them to a corner by a high window through which only the feet of passing people on the street above could be seen.

"My name is Ahmed," the man informed them. "I shall be your waiter for this evening. May I start by getting you some drinks?"

"I'd love a cider if you have one," said Franklin.

"No alcohol," said the waiter.

Verity squeezed his hand across the table. "It's very traditional, it's the authentic experience." She turned to the waiter. "Just a pair of sparkling waters, please."

The waiter nodded and turned away. Franklin screwed up his face in embarrassment.

"I hope you're not going to ask for a bacon sandwich," Verity smiled.

"I must look like some kind of yokel to him."

"I should've warned you ahead of time - trust me, the food's worth it."

"It'd better be at these prices," said Franklin as he surveyed the menu. "Sorry, it's just a tradition I have after funeral days. I have a drink in the evening, it's kind of like a toast."

"It's not too late," said Verity. "We can go somewhere else."

"No, it's fine, I'm sure it's nice. I just... don't really know what any of these things are."

"Perhaps we could find somewhere with pictures in the menu."

Franklin looked up at Verity, quite taken aback by what he took as an insult. He was no son of the soil and had no illusions about romanticising his origins. He'd grown up in a comfortably well-to-do lower-middle class family but in that moment Verity had let slip something significant in how she saw him. With no trace of malice on her face, Franklin decided to shrug the perceived snobbery off.

"What can you recommend?" he asked.

"I was thinking of going for something Egyptian. It's all so good that you can pretty much choose anything and it will surprise you."

Franklin decided to do just that. "The kushari sounds nice."

"Really?" Verity queried.

"What's wrong with that?"

"Nothing, it's just sort of street food really. I thought we were going for something a bit more formal."

Franklin could feel his temper simmering. "I said I didn't know what any of these dishes are. Rice, macaroni and lentils sounds tasty. If you're going to be embarrassed by me eating it at your table would you rather they serve me it in the street along with all the other commoners?"

Verity chuckled. "Franklin, you're so funny. Eat what you want, I was just going to try something a bit more... sophisticated."

"Sophisticated," Franklin repeated. The word bounced infuriatingly through his head as a frosty silence fell between the two of them and Franklin found himself gazing enviously up at the feet marching blithely by the restaurant. Verity was not like him, he reminded himself. Born in Dorset to one of those old money families that haven't had to work for generations and where nobody can even fully remember where their wealth came from, seeking education and employment had been the closest act of rebellion she was capable of. With both her parents dead that enormous nest-egg was hidden away somewhere while she played the role of free-spirited dreamer, ditching her job, home and former life for a new one in Bristol. How brave an act was it when there was never any risk of failure?

Franklin's silent, angry pondering continued for some time and was only interrupted by the arrival of his kushari. Verity had ordered a veal shawarma, the callousness of which had further angered him. Immediately identifying the angry silence between the pair, the waiter simply bowed his head before slipping into the kitchen.

Midway through the meal, Verity was the first to break the quiet. "How's the kushari?"

"Not bad for peasant food. How's the tortured baby cow?"

Verity dropped her fork onto the plate with a startling clatter. "What's up? Did I say something wrong?"

Franklin looked up at her, her face full of earnest concern. Was it really worth starting an argument over this? "It's nothing, honestly. Just feeling a bit chippy, I'll get over it."

"Good," she smiled. "Cheers."

The pair clinked glasses together and the tension between them seemed to evaporate.

"So how's Bristol treating you? Are you living the dream yet?"

Quite unexpectedly, Verity tossed her head back and laughed. "Believe me, I gave up on my dreams a long time ago."

"Oh. What dreams?"

"You know, the fast life - in London, or even Paris… New York. I would be one of the glamorous, beautiful people with features in magazines about my fabulous apartment decor and secret drug habit I was barely keeping in check. I was going to be one of those women other women pretended to hate but secretly envied and spend my evenings in exclusive nightclubs with vacuous people."

"That was your dream?" Franklin was bewildered by this stranger. "You wanted to be an *It Girl*?"

"Pathetic, I know."

"So what changed your mind?"

"Nothing changed my mind, Alf came along and my priorities had to be different, I had to be sensible and responsible. Get a job to secure my future and stop relying on handouts from Daddy. All the while I knew my life would be different though, that I wouldn't be stuck teaching for the rest of my life. I guess when I thought about moving to Bristol, it was a bit like grabbing a slice of life that I thought I was meant to have before I got diverted. It may not be London or Paris, but it's a city where I could start again. Bristol is kind of my backup plan."

"I see." Franklin finished up the last of his tepid meal before pressing her. "So what does that make me? Am I your backup boyfriend?"

"What? Don't be harsh on yourself."

"No, be honest. We've been on the same dating websites for years so I knew you were out there looking for someone, but it was never me. You'd throw me a bone once in a while, but was that just a way of keeping me close, so I didn't go running off with another woman?"

"Why are you trying to pick a fight, Franklin? I'm here, aren't I?"

"You're here because you decided you couldn't find anyone better so you'd settle for me. You're only here at all because you couldn't find anywhere better to live."

Verity wiped her mouth aggressively on a napkin. "If I'm honest, then yes, you're my backup - but that's true of everyone, isn't it? I didn't string you along, I was just playing the field, seeing what I could get. You must've been doing the same thing, it's not like you haven't been dating other people."

"I had no other choice," Franklin's elevated tone was alarming the staff so he leaned in closer to Verity and lowered his voice to a hushed, vicious whisper. "I only wanted to be with you. You were the best, but you kept shutting me out, or doing weird things like pretending to be someone else to chat with me online. What was I supposed to do?"

"I single-handedly raised our son, Franklin. I think I should be allowed a little freedom in my life and the chance of some happiness."

Franklin beat his fist on the table. "You *stole* Alf from me. You stole his childhood years from me and now we're never going to have a decent relationship. You didn't do me a favour, you never even gave me an option. I would've been a damn good dad, but you deprived me of the chance. I would've been there for you, and for Alf but you chose to cut me out of his life, so if I were you, I'd stop pretending to be such a bloody martyr."

Franklin's barely contained rage had drawn the attention of the restaurant manager who sheepishly drew nearer to stand guard over Verity's shoulder. "Excuse me, sir. Is there a problem?"

"No problem," Verity replied. "Could we have the bill please?" As soon as the manager was gone, she volleyed her attack at Franklin. "That was a *gift* to you, I let you have the freedom I never had - and what did you do with it? You blew it, you ended up working for your dad even though it was the last thing you wanted to do. I gave you a chance at a future and you squandered it. Have you any idea how difficult it is raising a child by yourself?"

"Pretty easy if your parents have bottomless wallets," Franklin huffed.

"That's it," Verity stomped to her feet and reached into her pocket before casting a handful of banknotes onto the

109

table. "I'm going. I don't want to see you again, I've never been so insulted."

"Then you obviously haven't been paying close enough attention," Franklin folded his arms petulantly.

"Do you know what your problem is, Franklin? You say I think of myself as a martyr? Look in the mirror. You're just another one of those men who believes he's a nice guy but secretly thinks the world owes him something. There's a reason why you've been single all these years and it's got nothing to do with the funeral home. You're single because you're a mean, spiteful man pretending to be one of the good people. Women see through that - and they know desperation when they smell it too."

With a defiant march, Verity thundered from the restaurant and into the bitter night.

21.

The sound of the TV was becoming a distraction to Rowan's task, so she switched it off without even looking up at the screen. What had begun as a simple exercise meant to order her chaotic mind had become a nightmarish take on her own sense of reality.

It had begun simply enough, a list of names of the people who had seen Ruby on the night she'd been murdered. It began with her, there was something almost pleasing about including her own name, simply because she had someone to discount from the start. Then came her mother and the three additional members of Morning Shiver, along with the still-unnamed videographer who'd been present at the bar that evening and the taxi driver who arrived to collect Kay after rehearsal. Writing down *"Dad"* on the notepad gave Rowan a tremendous sense of unease. It should've been no different than her mother being named on the list but she understood the weight of suspicion that accompanied her father.

On the coffee table in front of the sofa on which she lay, her phone buzzed to life as a text message arrived. It was from Jude. *"Hey babe. On my way home from work, are you in tonight? Xx"*

Rowan consulted the clock on the wall above her stove. It'd gone midnight. She was in no mood for niceties with her boyfriend, or to extend the night later than it needed to be, so she simply replied *"Working late again. See you tomorrow."* She considered adding a kiss at the end but knew Jude would regard that as some kind of sign, so sent it bare. She chewed on her lower lip as she composed another text message. *"Hi Gavin. This is Rowan from the other day at the prison, just making sure you have my number."*

No sooner had it been sent she heard the sound of the downstairs door opening, accompanied by the howl of rushing, wintry wind up the staircase. At first she thought Jude was talking on the phone but then another man answered him, a muffled, deep and refined voice. Creeping across her flat, she pressed her ear to the door to listen to the two men pass and heard their footfall followed by a hollow clack with every step, Rowan took this to be the sound of a walking stick.

She was instantly enraged. Had her boyfriend really been so nakedly conniving as to send a text message while standing on the street outside the building, just to check she wasn't around before he brought the mysterious man from the hotel into his flat? Was he so brazen that he would invite an old man home to have sex in the bed she had shared countless nights with him?

Livid to the point of panic, Rowan began pacing about her living room, listening intently for the tell-tale sound of a creaking bedspread or orgasmic moans but instead she heard nothing but the chill wind battering the windows in the frames of her tiny apartment. Briefly she considered marching upstairs and confronting Jude and the strange man but the thought of a mortifying encounter with the pair of them gave her second thoughts. It was then the chaos began.

"You can't make me!" A voice, unmistakably Jude's, thundered through the ceiling above. She had never heard her boyfriend shout like that.

"Hand it over at once!" the man roared in response.

"Get out of my house you old bastard, get out!"

A heavy thud from upstairs shook the bare light which hung from a wire in the middle of Rowan's ceiling as something was toppled. It was followed by the sound of two bodies dropping to the floor, tumbling over one another. Rowan reached for her door handle, unsure what, if anything, she should do. She decided to bolt the lock. Briefly, she looked at the ceremonial robe which hung from a hook on the door, the one Franklin's father had loaned him which had somehow ended up in her possession. She knew that in its pocket it still held the sheathed dagger of the Brotherhood of Brigstowe.

"Give it back!" Jude cried. "Or I'll call the police!"

The man laughed, cruelly. "And tell them what? You'll be in a hell of a lot more trouble than I'll be."

"Then I'll smash your face in!"

"Go on then, do it, you coward. Hit me right in the face, hard as you can."

112

The two men seemed to be wrestling on the floor again. Rowan had heard enough. She unbolted her door, grabbed her phone and pounced into the landing, just as she heard the door to Jude's flat open. Ducking out of sight she crouched behind the pile of old suitcases and broken bike parts the previous tenant had left behind. In the shadows she tried running through scenarios that would explain what was going on. Was Jude being robbed? Was the old man a loan shark, coming to collect some debt. She turned her phone on and considered calling the police, until she heard the heavy clomp of the man's footsteps draw closer. She extinguished the light and held her breath.

The man paused on the landing outside her flat and peered up the staircase to where Jude was roaring obscenities down upon him. He stood so close to where Rowan hid that she could smell the pipe smoke on his tweed jacket.

"I'll be back with this tomorrow," he shouted up at Jude.

"Why can't you just trust me?" Jude called back.

"Because I've made that mistake before and look what a mess it landed us both in."

"Just leave me alone. I'm trying to be better. I never asked to be like this, it's not my fault!"

Rowan had never heard her boyfriend sound so feeble or frightened. It was alarming. The man stepped past her and down the steps to the front door, his walking stick feeling the way through the darkness of the passage as he went. Rowan didn't move until she heard the downstairs door open and she was certain the man had left the building.

Her first instinct was for Jude. Whatever had just happened had left him devastated and frightened. She heard him withdrawing from the upstairs landing and slamming the door to his flat. She imagined him crying, perhaps even climbing into bed to escape the miserable state his home was in. Whatever was going on, the only thing that Rowan was certain about was that Jude wanted her to be no part of it, why else would he have ensured she was out of her flat when he brought the strange man into the building? Rowan decided to leave him alone for the time being and attempt to get answers in the morning when he'd calmed down a little.

Rising from the shadows of her hiding place, she tip-toed to her door and found her overcoat. After slipping it on she crept silently down the staircase, aiming her slippered feet at the edges of the crooked, old steps to silence the creaks which would inform Jude of her presence. She peered through the spy hole in the door but could see nothing but darkness. She opened the door slowly, allowing a whisper of the cold night in to adjust herself to it, and stepped out onto the street.

To her horror the man was still there. A car had been waiting for him, its engine idling while a middle-aged woman, with an expensive looking haircut of red tinted spikes, sat in the driver's seat. The man looked at Rowan and she looked at him. Knowing that she had no option to run or hide, she instead had to act indignant.

"Why have you got Jude's laptop? Give it back!"

The man just shook his head and ducked into the passenger side of the car. "Just drive," she heard him say to the woman.

"Who are you?" Rowan demanded.

The woman rolled the window on her side down. "You must be Rowan," she said. Her voice was kind, so were her eyes, but the statement jarred Rowan.

"How d'you know that? Who are you?"

"Just drive," the man repeated. "We've got what we came for. Let's get out of here."

"She has a right to know, Stan. She might even get in trouble if we don't tell her."

"Tell me *what*? I'll call the police if you don't explain what's happening at once."

The woman tenderly touched the man's shoulder and turned to Rowan. "My name's Olive Tyndall. This is my husband, Stanley. We're Jude's parents."

Rowan gasped so suddenly a cloud of steam billowed from her open mouth. "I know all about you… Jude's told me everything."

"Has he now?" Olive answered coolly. "What has he told you?"

"Everything," Rowan replied.

"It's getting late," Stanley urged his wife. "Let's go."

"There are very few people who know the full story," Olive went on. "I don't believe you would've been one of them."

"I know about your husband. I know he beats you and that Jude had to escape in the middle of the night, he stole a load of money and ran away."

"I beg your pardon?" Stanley leant across his wife to see Rowan. "*This* is the story he's been telling? That I'm an abusive monster? I've never laid so much as a finger on either of them - there's only one monster in our family and that's Jude!"

Rowan was bewildered. "But the money…"

"Forty-five thousand pounds, right?" Olive asked.

"That's right. He said he stole it."

Olive turned to her husband. "She has every right to know about Jude. She practically lives with him and we have no idea what her future plans with him might be - and we don't want her calling the police, for Jude's sake if not ours."

"Please. I need to know," Rowan found herself begging. "My whole life right now is questions without answers and it's driving me mad. If there's something I need to know then please tell me."

"He didn't steal the money," said Olive. "We gave it to him so he could get out the house and start a new life away from us. We couldn't bear to look at him any longer. If you want to know what's going on, then get in the car and we'll explain it all."

With those words in her ears, Rowan ignored a childhood loaded with warnings and climbed into the car with two strangers.

22.

On waking, and even before the memories of the night before returned to him, Franklin realised he'd made a mistake. His head felt huge and heavy, his tongue swollen and his eyes as bulbous as golfballs. With every heartbeat a searing dagger of pain split like lightning across his head. From the depths of this hangover came remembrance of the night before and the earth scorching, bridge burning row he'd had with Verity.

Heaving himself up from the sofa, he began to notice the detritus from the night before. One bottle of red wine stood empty on the coffee table, another had been knocked over and spilled most of its contents on the carpet. A chip butty had been half eaten and deserted, the sight of it now, oozing with congealed ketchup made his stomach turn. His TV was asking him if he'd like to watch yet another episode of *Neighbours*.

It had been a long time since he'd last poisoned himself to this degree but he was certain the rules of recovery hadn't changed. After emptying his painfully full bladder of alarmingly dark coloured urine, Franklin took two aspirins with a pint of water before climbing into the shower and gazing at his reflection miserably in the shaving mirror as more horrific memories of the night before emerged like ghosts in his head. Had he really been singing Kim Wilde at the top of his lungs at midnight? Had he really attempted to write a stage musical about life in a funeral home? It was halfway through brushing his teeth that he panicked and rushed to his phone – he'd not sent any bitter or pleading text messages to Verity in the middle of the night. This small mercy seemed to halve his hangover at once.

The lost night felt like a patchwork of moments. Arriving home, opening a bottle of wine, weeping over Facebook photos of him and Verity Duke at university, wondering where the years had gone, before uncorking another. As he forked cat food into Felicity's bowl he decided to reason with himself. This emotional breakdown was normal and

116

necessary, things had fallen apart and he needed a night of abandon - he just mustn't make a habit of it.

Downstairs he heard the door to the reception open and after swigging back mouthwash to dispel the last of the booze-breath, Franklin buttoned up his suit and went to meet Rowan.

"Jesus, Franklin. What happened to you?"

"I overslept."

"In a ditch?"

"I got drunk, by mistake," he sighed.

"By yourself?"

Franklin nodded. "Me and Verity broke up."

"What? You've been together for three minutes. Are you sure that even counts as a breakup?"

"I'm really not in the mood for your glibness today, can we please just get on with work?"

Rowan's face dropped from a smirk. "Oh my god, you're serious? What happened?"

"I really don't want to talk about it. Not right now, anyway. It's just too depressing."

"Well, I'm really sorry," said Rowan. "If it makes any difference, I'm breaking up with Jude tonight, so at least we'll have that in common."

"I can't say I'm surprised, if I'm honest. What was the final straw?"

"If you don't want to talk about your night, then I'm allowed to keep quiet about mine - at least until I've dumped him. Let's just say, I met his parents last night…"

"His parents?" Franklin's blood-shot eyes opened wide. "But wasn't his dad…"

"…I don't want to talk about it. OK?"

Franklin nodded his head and led the way to his office where he filled the kettle and prepared coffee for Rowan and himself. "So you know Edison's coming round later, with the last of the evidence?"

Rowan nodded. "Any other day I wouldn't be able to think of anything else but my head's all over the place right now. Would you mind looking over it first for me, just to check there's nothing too graphic in it?"

"Of course," Franklin handed her a mug of steaming, black coffee. "I think the worst bits have come out already."

"I don't know how much more stuff there can be out there, or what we can learn from it." Rowan settled into the office chair in front of Franklin's computer and began scrolling through the service itinerary.

Franklin bit his bottom lip and pulled up a chair beside Rowan. "There was something else Edison told me the other night. It's pretty important, it was part of one of the folders he'd shown me that had crime scene photos in it."

"Wait, what? You saw photos of Ruby? Dead?"

Slowly Franklin nodded. "Just two of them. I didn't want to but Edison thought it was important, it wasn't salacious or anything, it was evidence."

"Were you ever going to tell me?" there was a note of righteous indignation in her voice.

"Probably not. I wouldn't be telling you at all if there hadn't been anything significant to come out of it. It's quite horrible though."

Rowan took a deep breath. "My sister was stabbed to death at the age of nineteen. There's nothing about it that isn't horrible. But if it's something really nasty... are you sure I have to hear it?"

The comment took Franklin aback and he wondered if the revelation really was vital. "I think you do. Did you know that Ruby wasn't stabbed to death?"

She frowned, incredulously. "What are you talking about? She was stabbed multiple times."

"The investigators think she was strangled first - and that one of the killers stabbed her after she died."

"*One* of the killers? What are you talking about."

Franklin gulped hard, already regretting having chosen this morning to break the news. "There's a theory among the investigators that there could've been two killers. She was strangled from behind but was stabbed in the front."

Rowan turned to the computer screen and closed her eyes. "Two of them makes sense. All these years I wondered why she didn't put up a fight, she was just... overwhelmed."

"I'm sorry I didn't tell you sooner, I just didn't want Edison to let anything slip."

118

"I get it," she said. "And it's actually comforting in a weird way that she wasn't stabbed to death. I've thought for years what it'd feel like, to have a knife penetrate your skin over and over again and to know what's happening, to see who's doing it, but strangling… at least it would be quick, right?"

"I think so," Franklin whispered.

"Please don't lean too close to me, your breath smells like a pub carpet."

"Sorry," Franklin backed off and found himself unexpectedly laughing, to his surprise Rowan laughed too.

"Oh god. Am I losing my mind? There's too much stuff happening right now." There was a knock at the reception door. "Talking of losing your mind, is that Edison?"

Franklin opened the video camera window on his computer. As expected, Edison was standing in the driveway, hugging a folder to his chest as he hopped from foot to foot.

"He looks a bit manic to me," Rowan warned.

"I think he's just cold."

The pair met him at the door.

"Bloody hell Frank, were you up drinking turpentine last night?"

Franklin shrugged. "Good morning to you too," he said.

"I smell coffee. Is there coffee?"

"Follow me. Rowan, d'you mind waiting here for a bit?"

"No problem." Rowan grabbed one of Meredy's celebrity gossip magazines that she kept behind her desk and slumped into the reception sofa.

"How're you doing?" Franklin asked his brother after closing the office door behind him.

"Probably not as bad as you, but I'm on my way down."

"What does that mean? It doesn't sound good." Franklin poured his brother a cup of coffee and stirred in four teaspoons of sugar.

"I'm crashing out from the high. It's sort of like a hangover from the new drugs. I get a few days of euphoria and then weeks of nothingness. It's like turning down the colour bar on a TV set. I feel it happening, I'm kind of used to it by now."

"How about sleep? Alcohol intake?"

"Sleep's down, booze is up - though not as bad as you. What the hell happened last night?"

"Broken heart, that's all," Franklin replied. "I'm not going to dwell on it though."

"Ah, sorry about that Frank. I know the feeling."

Franklin nodded but was unsure if this was true of his brother. Edison's romantic history was even less interesting than his own. "So what do we have in the next set of dispatches from the evidence file?"

"Next and last," Edison reminded him. "If you can't find the proof you need in here then there's very little I can help you with."

"D'you know anything about the videographer? The cameraman? He was at the bar on the night of the murder."

Edison tapped a finger on the folder he was holding. "It's all in here."

Franklin took the folder and flipped through its contents. "Rowan wants me to check there's nothing too explicit before she looks over it." Franklin paused on a series of photocopied images. "What are these?"

"CCTV. Just walking from the pub to the warehouse Ruby was caught on camera at least a couple of dozen times - and don't go lecturing me about *1984*, Frank. Those cameras save lives."

"I didn't say anything, and I got one installed outside too. It's remarkable how much something as simple as getting shot by a serial killer with a crossbow in my own home can change a person."

"Rowan won't have seen all of these. They're video stills, so we only choose the clearest of the lot to show family members. No use traumatising them unnecessarily. I can send you original video of the clearest footage if you need it."

"I don't know if Rowan could handle it, so keep it quiet." Franklin flipped through a few more pages, they seemed to mostly consist of additional statements from suspects and would-be witnesses, until he stopped at a handful of photocopied sheets. "What's this?"

Edison peered over his shoulder. "It's nothing. Apparently the police have been receiving them for years. Some nutter."

120

Franklin grabbed the pages from the folder and darted out into the corridor.

In the reception, Rowan had found her mind wandering from the trivial goings on in the world of minor celebrities and had been reliving the most terrible moments from the night before. The sober tone Jude's parents had taken as they unemotionally laid out the full and horrible story of how her boyfriend had come to live in Bristol. She'd not wanted to hear any of it but had been powerless to resist the urge, and the more the tale went on the more the missing gaps began to fill in, until finally, like a horrid, sordid jigsaw puzzle, she was able to take a step back and see the full picture. Jude Tyndall suddenly made sense, and it was awful.

On her phone she typed a single text message to Jude. "*We need to talk tonight. I know everything.*"

Within a minute he'd responded. "*Mum told me. I'm so sorry. I'm really going to miss you. xx*"

It was then that Franklin came crashing into reception, his mad stare and tumbling words were like a torrent of nonsense until Rowan saw the sheet of paper he was waving aloft. "They've been getting these messages for months!" he blurted. "They never bothered telling you. It's just the same as your ones, look!"

Franklin dropped the paper and it fell on her lap. Across the sheet were photocopied reproductions of little notes with handwritten dates beside them which the police had added at the station. Each note had been typed on an old-fashioned typewriter.

"*Oscar Kaplan Murdered Ruby Kaplan.*"

23.

If Rowan had known that both her boss and his brother would be in her flat that morning, she would at least have put some minimal effort into cleaning. Instead she found herself apologising for the state of mayhem she had cultivated over the course of a fortnight. Dirty dishes overflowed the sink, clothes and underwear were discarded with abandon across the carpet and empty bottles of Jude's homemade cider were balanced in a pyramid over her recycling bin.

"It's not normally like this," Rowan told them. "I've just been a bit distracted lately."

"Don't worry about it," Franklin reassured her. This was the first time he'd seen inside her flat, and though he hadn't been imagining anything close to luxury, he was momentarily taken aback by it. It wasn't the mess, but the sheer gloom and unfinished baseness of the draughty, open apartment that seemed to be lacking both doors and walls, a flat that was completely open plan yet somehow felt cramped and oppressive.

Rowan reached under her immaculately made bed – she'd spent the past two weeks sleeping on the sofa in front of the TV. "Here it is," she handed a shoebox to Edison.

On to Rowan's wonky and stained coffee table, Edison emptied the box of notes. Several dozen of them tumbled out. "Jesus, Rowan. Why didn't you tell me?"

"Snap," she replied, as she waved the printed sheet of identical notes in front of him.

"How long have you been getting these?"

"One a month for about three years now. At first they were being sent to my old house - all hand delivered - and after moving here they didn't even skip a month."

"You should've told the police," Edison shook his head.

"What good would that do? My dad'd just wind up in trouble all over again."

"This is evidence in a criminal case, you must have been aware of that."

"It's evidence that someone's trying to frame my dad. Evidence that only works if you take the notes seriously. After a while I just learned to ignore them. It's odd the things you can get used to."

Edison compared the notes to the ones the police were in possession of. "The wording changed. Were you aware of that?"

"Of course I was. That happened about eighteen months ago. The notes used to say *"Your father murdered your sister"* and then they became *"Your father killed your sister"* and they never went back."

"The exact same thing happened with the notes sent to the police," said Edison. "A year and a half back *"Oscar Kaplan murdered Ruby Kaplan"* changes to *"killed"* for every note afterwards. Killed definitely implies less intent, but there's no way Ruby's murder could be an accident. Why did he change it?"

"Who says it's a he?" Rowan asked.

Edison shrugged. "You may think that I'm some chauvinistic fossil from the past, but I've never once heard of a female criminal bragging about her crimes."

"But we don't know if the person who sends the notes is the killer," said Ruby.

"True, but criminals are a wide spectrum of people, from shoplifters to serial killers. For someone to have insight into a murder, that not even the police are aware of… you'd better believe that their hands aren't clean."

"We've a theory about the wording," Franklin interjected. "In both cases whoever wrote the notes would have to change their content if the *M* on their keyboard stopped working. It's the only letter that doesn't repeat and without it they'd have to change the whole phrase. Those old typewriters were built to last, but they weren't indestructible, and getting replacement parts would be difficult."

Edison eyed the assorted sets of notes. "Well I'll be damned. You'd have made quite a detective, Frank."

Franklin frowned at his brother. It was still a bone of contention between them that the family business had fallen solely into his hands when the business itself was still known as Gallow & Sons.

123

"So how long have you known about Rowan getting these notes?" He asked Franklin.

"Long enough. We're not the criminals here and I'm sure you can understand why Rowan would want to hide them. Enough people suspect her father already."

Edison knew from the daggers in Franklin's eyes not to push the matter further. "Well, we're in a city of half a million people. How many working typewriters can there be here? Not many, I'd wager. On top of that, typewriter ribbons dry out and getting a new one has to be a bit of a faff. Do they even sell them anymore?"

"Online," Rowan informed him. "I've checked already. There're a bunch of places that sell them. There used to be a couple of stationers in the city, but they've both closed now."

Edison tutted. "Pretty soon all of Bristol'll be nothing but organic bakeries and fro-yo shops." A text message came through on his phone. "I've gotta get back to the station," he informed them. "There was a fight in Cabot Circus over the last Playstation 4 in stock. Bloody Christmas brings out the worst in people."

"Bah humbug, you old misery," said Franklin.

Edison departed in an exasperated hurry. Franklin and Rowan were left alone in the dinky, damp flat.

"How're you doing, Ro?"

"I'm keeping it together," she replied as she gathered up the notes and dropped them into her shoebox. "I sort of feel like If I stop what I'm doing I'm going to get crushed under the weight of it all, so I have to keep on going. How's your hangover?"

Franklin rocked his hand from side to side. "The headache's gone now, I'm just feeling queasy. If I remember right the next stage will be existential anxiety."

"Well, that's something to look forward to. Are you up for a journey to the seaside?"

"Um, what are you talking about?"

"It's another little theory I want to put straight, about Douglas."

Franklin checked his watch. "I'm meeting his mum later on, but that's not until mid afternoon. Where d'you want to go?"

Rowan shrugged. "I'm not really sure, but I'll know it when we get there."

"Good enough for me," said Franklin and he followed her out of her flat onto the landing beyond.

"I think we're going towards Clevedon," Rowan said, as they made their way down the stairs, and before Franklin could reply, she'd opened the front door to reveal a man standing in the street, reaching for the buzzer.

"Stan!" Rowan gasped, taking a step back.

"I thought you were out," the man replied, hurriedly.

"I think Jude's upstairs," the moment was frostily awkward in a way Franklin couldn't understand.

The distinguished looking man in a tweed jacket turned to look at Franklin. "Is this... your father? No, of course not. Sorry."

"I'm Franklin," he introduced himself with a handshake. "We work together. I just got here. I mean, I didn't spend the night or anything..." the weird tension was clearly contagious.

"So you're bringing back the laptop?" Rowan asked Stan.

The man leaned in to her and whispered something in her ear to which she simply nodded and offered him a compassionate smile. "Please don't say you saw me here," she said.

"Of course," and with that he brushed past her and went up the stairs to Jude's flat on the top floor.

"Am I going to be privy to any of what that was about?" Franklin asked before he and Rowan got into his Smart car.

"Eventually, yes. I'm just processing it myself, and it's very... sensitive."

"Say no more, but if you want to talk...."

"I'm fine, for now. I just have to keep on moving."

Rowan had asked that they drive to the pretty seaside town of Clevedon not by the traditional route of the motorway, but via a series of winding country lanes that made Franklin feel nauseated with every lurching hill and spiralling turn. It was only when she touched his shoulder and asked him to stop that he realised why she'd insisted on this route. At a gateway entrance to a field where Franklin stopped the car, there was a small memorial of flowers and ribbons. With a gulp in his dry throat he saw that this makeshift shrine was in honour of Douglas Bennett.

"So this is where it happened." Franklin said.

"It definitely looks like that. I followed the route of the train tracks and this seems the most likely spot. Probably walked all this way, because he didn't have a license."

Beyond the gate a small field sloped towards a single railway line with a hedgerow of thick and spiky gorse on either side. Yellow police tape had been stretched across a section where it appeared someone had clipped their way through the undergrowth to meet the track.

"That must've been how he got through," said Franklin.

"I didn't know he had to cut a path, he must've really wanted to kill himself."

Franklin nodded. "Have you been thinking what I've been thinking?"

"Did he jump or was he pushed?"

"Exactly. It's definitely possible that someone could've hidden down there in the hedgerow and pushed him in front of the train. The driver would be none the wiser, but how d'you lure someone into the middle of a field in the early evening? Douglas wasn't a small guy, I bet he would've put up a fight."

"Maybe he was drugged?"

"The report from the coroner said he had drunk most of a bottle of vodka. Whatever happened, it happened when he was pretty leathered."

Rowan stared contemplatively at the sinister bandage across the injured hedgerow. "It could've just been suicide then. Plain and simple, he couldn't get over Ruby. Maybe a bottle of vodka to find the nerve to jump."

Franklin nodded. "His mother seemed to think so. I've met the parents of suicide victims before, and believe me, if there's any doubt at all that their kid could've died any other way, then that's what they would believe."

"Unless she pushed him," Rowan said, bluntly.

"Don't say things like that, the poor woman's devastated - but I think she knew this was coming and could do nothing to stop it. I know we've seen our fair share of monsters, but most people are good, most people are kind and love their children."

"Just like my dad?"

"Exactly. There aren't mysteries everywhere, sometimes things are just what they seem – tragedies - stupid, pointless wastes of life, but still tragedies. Poor chap, imagine living with that inside your head."

"Edison's getting better," Rowan was getting very good at reading her friend's mind. "He seems to be managing it a bit better, at least. This won't be what happens to him."

A gentle, cold breeze rustled through the overhead branches and sent the little ribbons tied to the fence fluttering. Among the tributes of flowers was a laminated pamphlet bearing the number of the Suicide Prevention Hotline, alongside images of the young man smiling, singing karaoke and holding a pint of beer in front of his laughing face.

"It's funny how cameras can't ever catch what's really going on," said Rowan. "He looks so happy here."

In a line along the bottom of the fence lay little bouquets of frost damaged flowers, burnt colourless under the winter sun. Rowan found herself reading the heartbreaking tributes on little cards tied to them, until her eyes fell upon the face of her sister. The image, glued onto paper and tied with a length of string to single red rose, showed Ruby sitting next to Douglas, his arm protectively, possessively, across her shoulders.

Two young people who would never grow old.

24.

"Can't we even have a wreath on the door?" asked Meredy. "Christmas is a week away and it feels like a…"

"A funeral home?" Franklin answered. "I'd love to cheer the place up a bit but we're a secular business that deals with all kinds of religions, it's not professional to be seen to favour one over the other."

Meredy threaded a scarf intricately about her neck before hauling a coat across her shoulders. "I know, I think I'm just looking for distractions at the moment, or at least something to cheer me up."

Franklin adored his receptionist, the no-nonsense but kindly face with almost twenty years of loyal service, she was as dependable a fixture as the constant arrival of corpses, and as such, he often forgot how troubled her life away from Gallow & Sons was. "Is that son of yours still being a tyrant."

Meredy threw her hands up, exasperated. "Honest to God, it's a good thing I'm his mother as otherwise I'd have throttled that boy by now. He's on a two week suspension from school which means he won't be back until after the Christmas holidays and by then I'd imagine the teachers will have all but given up on him. He'll be leaving school in May without so much as a GCSE to his name. Good grief, the worry. You're lucky you never had any of your own."

"I've got Alf."

Meredy blushed at once. "Oh Franklin, I'm sorry, I didn't mean it like that, I just meant… I don't know what I meant. I guess teenage boys are as alien to me now as they were when I was a teenage girl."

"They were pretty alien to me back then too," Franklin smiled. "Boys were always hitting each other, or pretending to hump each other… causing mayhem. I was a just a square."

"Can't say I'm shocked to hear that," Meredy laughed. "Anyway, I'll be off. First thing Monday?"

"Of course. Enjoy your weekend."

Meredy just gave him a withering look of cynicism before she let herself out the door into the cold. Of course she wouldn't enjoy her weekend.

Upstairs in his flat, Franklin made himself a cheese and pickle sandwich and was just about to pour himself a glass of wine when his phone rang. The screen informed him that Alf was calling, but he'd been tricked by Verity using her son's phone before. He considered ignoring it, then even erasing Verity's number and email from his phone, but pushed such silly thoughts aside and opted to answer it.

"Dad, it's me. I'm outside your house." The line went dead.

Only mildly irritated, Franklin replaced the screw top on his bottle of wine before pulling on his overcoat and jogging down the staircase to answer the door.

"Alf!" he began, attempting to sound cheerful as opposed to alarmed. "Come inside, it's freezing."

"I can't do that," he replied, his face an inscrutable mask. "It'll look like I'm taking sides."

"What are you talking about? It's near freezing, and it's dark, I can make you some soup."

"Franklin, I'm not saying if I think you're in the wrong, or mum's in the wrong, or you're just both a couple of babies about all this, and I'm not going to your flat to have soup and a nice chat, but I *am* going to go for a walk and while I'm walking I also might just happen to start talking to myself. It's a free country and I can't stop you walking at the same time, and if you happen to be doing so close enough to overhear what I'm saying, then there's nothing I can do to stop it."

Understanding his barely disguised instructions, Franklin nodded and closed the door behind him. "OK. Let's walk."

It was almost six in the evening and bitterly cold, the kind of cold he could feel in his lungs with every intake of breath, but the night was clear with countless stars twinkling overhead, on the breeze the sound of early drunken revellers could be heard, singing "All I Want for Christmas is You."

"I hate this song," Alf huffed.

"How can anyone hate this song?" Franklin asked. "It's like distilled euphoria. It's perfect."

"It's cultural appropriation. They just stole from a bunch of Motown hits and got a white woman to sing over the top."

"Mariah Carey's black," Franklin informed him.

"No she isn't. Wait, what?"

"Trust me Alf, as someone who's spent his life analysing everything and dissecting it until there's barely anything left, it's fine just to enjoy something for what it is. Sometimes art can just be for fun."

Alf was a fast walker, something which Franklin had always appreciated as he was one himself, and the bitterness of the night was softened by their brisk pace. At the corner of North Street, a young couple were loudly arguing while the last of the evening's Christmas shoppers scurried past, arms laden with gifts.

"I was much worse when I was younger," Alf conceded, much to Franklin's surprise. "A year at uni sort of loosened me up a bit."

"I've noticed. Bristol does that to people too, it's very laid back."

"It used to be," Alf said, cryptically.

"Yes, the second year of university is a bit more serious. The first is easy; it's very hard to properly screw up."

"I'm not talking about that... it's Mum."

Franklin held his breath. Was he about to become a confidant for his son's woes? He knew he had to proceed with caution. "Really? How so?"

"She never asked me about her moving to Bristol, she just turned up one day. I love Mum, I really do, and I miss her, but at the same time, I spent years dreaming of leaving home and starting out by myself, not because I wanted to escape but because I wanted to do something that was just me. All my life it's just been me and her and it was great, but also... kind of intense. I was having fun with my freedom, going to bed when I want, getting off my face on whatever substance I could get hold of. The other day I ended up snogging the face off a total stranger on Park Street, and now I just think I'm going to be running into her wherever I go, or she's going to be checking up on me. It's like I got a gap year and now she's forced me to come home."

Franklin was astonished. It was the most nakedly honest his son had ever been with him, yet he was also aware that he was supposed to be his father. "What kind of substances are you talking about?"

"I don't need the *Just Say No* lecture, Dad, I'm not a moron, I'm responsible. Anyway, I'm supposed to just be walking along, talking to myself. You're not allowed to judge. Forget it, d'you want a pint?"

The pair had stopped outside the Spotted Cow on North Street. The windows were steamed and inside looked warm and welcoming. Stepping through the door they were at once surrounded by the chatter of workers who had stopped off on their way home and members of Christmas parties wearing paper crowns and quaffing down mulled wine.

"What d'you want?" Franklin called to his son over the din.

"A pint of Ashton Press," he replied.

As the drinks were poured, Franklin found himself taken aback by the importance of the moment. It wasn't just that Alf was fond of his own favourite cider, but for the first time he was buying a drink for his son.

Reading his thoughts, or merely noticing the tears pricking at his dad's eyes, Alf leaned in and said, "Don't over analyse it, Dad. It's just a pint."

Finding a corner away from the rowdier customers, they slumped into a leather sofa in front of a roaring fire. "Cheers," said Franklin and father and son clinked glasses.

"Don't tell Mum what I told you," Alf said.

"Of course not. I get it though, I really do. When I was your age and I went to university it was like escaping into a new world, except for me it was also escaping the funeral home, and I thought, for a little while at least, I'd end up never returning. Fat lot of good that degree did because I ended up returning anyway and all that potential was gone to go off to some alternate universe where I don't live with the smell of death all day long."

Alf stared into the fire. "That does sound pretty grim, worse than my situation, anyway. Are you going to call Mum soon?"

Franklin shrugged. "It felt pretty final the other night. All those years of waiting and we blow it as soon as we give it a shot."

"Maybe the idea was better than the reality," said Alf. "I saw this documentary the other night about these two guys before World War Two. They met in this queer cinema and hit it off, but then they got conscripted and sent to opposite sides of the world, but they kept in contact, writing letters and planning a life together. For six years they pined for each other and then the war ended and they finally reunited and moved in together. They lasted two weeks before they split up."

Franklin laughed. "I see what you mean. Sometimes the fantasy is better than the reality."

"Don't give up on her though. She can be a pain, maybe even a bit of a snob, but she's a good woman."

"I see you've been talking about last night," said Franklin.

"She wants me to go round for dinner every night. I don't want to hurt her feelings."

"So you came straight from her's to mine?"

Alf nodded. "Thought I'd check up on my old man."

"So how about you. How's your love life?"

"All over the place," Alf replied. "Literally, at times. Bristol's a lot bigger than Cheltenham and I'm young and single."

"And safe, I hope," Franklin could not prevent his paternal reaction.

"And safe," Alf reassured. "Mum says you're pissed with her for not telling you about me. Is that true?"

Franklin shrugged. "I'm a bit resentful but she made her choice and that's the past. Not much use in crying over it now, and maybe it was the kind thing to do, letting me skip out on the sleepless nights and nappy changing and go straight to the pints of cider in the pub with you, but I would've liked the choice."

"I resent it a bit too," said Alf. "It might've been different, knowing who you were, but I never had the chance. She kept you so vague until I turned eighteen, that I thought you were some kind of deadbeat dad. That's why I treated you like one when I met you."

"It's fine,"

"It's not. I'm sorry, Dad, I was a total arsehole. I treated you like dirt because I knew I could get away with it and you'd keep on coming back. What a horrid little kid I was."

"You're like me," Franklin declared. "At least like I was when I was your age. You've got some fire in you and I like it. Don't let that venom completely drain from your blood just because you're growing up. You're very moral and I think that's about the best compliment I can give anyone. I'm proud of you, son."

Alf looked away, allowing both men a chance to wipe their eyes before returning his gaze to his empty glass.

"My shout. Can I get you another one?"

"Same again, please." Franklin replied.

Alf stood up. "Great, let's keep this thing going."

"I really hope we do."

25.

Rowan had hoped her parents would be out when she let herself inside the kitchen of her former home, but her father was sat on the sofa in front of the TV, half way through a bite of a chicken patty, when Rowan walked past the open door.

"Ro?" he asked, surprised.

"Dad, I thought you'd be working."

Oscar shrugged. "Got off early, even though it's madness at the moment. The number of people coming to the pharmacy for cold treatments is just ridiculous. What do we say Rowan?"

"There's no cure for the common cold," Rowan repeated the words her father had claimed were the core ideology of the pharmaceutical business.

"That's my girl. We're just selling junk treatments and nicotine patches at the moment."

"Why nicotine patches?"

"Christmas is coming and people are realising they're going to have to spend time with their families who don't know they smoke."

Rowan smiled at this revelation. "I was just stopping by to pick some things up. Can't keep it all in the attic forever."

"Can I tempt you with a patty? There's another in the fridge if you want one."

"I'm fine, I ate earlier." Rowan replied.

"You should've tried your grandmother's patties. Nothing like it in the world, my mum could whip up proper Jamaican food like magic."

"Jamaican food's always been a bit too reliant on goat meat for me."

"Suit yourself," said Oscar. "You just missed your mother. She's gone off to her Friday night meeting with Gordon. She shouldn't be back for another couple of hours. Is there anything I can help you with?"

Rowan slipped into the living room and sat on the couch beside her father. "There was something, actually. It's about Ruby."

Oscar's face turned to stone, he loosened his work tie and sighed. "Your mum said this might happen, she said you've been snooping around a bit. You'd better not be getting into any kind of trouble again. I listened to that podcast with your boss about the Blackbeard murders; I hope it's true that you weren't involved at all."

Rowan's role not just in the amateur investigation, but also in capturing one of the culprits, had been kept secret from her parents and she had no plans to change that. "It was nothing to do with me, Franklin takes on these side projects."

"So, is that what's happening here? Ruby's his latest project?"

The bitterness of his tone had not gone unnoticed by Rowan. "I'm just trying to get a few things straight about that night and what happened... where everyone was."

Oscar had stopped eating his patty and was now staring at Rowan. "I trust you'll be a little more sensitive than that bloody Murder Club podcast. They're all but celebrating Ruby's murder tomorrow night."

"How d'you mean?" Rowan asked.

"That pair of morbid losers are recording a live podcast in the pub. On Christmas Eve, of all times, they're charging people for tickets to come and watch them discuss Ruby's murder and whatever kind of nasty little rumours or theories they have."

Rowan was astonished. "What? They can't do that. Can they?"

Oscar shrugged. "They seem confident that they can. As long as they don't accuse anyone of being responsible, they're within the law. It's just common decency that they're falling foul of."

"I've got to get one of those tickets and crash it. You said they're holding it in a pub?"

Oscar nodded. "No, they're holding it in *the* pub, where Ruby was rehearsing that night. Sounds pretty tacky, don't you think? This is how they choose to celebrate Christmas, by turning your sister's murder into some cheap puzzle to be solved. No doubt they'll be going over the usual suspects, so I'd imagine my name will be coming up a few times."

This was the first time she'd heard her father so brazenly admit that he was among the list of suspected murderers and Rowan found it disarming. "But you were playing dominoes," she said. "And the phone records put you way over in Dundry."

Oscar's eyes narrowed. "What're you doing Rowan?"

"I was just saying that there's no way you could've done it, so they can't suspect you. I mean there's evidence."

His face had not changed. "And if there was no evidence?"

"What d'you mean? You have an alibi, for most of the night."

"But if I didn't, if there was no evidence and no record of my movements, it'd be fine to suspect me?"

"That's not what I'm saying."

"Would you suspect me?"

"Of course not!"

"Do you suspect me?"

A silence fell between them. A Question of Sport ran obtrusively and annoyingly in the background. "I don't suspect you, Dad. But some people do and you can't entirely blame them. Most of the time it's someone close to the victim."

"This isn't about *a victim,* Rowan. This is Ruby, your sister, my daughter. It doesn't matter what the statistics tell you, this is *our* tragedy and *our* story. It belongs to nobody else but us and I need to know that you trust me."

Rowan didn't know where the tears came from but they rushed upon her in an unstoppable torrent and she erupted into sobs. "I trust you!"

Oscar looked away from her, his face caught somewhere between rage and regret. "I didn't mean to get angry, Ro," his voice was calm. "I've got a lot of stuff going on at the moment. I hate Christmas, every year when it returns, I hate it just because Ruby loved it."

"I know," Rowan wiped her eyes on her sleeve. The tidal wave of emotion had subsided in an instant. "It's hard, and it'll never be the same again."

"This podcast thing has put me in a foul mood too. Have you any idea what it's like to know that everyone suspects you of something so terrible? Living with the grief is unbearable, but to have people looking at you and *wondering* all the time if I did it, I can't take it, the police have to catch that bastard."

"I know," she whispered. The police will clear you soon, I just know something's around the corner." Even as the words came from her lips, Rowan knew they were a lie; the kind of soft lie people who love each other tell all the time, the kind that plasters over cracks and softens harsh words, the kind that lets a man sleep more peacefully at night. To say that the police were soon to vindicate her father's innocence was a tender lie. To say that she had never suspected his guilt was a terrible one, because though she believed in her heart that her dad was incapable of murder, a small, yet relentless, voice inside her questioned how much anyone can really know someone. The dark corners of a mind can be a dangerous place and she'd no way of knowing how the man who was Oscar Kaplan truly felt inside.

"Would you like some help in the attic? It's a bit chaotic up there," he asked.

"I'll be fine," she replied, before rising from the sofa and leaving the room without another word. Remorse for her actions had turned the air in the living room sour. The staggering act of betrayal, to go from reassuring her father, to snooping through his private things in a matter of minutes, felt like an unforgivable sin, yet she felt as if she had no other choice. The sense of distrust of the people closest to her was at a point where it would drive her insane, so she needed an answer.

With a hook on a stick from the now empty, neglected airing cupboard, Rowan opened the latch in the ceiling and a ladder slid down invitingly. She scaled her way upwards and through the hole and entered the mysterious world of the unvisited room. It was always a peculiar experience, the realisation that all the time, in the most familiar home she had ever known, was hidden a near secret space full of memories of the past. Beneath a veil of dust and the skeletal remains of spider webs sat folders full of her and Ruby's old school books and report cards, alongside forgotten toys, once loved but abandoned when boys and hormones made their presence known.

These were artefacts from a happier time, and Rowan could have spent days reliving the past in this dark and musty space, but she was here in search of something else, something half remembered in a near-waking daze of that morning before the full horror of Jude's parents' confession had coming rushing back to her. It had to be here still.

Pulling away a dust cloth which covered a pile of stacked cardboard boxes revealed more treasure troves of memories. In a tangle of wires sat Ruby's old Nintendo Gamecube, with Mario Kart still in the drive. A full collection of Famous Five books were bound up in string alongside the ballet shoes Rowan had begged her mother for during the fortnight she'd been enchanted by ballerinas.

Beneath another was a collection of photo albums. Part of the pharmacy her dad worked at was given over to a camera film processing unit, and owing to a sense of loyalty to the company, the Kaplans continued with film photography well into the age when digital had taken over. Inside Rowan knew she would see page after page of her sister, full of life and the promise of a future that would never come. Mournfully she dragged the sheet back across the albums, much like she did to the corpses at Gallow & Sons when she'd finished painting their faces.

It was beneath the third dust cloth that she found what she'd been looking for. Glinting at her in the half-light, and in the same pristine condition she had remembered it, sat the typewriter. It was a gloriously robust invention, reassuringly heavy and near bomb-proof in its 1920s construction. As a child, Rowan had enjoyed the clatter of typing a line of nonsense until the ding of the bell, now it seemed framed in menace.

There could only be one reason why her father would have used this contraption to write notes to the police and to his daughter, as a confession. The guilt becoming too much of a burden, his monthly attempts to admit culpability would assuage him for a while until those thoughts returned to haunt his mind. With a trembling hand, Rowan reached for an old bank statement bundled in elastic bands and shoved haphazardly into an overflowing folder. As she threaded the paper through the rollers, the ancient, dried ribbon crumbled away like dead leaves. She located "M" and pressed it. At once the corresponding type bar launched like a trebuchet and hit the paper with a satisfying snap where it left its unmistakable mark. Triumphant, Rowan rapped away at the key to leave a line of identical letters before gleefully smashing at random buttons until the bell sounded. This was not the machine that had plagued her for years, and in an instant she felt euphoric - it was all the proof she needed that her sister's killer had not come from within her own household.

Suddenly the voice of her father calling up from the landing brought her back to the moment. "You're not playing with that old Remington are you?"

"Just wanted to check it would still work," she called back.

"You're welcome to have it. Kind of steam punk, don't you think?"

Rowan simply smiled at the old, familiar and near-antique contraption. It did not prove her father's innocence but it had not proven his guilt, and in a world where there seemed to be fewer and fewer certainties, that in itself felt like enough.

26.

Rowan knew that all jubilations were short-lived. She could find herself in fits of uncontrollable laughter or enthusiastically anticipating a dance event when the words *"but she's gone"* would return to her mind and once more she'd be dragged down into the darkness.

Opening the door to her apartment block Rowan stared up into the darkness that waited for her at the top of the stairs. Without unbuttoning her duffel coat, climbing higher, past her flat, after dropping off the old diaries she'd used as her excuse to visit the attic, ascending to Jude's door. Beyond it was a man once so familiar but now little more than a stranger. Jude had scrubbed his flat to an eerily precise sheen, the smell of cleaning fluids reminded Rowan of Gallow & Sons. The space was alien, and cold, the door to the roof garden had been left ajar and was swaying in the harsh December breeze. Rowan ducked through the opening and climbed the coil of stairs until she was standing in the bitter wind on the flat roof of the building.

Jude had once cared for this place with the tenderness of a new parent, doting on every leaf and flower, feeding and pruning to exquisite perfection, but autumn had hit hard and fast, just as Ghurt Lush had opened, and soon the roof garden was dying faster than he could save it. All that remained now were the frost choked corpses of dead plants. Jude himself was leaning against the far, low wall, gazing across the city with his back to her.

He turned and nodded to her. "Thanks for coming," he said.

"I had to speak to you," said she.

Jude had in his hand the final bottle of his Christmas cider. Around his feet were the toppled and discarded empties. "I needed a bit of courage to do this."

Rowan simply looked up at the sky to where Venus shone high and bright, ice crystals forming a halo around it in the stratosphere. "You could've saved me some," she half laughed.

"You must hate me." Jude's face was blank, his eyes would not meet hers.

"I don't think I do, but I need an explanation. Anything at all."

Jude didn't appear to have heard her. "I'm really going to miss this. Up here, you and me, I'm gonna miss all of it. I always knew I was doing better than I deserved, you were this kickass girlfriend with a cool job who caught murderers, and I was just this wannabe musician who knew he was never gonna make it. Thank you for giving me a try though, it was so great while it lasted and I was like… happy."

Rowan knew what he was trying to do, turning the situation to make her feel pity for him. "This isn't going to work on me, not tonight. You can't manipulate me, I've heard everything from your parents."

"You haven't heard my side of the story yet."

"You were looking at child pornography on the internet Jude. What possible other side to the story could there be?"

Jude's head fell and he turned back to face the city.

"Aren't you going to say anything? Speak up, you coward!" Rowan raged at him from across the roof.

"You can't insult me, it doesn't work. People use the worst word of them all to describe me, nothing else matters after that."

"And are you one?" Rowan inched closer. "A paedophile?"

Jude caught her gaze. "How can I answer that? You know already."

A wave of nausea rushed over Rowan as she recalled how just a few nights ago her boyfriend had claimed *"I'm up for pretty much anything, but mostly girls." Girls* he had said, not women. How many times had he cushioned himself and his true desires in this double-speak? "So the bisexual thing, that's just a cover, right? You're not bi-curious at all."

Jude wiped his eyes, his back still turned to her. "What d'you want me to say? I'm a liar, and yeah, that bi bullshit was just to throw people off. If they think you're being open about your sexuality they never suspect that anything dark could be going."

"So what about me? I'm not a kid."

"I'm not just into kids," Jude blurted defensively, until he realised just how sickening his words sounded. "I mean, I've been with women before - *adult* women. There's lots of us out there like me."

"*Us?*" Rowan spat. "So you've been in contact with other people?"

Jude nodded and upturned the last his bottle. "It's not what you think though. We need each other, it's important that I stay in touch with the rest of the... rest of them out there."

"Why? What possible good can it do, being in contact with each other, swapping nasty videos and..."

"...It's not like that!" Jude spun on his feet to face her. "I've never touched a child, *ever*. I'd never do that, I don't think I'd even want to do it, it's all just... watching."

"If you're going to defend yourself by saying all you ever did was watch videos then you can just shut the fuck right up. You know those kids are being exploited because pervs like you are creating a market for it. You're not abusing them yourself, but you're ordering it on demand."

"I know," said Jude, his voice was disconcertingly placid. "It's like an addiction."

"Mum's alcoholism is an addiction, that's just depravity."

"And that's why I need the other guys. D'you know what happens if I go to a therapist and tell them that I'm thinking about kids? The therapist is bound *by law* to report me to the police. So there's nothing, no help, no sympathetic ear. I never wanted to be like this? D'you think when they were handing out perversions I was standing in a queue hoping I'd be the one attracted to children and have the hatred of the whole world upon me."

Despite her expectations and intentions, in that moment Rowan found herself feeling sorrow for the man. "Tell me everything that happened," she said.

Jude took a deep breath and his eyes seemed to shimmer with tears as he reflected on his past. "It started when I was a teenager, and the kids weren't much younger than me then. I kind of thought as I grew older, the girls I found attractive would too, but they didn't, and that started to get really scary because the gap between me and them was getting wider and wider. I'd thought about it and fantasised about it... a lot, but it was when I went to university and I got my own laptop and internet connection that I started looking for the... stuff. At first it was stuff from the seventies and eighties, I don't know why, but it happening in the past seemed to make it... sort of less evil, like there was no way to intervene and those kids were all grown up now, but it wasn't working, in fact it was just getting worse."

Rowan would not let her revulsion cloud her judgement. She stood beside Jude but made certain the two were not touching. "How did your parents find out?"

"It was when I came home for the Easter holiday. By then my laptop was pretty loaded with stuff, really vile, twisted stuff that this monster inside me was craving all the time. I thought I'd been smart and had hidden everything away in an unmarked folder deep on the hard drive, but one day the wifi in the house went down and Dad wanted to check it wasn't just his computer... he must've been rooting around for something. It hadn't even crossed my mind that he could find anything, but as soon as I heard him shout "*What the hell*" I knew exactly what it was, and life as I knew it was over. He was furious, but Mum, she was heartbroken, it was like she could never look at me in the same way again, and she still never has. They were up arguing all night, and in the morning Dad told me they wanted me out of the house, but not just out of the house, I was supposed to drop out of uni and leave Yorkshire altogether. That was where the money came from, they gave it to me, not even a loan, that's how much they wanted rid of me. So I packed my bag and headed south. I tried London for a bit, then Cardiff and by autumn I was in Bristol."

"So that's where I come into the story," said Rowan.

Jude nodded slowly. "If I could do anything to not be like this, I would. If only someone could help me instead of just hating me."

"I don't hate you," Rowan cursed her impetuousness. "I think I might pity you, and I don't think I like you. A better man would've been able to resist it."

"I know, but it's easy for someone to say that when they haven't been living with this for years."

"You're not the victim here, Jude. Don't try painting yourself as one."

"I know," a single sob erupted from him like a convulsion. "It's just been so hard to fight, and I want help."

"Did your parents know you were living down here?"

Jude nodded and wiped his eye. "Soon after I moved in I sent them a letter, a real handwritten one because I didn't want them to know I had a computer. I didn't hear back for months, but Mum was the first to break. Eventually it became sort of a regular thing, and then a few weeks ago they said they were coming to Bristol and wanted to see me. First I was meeting them in a hotel, but last night I brought Dad round and as soon a he saw my laptop he got into a rage. We ended up fighting, actually *really* fighting on the floor, but he took it from me anyway. I got it back from him this morning. He'd been up all night going at it with tweezers and a fine tooth comb and found nothing."

"I know," she said. "I ran into him earlier and he told me the same. Why didn't you just let him have the laptop if it was clean?"

"I was pretty enraged that he'd just take it, I suppose. Plus, I actually do have some pretty freaky porn on there and it's just embarrassing for your parents to see that. Don't worry, it was all with adult humans and nothing freakier than stuff we've done."

Rowan shuddered with disgust, thinking of the handcuffs and the times he'd wanted her submissive and helpless in bed. "Jude, I don't think I hate you, but you do know it's over between us, don't you?"

"Of course."

"Maybe someone else, another, better woman, or someone more forgiving, could stick this one out, but she isn't me. Every time we were out and there were kids around I'd be giving you the side eye, wondering what was going on in your head, or every time you were at your computer I'd be peering over your shoulder. We both know the end's been coming for a while."

"That's true," said Jude.

"You may think it's like a monster inside you, but your choices are ultimately yours and what you did was... *unforgivable.*" Rowan looked over the edge of the wall to the precipitous drop below. "You're not going to do anything idiotic, are you?"

Jude didn't have to ask for clarification. "Of course not. I don't want to die."

"Good. I may not have a very high opinion of you right now, but you're worth more than that."

"Well," Jude half smiled, "you have more compassion for me than most of the world would. Can I ask you a favour, just something small."

"I don't think I owe you anything, but go on."

"Once in a while, could you just check in on me. Make sure I'm safe and just talk to me for a little bit. Ask me straight about how I'm dealing with *it.*"

"I can manage that, if you're honest with me."

Jude nodded and turned back to the city. Rowan shivered against the cold before returning inside, leaving her former boyfriend to his darkness.

27.

Beneath a blistering midday sun, Ruby and Rowan paused from their walk around the harbourside to gaze down from the walkway to a floating, wooden jetty upon which a line of young women in bikinis were lazing in the heat.

"White girls are nuts," said Ruby. "All that effort just to make their skin look darker and all it gives them is melanoma."

Rowan chuckled. They were at a small marina, flanked on three sides by eateries and bars, currently filled with office workers on their lunch breaks. In the shimmering water a line of narrowboats bobbed and creaked while barbecues were sparked up on their sterns. "Should we get something to eat?" she asked.

"I don't know, I'm watching my weight," Ruby replied.

"What are you talking about, you look great."

"Don't you think I know that?" Ruby smiled. "I've got curves, I just want to make sure they stay in all the right places. If we're gonna get that recording contract I have to be looking my absolute best, I'm the star of the band."

Rowan nodded. Her sister's confidence was not misplaced, she'd seen Morning Shiver perform and Ruby's magnetic charisma was enough to wash all other members of the band beige and lifeless. "You shouldn't skip meals though, it isn't healthy."

"Thanks Mum," she said.

"So how are things with Douglas?"

"Who?"

"Doug... your boyfriend. Have you told Mum and Dad about him yet?"

Ruby shook her head, her tight curls bounced around her face. "You know what Mum's like, she'll start giving me lectures about safety and consent like I'm a teenager."

"You're nineteen," Rowan reminded her.

"That's not a teenager anymore. Teens lock themselves in their rooms and listen to miserable music and slam doors in their parents' faces, I'm a *woman*."

"Would a woman be scared of telling her mother that she's seeing a boy?"

Ruby nudged Rowan's shoulder with her own and the pair began walking away from the harbour to Millennium Square. "It's not Mum I'm worried about, it's Dad. You know how protective he is of me. He'll want to meet Doug and then he'll have to come round for dinner, and they'll just see him as this little dweeb."

"He's not a dweeb. He seems nice."

"Dweebs usually are nice boys. He's not exactly exciting though is he? The other night we went on a date to the cinema. So I thought, great, we'll go and see some crappy horror film and I can pretend to be scared, and just, stick to the script, you know? But instead he takes me to the Watershed to watch *Seven Samurai*, which is over three hours long and in Japanese. I thought I was going to lose my mind with boredom."

"I think I'd quite like a highbrow boyfriend," said Rowan. "Someone to discuss art with, and I can pretend to know about wine and politics."

"Trust me, it's not fun, and it's all a trick anyway. He was as bored as I was but he'd never let it show, because the only reason he'd taken me there was to show off how smart he was. It was like an endurance test to see which one of us would break first, but I stuck in there, until my bum got numb and I ended up counting ceiling panels to escape the boredom."

"But he's a drummer in a band, that's kind of cool."

"Is it though? Half the men my age are in a band, and the other half are DJ's, trust me, Rowan, stay away from musicians."

"So, things aren't working out between the pair of you?"

"It was never really supposed to, we both kind of knew this was just a temporary thing. I think he's still into Lily a bit, but he'd never say so. When we're together there's no spark, it's like rubbing two wet sponges together."

"What're you going to do?"

Ruby shrugged. "I'm a bit screwed, really. If I dump him it might ruin the band, so I'm just going to string him along for a bit. It's mean, but I have to think about my future. It's not like it was going to last anyway, besides, loads of bands have relationship breakups and stick together afterwards. Did you know *Go Now* was written by Bessie Banks' ex-husband?"

"Yes I do, you've told me hundreds of times."

As they reached Millennium Square, Ruby helped herself to a handful of nasturtiums from the Edible Garden. "There you go, I've got my lunch. Are you happy now?"

The pair sat on a bench next to the statue of Cary Grant and distractedly watched a display on the Big Screen which was counting down the minutes, hours and days until the start of the London Olympics.

"Here's the thing, Ro," said Ruby, once she'd finished eating the leaves. "You need to get yourself a good man. The right kind of a man. Stay away from musicians, they're more interested in themselves, or looking cool, than they ever will be in you. You deserve someone better - and hotter."

Rowan distractedly agreed, her eyes still fixed on the countdown clock on the screen. There was something disconcerting about watching time be consumed, second by second, the present being tossed into the past with every moment. That day would be the last walk the pair of them would ever have together, for in less than two weeks, Ruby would be dead.

28.

Rowan could not quite fathom why, but the morning after her rooftop confrontation with Jude, she found herself scrolling through the contacts on her phone before stopping on Lise Nielsen. It had been several months since she'd even thought of the girl, but the compulsion to contact her was as overwhelming as it was surprising.

Lise had been sixteen when her older brother Henrik had been murdered by Martin Maybridge. The teenage girl had been the only one, besides Rowan, to suspect that his death had not been a suicide, and the pair, both grieving siblings, had bonded over their shared loss. Lise agreed to meet her in a cafe in St Nicholas Market.

Every time Rowan saw her friend she seemed further removed from the Lise she'd once known. The first time they had met, she was a shy, devastated girl with pigtail-plaits that seemed too young for her. In an act of defiance to her old life, she had chopped her locks down to an elfin, boyish cut and had now styled them into a choppy, blonde halo. Lise greeted her with an expected cheek kiss and placed an expensive looking handbag on the table before taking her seat in the cramped coffee shop.

"How've you been?" Rowan began.

"Exhausted," was her reply. "My publisher wants me to do some promo for the book, so I've been going around the country, doing the publicity circuit. Honestly, it's a nightmare. If I had my way, I'd just write a book, have it on the shelves for Christmas and get a nice royalty payment in the new year."

Rowan tried to hide her astonishment. "You wrote a book?"

"Oh honey, have you been living under a rock? I've written a memoir - at seventeen. Can you believe it?"

"I honestly can't," Rowan replied. Who was this person sitting opposite her? The young woman who'd affected a mildly posh accent to mask her Danish lilt and dressed like a shop mannequin in a Clifton Village shop window.

"I must forward you a copy, I think you'll find it fascinating. There might even be a few pages you could find useful on how I dealt with Henrik's murder. Mostly it's about my work exposing fraudulent mediums though. Did you know there's talk of a TV series? Maybe even chat show appearances in *The States?*"

Rowan was relieved by the interruption of a surly looking waitress in a Nirvana T-shirt who took their coffee orders without saying a word. "You really have been busy. No wonder we haven't seen that much of each other."

"And how about you? What wonders have you moved onto after that ghoulish stuff at the undertakers?"

"Gallow & Sons is a funeral home, not an undertakers. I'm still working there."

Lise gasped theatrically and threw a hand to her mouth. "Honey, I'm so sorry. I had no idea, I just assumed that you'd be moving on by now."

"It wasn't meant to be a temporary position."

Lise frowned. "Oh you sweetheart. You mustn't do this to yourself, you can't live in the shadow of death forever, you have to move on and make something of yourself."

Her friend, of course, had been allowed the chance to move on. Henrik's killer had been caught and imprisoned. Ruby's was still out there somewhere. "I actually find it very fulfilling work. It may be hard to understand but I've enjoyed it there."

"Oh, I feel like handing you the little sad-face emoji right now. I'm sure things are going to work out for you."

"I went to visit Maybridge the other day," said Rowan. She hadn't entirely meant to say it but she knew that doing so would silence her friend in her tracks.

"You did what?" Lise whispered, leaning in. "Why?"

"I was invited onto a prison programme where victims and perpetrators meet under supervision. I think it's meant to be some kind of therapy or something. I just went because I wanted to know what someone like that was really like, that maybe there was something in his eyes I could spot that I'd recognise in a killer."

"And what did you see in his eyes?" Lise asked, dramatically.

"Nothing at all. There was no remorse or anything, just a lot of anger he's been keeping hidden for a long time. I won't be doing it again."

"I'm amazed you had the courage to do it in the first place." Lise seemed genuinely impressed with her.

"There was another thing. Has anyone told you that he's got engaged?"

Lise's smile appeared bewildered. "He's engaged? How?"

"Apparently it's a pretty mundane event in prison. Inmates make pen pals with desperate or broken women who somehow fall in love with them. Don't worry, they won't be getting married, he'd have to be in a licensed building for a ceremony and he's never getting out of prison."

"Are you sure about that?" Lise's voice cracked temporarily into her native tongue.

"Trust me, he's going nowhere. Edison, my boss's brother, is a cop and he reckons the Home Office would intervene if he even applied for parole and slap a whole-life tariff on him."

"I wish they'd do that now. I'd love to see him locked away forever with no hope of freedom. That's as close as we'll ever get to punishing him for what he did."

Rowan nodded. "But have you ever thought of what you'd do, if he got out. If you met him, just walking down the street like he had the right to be there."

"Would I kill him?" Lise asked bluntly.

"Would you?"

She thought for a moment before replying, "I think I would. I don't think I'd have any choice in the matter. Something would take over. Mum and Dad would, in a second. How about you? If you found out who killed Ruby?"

"I think about it all the time," said Rowan. "I imagine what it'd feel like to stab him over and over and look him in the eye as he died, but I don't know if I ever could."

The change that had come over Lise was astonishing. The mention of Martin Maybridge had cracked the body suit she'd put on herself as armour, and beneath was revealed the angry, frightened, devastated girl, only three years younger than Rowan. When the waitress returned with their coffees, Lise at once rebuilt her shell and hid her frailties behind her synthetic accent. "Oh that is just divine," she said after taking a sip. "I tell you, I've been all around the country and it's turned me into something of a connoisseur of coffee, and this place is just perfection."

Rowan's heart sank. "So your book. What's it called?"

"*Coins in a Wishing Well*," she replied. "It's ghastly isn't it? I begged my publisher to offer an alternative and all they did was add a subtitle: *From Grief to Glory, A Sister's Story*. They said it has to sell and true crime is big right now... but the content is still the same. They put Henrik's face on the cover though. It's the whole cover and nothing else. It's really hard to look at it."

"Oh Lise, that's awful."

"It's business," she replied, firmly. "Like I said, the content is still all my own. I didn't use a ghost writer so I was able to keep it in my own voice. They did ask me to write a few extra chapters about Henrik and the murders so I had to. What's the point of writing about my success taking down fraudulent mediums if nobody's going to read it? It needs a hook."

Rowan felt sorry for her friend, she seemed to be trying to persuade herself that her endeavour had not been exploited by business interests and had remained as sincere as she had intended. "I'm sure it'll be great. I'll read it, I'd even like a signed copy if you don't mind. I was in it at the start, remember the night at the Picture House with that spiritualist?'

Both women smiled at the recollection. "Tegwyn Jones," said Lise. "You're in the book. A couple of chapters, actually."

Rowan's eyes widened. "Wait, did you use my name?"

"Don't look so alarmed. You're under a pseudonym."

"What am I called?"

"Erin Johnson," answered Lise.

"Oh. I was hoping for something a bit grander... like," Rowan looked at the ceiling as she thought. "Drusilla DuMontfort."

"I was writing about a nineteen year old, not a drag queen!" both girls laughed unabashedly and for a moment it felt as if their friendship had somehow travelled back through time to the days when Lise had not escaped her grief with

152

ambition and the pair were just ghosts in a city they couldn't quite understand, who had somehow managed to find each other.

After the coffees, Lise settled the bill and the pair headed out into the busy market. The smell of sizzling food from far away countries filled the air, as fashionable students draped in scarves, rifled through clothes hanging from frames. Lise slipped a £10 note into the pocket of a homeless man in a Father Christmas hat who'd fallen asleep next to a cash machine.

"What are you doing for Christmas?" Rowan asked her.

"Going back to Øresund for a family reunion," Lise laughed at herself. "Family reunion will never make sense to me. How can we be reunited when one of us is gone forever?"

"I know just what you mean. So are you planning on a hygge Christmas out there?"

Lise rolled her eyes. "It was a lot easier when you Brits had no idea of that word. Do you know how many times I've had to explain the concept to people this winter?"

"Sorry," Rowan smiled. "I do have to ask though, what's up with the accent?"

"That was my choice. Hygge and BBC4 murder mysteries are all this country seems to know about Denmark. When the tabloids started reporting on me investigating psychics they all called me a *real-life Sarah Lund* and wanted to dress me in Fairisle sweaters, so I thought, I'm not playing along with this, I'll sound like the most English of English roses."

"I prefer your real voice," said Rowan.

Lise sighed. "Well that's all in the past now, like so much other stuff. Anyway, what's your plan for today? Fancy a spot of shopping?"

Rowan shook her head. "D'you see this charity-shop chic I'm wearing and think I could afford any of the clothes around here?"

"I can treat you, I have my advance to burn through and I'm counting on my book being a hit this Christmas."

"I'll go and check it out. I'm sure I can find it in Broadmead."

"I'll get you a copy... I'll send you one." Lise's correction put into words what had been unspoken between the two of them. This would likely be the last time they would ever meet, they'd grown apart and Lise no longer needed Rowan.

Lise pointed to a vintage boutique called *Stupid, Sexy Flanders* and said "I best get going, it was nice seeing you though." With another kiss to the cheek, she was gone.

Smiling at the shop's slogan *"Feel Like You're Wearing Nothing At All"* painted over the door in a graffiti scrawl, Rowan watched her friend vanish inside and found herself surrounded by a hustle of Christmas shoppers as a wave of sadness washed over her. Despite the crowd, she felt horribly alone. Lise had been right about one thing, the time to move on really had come. Bristol could not be her home forever.

29.

Rowan knew she was in search of something that day. While the streets of Bristol were frantic with Christmas shoppers, hunting for last-minute gifts, Rowan found herself in pursuit of a friend, or at least a friendly ear. Perhaps she was simply in search of a shelter from the cold afternoon. Whatever urge had led her there, Rowan found herself at the door of Wandering Lily.

The window display had been provocatively redressed for Christmas, with a nativity scene depicting two mannequin women in the roles of Mary and Joseph, cooing over a plastic Jesus. Rowan pushed her way through the door to find Lily seated at the counter with Kay standing beside her. The pair were engaged in solemn conversation which was interrupted by her arrival.

"Rowan!" Lily bounded to her feet and threw her arms around her. "We were just talking about you? What a wonderful surprise!"

"You were talking about me?" she asked, as Lily dropped her arms from around her.

"You should've said you were dealing with Doug's funeral. Oh, sweet pea, it must be awful!"

"How did you know?"

Kay held up one of the notification cards Franklin had sent at the request of Douglas' mother. "We got these this morning. I've never received an invitation card for a funeral."

"I'm not working on it, Franklin's doing it by himself... I saw the body though."

Both women threw their hands to their mouths and Lily spontaneously hugged Rowan again. "You should've said, baby girl. It must've been *awful.*"

"It wasn't one of the best days on the job. Sorry I didn't tell you, I didn't know what to say. People get weird about funerals and what happens with the body."

Lily simply nodded and pushed her oversized glasses up her nose, but Kay spoke up. "So if you saw Doug's body, are you sure it was suicide, and not... you know."

Rowan found the eyes of the two women fixed on her with such sincere intensity, she could almost feel the heat of their gaze. "I thought the same thing - at first anyway. In fact me and Franklin even visited the tracks were he died. I honestly think he did it himself. His mum thinks the same and that has to mean something."

Lily and Kay both sighed with relief.

"I hope you don't think we were being dramatic," explained Kay. "But I can't pretend it hasn't crossed my mind that Ruby's gone and now Doug, it kind of felt like, who's next out of the four of us?"

Lily gently stroked Kay's back, an assortment of bangles jangled on her wrist as she did so. "We can't think like that, Kay. This was a tragedy, a completely different one to Ruby, but every bit as tragic."

Rowan found herself stiffening at these words. She could not comprehend how the two were in any way equivocal. Ruby thought she had her whole life ahead of her. A young woman just starting out in life, wringing joy out of every day with the expectation that countless more were to come. But she hadn't been allowed that chance, her life and those countless days were stolen from her and a void within the Kaplan family was opened forever. It was a tragedy of unsurpassed magnitude, for though Rowan often thought of what she and her parents had lost, it was nothing to what Ruby herself had been robbed of; her life, her future and the world had all been taken from her. Doug should have lived a life his former girlfriend had never been allowed, but instead he squandered it on self loathing. Ruby's life had been snuffed out like a candle by a stranger, but Douglas Bennet had snuffed his out himself.

"What can I help you with, sweetie?" Lily turned to Rowan. "Looking for some vintage fashion?"

Rowan hadn't expected that her unannounced visit would need an explanation, and elected to be truthful. "I've just been having a weird day. Sometimes, if I'm not working, I don't know what to do with myself. I thought I'd just drop by and like, see what's happening."

Lily offered her a pitying look, as if Rowan were a simple child. "That's so *sweet!*" Her smile seemed sincere in its warmth.

"So what are you two doing here, together?" Rowan asked.

"It's the last of the slaughter days," Kay said matter-of-factly. "I never like being there when it happens. Much easier just to be out of the place and come home to an empty shed. I thought I'd drop in and see how Lily was coping. I guessed she would get the card on the same day."

Lily sighed. "It's gonna be a weird Christmas with the service happening the day after Boxing Day."

"Franklin tried holding it back until after New Year but the... storage costs would've been too much for Doug's family."

Rowan caught the briefest glimpse between Lily and Kay and felt a stab of remorse for the business practices of Gallow & Sons. Turning a profit out of tragedy rarely felt like a noble pursuit but it was particularly troubling when the minutiae of a service was broken into units. Extortionate costs for flower arrangements, vehicle hire, home meetings and the storage of a corpse. Body cleaning, body dressing, hair and make up, all contributed to the shocking cost grieving families had to add to their list of woes. Even a budget service at the cheapest rate offered by Gallow & Sons could be financially crippling.

"Well," Lily smiled softly. "I'm sure you're taking good care of him."

"I can promise you that he's being well looked after." It was a line that, while true, felt empty from overuse.

"D'you know who else is going to the service?" Kay asked.

"Franklin has a list, but I didn't want to look over it. I've stayed well away from all of this."

"I wonder if that crazy witch is invited," said Lily.

"D'you mean Orlagh?" Rowan asked.

Lily nodded. "Did you know she thinks she killed Ruby? With magic," she said to Kay.

"Jesus Christ, what mad stuff is she smoking now? I told you she was trouble as soon as she joined Morning Shiver. I just knew it was a bad idea. She was too intense, and she just stood there on stage with this full-on stare like she was singing about genocide or something."

"D'you know she sent me a friend request on Facebook last night. I was like, who are you? Why now?" said Lily.

"That's a bit strange. Did you accept it?"

Lily shook her head. "Things are crazy enough in my life right now without inviting more of it in. You don't think she contacted me because she's coming to the service do you? God, imagine the state of her in mourning clothes. Can a goth even do mourning properly?"

Rowan watched the two women chuckling at one another. Orlagh certainly was crazy, or at least her brain had been addled to the point of craziness by drug use, but she couldn't help but think there was something significant in this unexpected attempt to contact a long-forgotten friend.

"I've no idea who I'm going to take as my plus one," said Lily to Kay. "It's fine for you, you live with your wife. My boyfriend's out of town for Christmas. I really don't want to show up on my own though."

"It's a funeral, Lily, not school prom. I don't think anyone will even notice if you show up without anyone. You can arrive with Ruth and me if you want."

"Thanks, I might need a shoulder to cry on. Can you believe I've only ever been to one other funeral, and that was Ruby's."

"Same here," said Kay. Both women turned to face Rowan.

"I've been to loads," she said. "Hundreds. Because of work."

"Oh yes, of course," said Lily. "I was thinking I wanted to bring some token from here to the service. D'you think that'll be allowed? I don't know what, just something that I think Doug would've liked, I think he really enjoyed working here."

"How long did he work here?" Rowan asked.

"Off and on for about two years. He was only ever part time, and he was always looking for work elsewhere, but he was never any good at holding down a job. His moods made him too unstable and hard to depend on. I never really needed him here but I felt too protective of him to let him go. He mostly just kept the basement in order. Which reminds me, did you ever hear about the engraving he made in the wall?"

Rowan shook her head, perplexed as to how she could be privy to that information.

Built into the wall at shoulder height behind Lily was a small safe with a digital touchpad. Lily turned and hastily entered a four-digit code which opened the door, revealing a single wooden box inside, from which she produced an old-fashioned looking brass key. "Follow me, you have to see this."

Rowan did as she was told and followed Lily through the maze of bric-a-brac and vintage treasures to a narrow green door in the far wall between two shelves of ladies' shoes.

"I keep this locked even during business hours. Even if it says no entry you'd be amazed how many people think they can just potter about wherever they want to go. The stuff on display in the shop is probably about 10% of all the goods I have, so in a way it's the most precious part of the whole place. People don't care though, they think it's their right to go wherever they want." Lily turned the lock and pushed the door open. From the blackness beyond came a gust of cold air and a stench of musty dampness. She flicked on a switch and the space was illuminated in a chilly fluorescent light. Lily led the way down a coil of stone steps with Rowan and Kay in tow.

"It's like a museum," Rowan marvelled. Before her stretched rows of high wooden shelves, stacked with oddments and curiosities. An entire aisle was dedicated to taxidermy and preserved animals in jars of formaldehyde, another heaved beneath the weight of unsorted watercolour paintings. A fox head dangled from a box of fur stoles and seemed to stare at Rowan with its beady eyes as she passed it.

"A museum is the right word," said Lily. "Everyone knows that all the really good stuff is kept backstage. This is my nest egg. I hold it back for the slender months, or when the wolf is at the door. I inherited it from the woman who ran the shop before me and her family weren't interested in any of this, I think they thought it was all just junk. I shall probably wind up retiring on this."

"Or getting crushed to death beneath it all," Kay added.

"Yes, there is that. Doug was working on sorting this into some kind of order. Believe it or not, before he started it was even more chaotic than it is now. I think he enjoyed the task. It was good for his mind to bring balance to disorder. Kind of like doing a jigsaw puzzle. Soon after he started working here it was actually accessible and I could see just how much stock there is, and it was about that time that he left his mark." Lily gestured to a tea chest that was resting against one of the bare, stone walls. "Can you help me shift that?"

Rowan pushed and Lily pulled and soon the chest was crunching and grinding its way along the concrete floor. Lily pointed it out but Rowan had seen it already.

Etched in the wall were the words *"I MISS YOU RUBY"*.

30.

Midway across the Clifton Suspension Bridge, Rowan looked up at the huge, iron chains which held the gargantuan construction aloft. Two men had died building the bridge, she recalled, but countless more had lost their lives intentionally, plummeting to their deaths into the River Avon, far below. The first suicide was a mere 18 months after the bridge had opened, a middle-aged local man leapt from the railings and into history, founding a deadly tradition that would claim hundreds.

The barriers which had been put in place in 1998 at either side of the span had halved the number of suicides, and additional work had made jumping virtually impossible. The mighty structure loomed over the city as its most iconic monument, and testament to Victorian ingenuity, but also as a stark reminder of death and despair. Rowan had not come here to contemplate mortality, but had found herself doing so regardless. The dark thoughts of a woman who has been touched by death were only ever temporarily retired to the wings, waiting for their cue; the sight of flowers taped to a lamppost; the crushed remains of an animal rendered unrecognisable as roadkill; even the persistent ticking of a clock, counting down the seconds until oblivion.

Rowan studied the colossal towers at either end of the bridge, taking notes in her mind of the irregularities of its construction, documenting them with her phone camera. Above her head she watched as a spherical camera swivelled its lens like an eye to point at her, and she took a couple of steps backwards to be out of its gaze. After capturing a few more images of the bridge, and allowing the theory in her mind to solidify into something comprehensible, she peered over the edge to the water below, to where sheets of ice, like glass, were drifting on the river, reflecting the amber sky overhead. She felt a gentle tap on her shoulder.

"Excuse me, Miss," said an elderly gentleman.

Rowan turned to face the man. He was white-haired and round faced, and wore a high-visibility jacket which brandished a name tag with "*ELVIS*" printed in block capitals. "Yes?"

"I work in the tollbooth on the Leigh Woods side and noticed that you've been standing on the bridge for quite some time. Is everything alright?"

Rowan did n't at first understand the man's concern. "I was just taking pictures. It's for a project."

"Is there anyone I could call? Perhaps a friend? Or maybe you'd prefer to talk anonymously to someone, I can get you in touch with a sympathetic ear. I know things may seem bad, especially at this time of year, but trust me, it's not worth it."

Rowan stifled a startled laugh. "Oh no! I'm not thinking of jumping, honestly. I was just taking photographs, that's all."

Elvis looked at her suspiciously. "I have a kettle in my tollbooth if you'd just like to sit down for a while with tea and a biscuit. I'm told I'm a very good listener."

"I'm not going to jump, sir," she informed him, kindly. "I just haven't ever had a really good look at the bridge until now."

"The lights will be coming on soon. It's hard to photograph at dusk with the lights on, perhaps it'd be better to get on your way."

"I'm almost done," she said.

"Please, Miss. I've seen it happen too many times and I couldn't bear another. It's always the same, people loiter about, pretending to take pictures and trying to look inconspicuous and then... it's all over. I got worried when I couldn't see you on CCTV anymore."

"Wait. You can't see me here?" Rowan asked.

"It's a black spot at the moment. One of the cameras has gone out. Look, if you don't mind, it would make me feel much better if you walked with me to the end of the bridge. I can give you a pamphlet."

Rowan sighed and consulted her watch. "Fine, I have to get to my work Christmas party in a bit anyway."

"Are work problems getting you down?"

"Elvis, I'm not suicidal. I'm not even close, I'm just appreciating a bit of architecture."

Elvis seemed unconvinced. "Is it boyfriend troubles?"

"Come on then," Rowan picked up her Brompton bike which had folded at her feet. "I know you mean well, and I do appreciate it, but I'm not going to commit suicide."

"Actually the preferred term now is died by suicide as it's no longer a crime."

"Fine. I was going to go anyway, I have quite a busy evening planned."

Elvis followed her closely as she led the way to the Clifton side of the bridge. "Just two more days to Christmas and then New Year isn't far behind. That's always a great time to make a fresh start, new beginnings and all. It's like turning over a new leaf."

"Yes, I'll bear that in mind," Rowan had given up trying to convince him that she wasn't attempting self-destruction.

After reaching the tower and unfolding her bike into shape, she was about to cycle away when Elvis hastily blurted, "I hope I made a difference."

Rowan turned to look at the kindly-faced man, whose cheeks and nose were turning red in the cold. His eyes were full of sorrow and she wondered how many tragedies on that bridge he may have witnessed, incapable of preventing them, powerless in his little tollbooth. Perhaps he needed to hear that, for once, he had made a difference. "Thank you, Elvis. You were very helpful indeed. Merry Christmas," before she cycled away she saw the man exhale deeply and a smile break out across his face.

She barely had to pedal as she made her way downhill from Clifton Village to Park Street. She didn't even offer Ghurt Lush a sideways glance as she whizzed past to St Augustine's Parade and onto the ancient cobbles of Corn Street. Outside the Elephant Restaurant, so named as the grand, old building bore the plaster-cast likeness of an elephant on its exterior wall, she folded up her bike and stepped inside.

Franklin was seated opposite Meredy at a long table which had been draped with a festive tablecloth and dressed with Christmas crackers and miniature snowmen which held their knives and forks from extended, twig arms. It was charming.

Franklin and Meredy cheered her arrival as she sat beside Franklin. It had only been a day since she'd last seen him but it felt much longer and she couldn't quite explain why. At an adjoining table the assortment of day labourers offered her a half-familiar nod to which she responded in kind.

"Franklin's sitting under the mistletoe," Meredy informed her with a rich giggle, before she upturned her wine glass and finished the last of its contents.

"I didn't know," said Franklin, who was helping himself to another glass from one of the bottles which stood on the table. Rowan got the sense at once that the pair had been drinking for some time. "So, how are things with you?"

"The deed's done," she shrugged. "I broke up with Jude."

Meredy gasped. "You dumped your boyfriend two days before Christmas? That's stone cold, Rowan. I like it!" Meredy held out her empty glass to her and Rowan clinked her own against it.

"Trust me, you would've done the same if you knew what I did."

"Mysterious," Meredy added.

"Are you alright?" Franklin poured her a generous helping of red wine.

"I'm better than I'd be if I was still with him. I'm glad it's over but I was with him for almost a year and a half, that's longer than anyone I've ever been with. It's kind of strange."

"Don't look back, Rowan, that's what I say," Meredy slurred. "Enjoy being young and single. Don't tie yourself down with anyone and don't marry some man just because he's the only person to ask you, and for the love of god, don't have any kids, they're more hassle than they're worth."

Rowan smiled at Meredy. She'd never seen her drunk before. To Franklin and Rowan, the Christmas party was little more than an annual formality, the social gathering which was attended only because it was expected of them, but for Meredy, whose home life was problematic and nights out were rare pleasures, this party was a chance to have some fun.

"Are we waiting for Peterman?" Rowan asked.

"He says he's coming, but I'll believe it when I see it. I've never known him make it to one of these things before." Franklin replied.

"You shouldn't have invited him," sneered Meredy.

"That would've guaranteed he'd show up, just to spite us. Like the ghost at the feast."

"Or Maleficent in Sleeping Beauty," Meredy added.

It was at that exact moment that Peterman chose to make his entrance. He was dressed in his work suit which he had matched with a surprisingly merry tie which bore a cartoon Christmas pudding. His tangled wiry hair had been tamed into a waxed flat comb-over. "Evening all," he chirruped as he took his seat. A broad smile stretched his face disconcertingly. "Under the mistletoe are you, Franklin? I would've brought a breath mint if I knew I was going to be kissing you."

Repulsed by the idea, yet perplexed by Peterman's demeanour, Franklin replied, "I didn't know it was there when I sat down."

"A likely story," he turned to Rowan. "Well, it seems I'm rather overdressed for the occasion. I didn't know we were keeping things casual."

Rowan had dressed in layers for the cold, with one of her granddad's old knitted jumpers pulled over a plaid shirt. She refused to take Peterman's bait and simply smiled at him. "You're looking very nice this evening."

He offered her a grotesque wink before staring directly at Meredy's cleavage. "Evening Meredy,"

"You know they don't do tricks if you keep on looking at them, don't you?" Meredy replied, with a filthy laugh.

"Well, isn't this nice. A cosy little reunion of friends. I wonder why we don't do it more often." Peterman's statement was heavy with sarcasm.

Upon seeing his arrival, the wait staff began piling the two tables with gravy boats and bowls of bread sauce, before bringing out huge plates laden with Christmas dinners from the set menu.

The sound of Christmas crackers being pulled filled the restaurant, followed by the rustle of paper hats being placed on heads. Rowan was surprised to see that even Peterman had put his on and was unfurling the joke which had landed on the table.

"What does James Bond eat at Christmas?" Peterman didn't wait for speculation. "Mince spies. What utter nonsense, who writes these things?"

But Meredy had been tickled by the pun and threw her head back in a raucous burst of laughter until tears began rolling down her cheeks. The laughter descended into a hoarse cough before collapsing altogether, leaving Meredy heaving with desolate sobs. "I didn't mean to say my kids were a burden! I love them, and I never regret having them!"

"Ok," Franklin slid her glass of wine away from her. "Perhaps it's best that you eat something before you drink any more."

Meredy nodded, wiped her eyes and then, as if nothing had happened, straightened her paper crown and began forking Brussel sprouts into her mouth.

Rowan had received a minuscule plastic car in her cracker which she placed beside her dinner plate, on spotting it Peterman commented, "There you go, Gallow, your next car. Damn sight roomier than the one you drive now!"

His attempts to shame her for her old sweater aside, Rowan couldn't help but notice a change in Peterman. He seemed festive, even happy. Perhaps, she thought, he'd been visited by three ghosts the night before, who'd told him to mend his ways.

"Someone else's Christmas dinner is never as good as the one my mum used to make," said Franklin to Rowan, as he tucked into the feast.

Rowan nodded. "It was my dad who used to do the cooking, especially on Christmas day. We were all banned from the kitchen until it was ready because he approached it like a scientific experiment with a spreadsheet and everything. He'd even do a trial run the week before and take it down to the homeless shelter in St Pauls."

Franklin nodded his approval. "Me and Edison used to spend the whole day fighting, it must've driven my parents nuts, it was chaos."

"I was always the one up at dawn, but Ruby was always too cool to let on that she was excited about presents, even when we were really tiny."

"Who's Ruby?" The voice cut across the table and sent everyone around it into a state of frozen shock. Peterman looked oblivious to the reaction his comment had made.

"Ruby's my sister," Rowan said.

"Oh yes. Older or younger?"

"Let's change the subject," Meredy slurred. "What's everyone getting for Christmas?"

"Older," Rowan continued.

"How old?" Peterman couldn't have been really interested. In all the time she'd worked at Gallow & Sons he'd not enquired about her life even once, but something about the tension in the air his question had caused seemed to be driving him on.

"Nineteen."

"But..." Peterman's eyes dropped and he looked momentarily lost for words. "I'm very sorry. What was it? A car crash?"

"Don't be so insensitive," Franklin interjected.

"She was murdered, actually. Three and a half years ago."

"Crap." Peterman looked genuinely mortified by his crass questioning. Perhaps, Rowan wondered, the old man never *tried* to be offensive, it just seemed that way to others. Like the way some people can go through life being utterly unaware that they have terrible body odour, as everything smells fine to them.

"Did these two know?" he asked and Rowan nodded. "Well, I suppose it's to be expected, I'm not the easiest person to get along with, or work with... or spend any time around. I'm sorry, really I am."

Rowan didn't know what was happening, she'd never seen Peterman the slightest bit concerned about what she thought of him, let alone contrite. "It's fine," she said. "Honestly."

He seemed not to have heard her, as he rose to his feet and clinked a dessert spoon against the edge of his wine glass to get the attention of both tables. He cleared his throat. "I'm not one for speeches most of the time. In fact, I'm a man of

167

few words, because every time I do say anything somebody winds up upset, but I would like to say something, an announcement really. Some of you may be aware that I've been working on a service for two young kids - babies really - and I think it's best that all of you hear it from me, that this will be the last service I work on. I'll be retiring soon after New Year."

The day labourers on the adjoining table knew nothing of Peterman except for his reputation as a difficult man, so they merely mumbled empty platitudes like "Good for you" and "Shame to see you go" but Rowan didn't quite know how to react. They had all longed for this moment, of course, but manners prevented them from celebrating.

"Why now?" Franklin was the first of them to speak. "Why not years ago?"

Peterman sighed. "I know you'll all be pleased to see me go, and maybe with good reason. It's not nice to think that nobody will miss you and the only cheer you can bring to other people is by buggering off out of their lives for good. You see, I got some rather bad news this week. It appears that I've gone and got myself a pretty aggressive bout of cancer. Colonic, if you must know."

To this, Rowan's table did know how to react - with gasps.

"They haven't given me a timeframe but the prognosis isn't great. If I'm here this time next Christmas it'll be nothing short of a miracle. It's made me think about how I want to spend the last of my time here on earth, and I don't think I want it to be surrounded by corpses. I have some people I'd like to apologise to - not any of you lot, of course, but some people I need to mend some bridges with. I hope you don't mind the short notice, Franklin but I hope you can make an exception for me."

"Of course," Franklin said, solemnly. "Peterman, that's awful. I don't know what to say."

Meredy was far less reserved in her response, bursting into tears and throwing her arms around his shoulders. "Oh Peterman! We can beat this thing, I'll be at your side every step of the way. It takes a positive mental attitude and I just know that…"

"...There isn't much that can be done," Peterman said. "Any treatment is just prolonging the inevitable, but I'll take whatever extension I can get."

The rest of the dinner was eaten in a mirthless silence as each reflected on what Peterman had meant to them. Rowan had disliked Peterman, and thought that she hated him, but she could not find it within himself to feel anything but tremendous sorrow for him and his mortal predicament. As the workers of Gallow & Sons began to depart one by one from the table and disappear into the cold night, Franklin and Rowan bid Peterman a good night as he left, both in tones that felt too heavy with meaning. Soon only the pair of them remained seated at the table.

"I never thought I'd end up feeling sorry for Peterman," said Franklin.

"I know. Poor guy, I'm not even going to mention anything about the irony of him getting cancer of the arsehole."

Franklin winced. "He may well be an arsehole, but I think I'm going to miss him being around the funeral home. Is that weird? Not to mention how difficult it'll be finding a replacement."

"It's not weird. I kind of know what you mean."

"It might be inappropriate to ask this right now, but if there's going to be an opening, there's nobody I can think of who's more qualified to fill it. What d'you say? How about becoming a funeral director?"

Rowan blinked, and thought.

31.

The numbness Franklin felt at Peterman's revelation broke the shock of the cold and as he wandered home alone across the frozen city, he found himself reliving memories of his disagreeable foe like an orchestral overture, highlights from years of dreadful, often drunken, behaviour, which were now tinged with a sadness that he could never have anticipated. He had once read that memories weren't replays of what genuinely happened, they were closer to reconstructions, and every time a memory was recalled it was restaged, with all the players taking their cues but each time slightly changed from the time before, tainted by the present and forever altered. Perhaps there would come a time when Peterman was long gone and Franklin would think of him and smile, such had his memories of the terrible man been corrupted by his impending death.

He thought of Rowan and her reticence to give an answer to his proposal. He knew she was ready for the job and there was nobody he would have trusted with it more. Of course she would need extra training and to obtain a driver's licence, but they were trifling issues for the future, what mattered was that she could and would be fine replacement for Peterman, who, regardless of his failings as a person, had been a near flawless funeral director.

So why had she not said yes? Why had she asked for time to think about it? Franklin tried to shrug his doubts away and instead reflected on what would have been, had it not been for Peterman's doom-laden prognosis, a moderately enjoyable Christmas party.

The first snow began to fall as Franklin entered Queen Square. A pair of drunken men of student age began cheering its arrival as if they were excitable children. It fell in big, pretty flakes which drifted on the gentle breeze and settled on the dry, frosted ground. At first it was light, just a gentle dusting which fell on the lapels of his overcoat, but soon it was coming down in white curtains, surrounding him on all sides and making it difficult to see the mighty, grand statue of

William III on horseback which stood proud over the ancient park. Snow was pitching around its hooves.

"Mr Gallow?" The voice of the man he had come to meet spoke through the flurry of snowflakes and stepped into the pool of light created by a streetlamp. "Is that you?"

"It is. Thank you for meeting me here. I'm sorry I'm a bit late, there was a work thing - well, a work party, and it went a bit sour towards the end."

"I understand," said the man. "I had my works do a couple of nights ago. Things got pretty rowdy…"

"Well, if the cold doesn't kill us I'm sure this snow will have us buried in no time. Can I treat you to a pint in the warm somewhere?"

"Please. I'm gasping. How does the Llandoger sound to you?"

"Perfect."

Franklin had only ever seen Oscar Kaplan once, at a dancing competition where he and his wife had come to watch Rowan and Jude lindy hop their way to an award. They had exchanged nothing more than a knowing glance and a nod, each reciprocating the knowledge that the other had recognised them. He had thought Rowan's father was a handsome man but hadn't quite appreciated just how striking he was. The man towered over him to an imposing degree and wore a long coat open in spite of the cold, under which he had intentionally mismatched lurid, bold colours in his jacket, tie and trousers, a look Franklin knew would look ridiculous on himself, but offered Oscar Kaplan an air of tremendous confidence.

"Not a word about this to Rowan, alright?"

"Of Course. I don't like keeping secrets from her, but this is for the best. I don't know how she keeps it together sometimes. She's remarkable."

"I don't know how any of us keep it together, but you're right. Four years ago you would've met a girl who was very different to the Rowan you know now. She was quiet but that was because she was thoughtful. She was in awe of Ruby, but everyone was. Sometimes when I think back to who she is now and who she was then, it's like I lost two daughters that night. She keeps everything locked up inside her, she doesn't talk to us like she used to. One of these days it's all going to become too much and she's going to... explode or something. It can't be healthy."

"Mr Kaplan?"

"Oscar."

"Oscar, can I be completely level with you this evening? I have no opinions about anything that happened that night, I have no theories or suspicions. I just want to know everything and for you to be as honest as you can be, please tell me everything, no matter how small it may be, even if you thought it was too irrelevant to mention to the police. I want to know everything, to piece that night together and to find out where everyone was and what they were doing."

Oscar pulled the door to the Llandoger Trow open and stepped aside to let Franklin in before him. "You mean you want to know where I was and if I killed my daughter."

"If we're being completely honest," Franklin replied. "Then yes."

The Llandoger Trow was among the oldest pubs in Bristol and wore its antiquity with much character. For centuries it had been the meeting place of crooks, scoundrels and pirates, of prostitutes and privateers and the target of temperance societies who saw it as a beacon of all that was wrong with the sinful docks. Its fortunes had risen and fallen with those of the city, but still it remained, a quaint muddle of Tudor cob and wood, warped and buckled with age, but still standing as a proud relic of a bygone age; even an incendiary bomb dropped by the Luftwaffe had not destroyed the Llandoger.

In a quiet corner, far from the drunken patrons who were singing Christmas songs around the bar, Franklin and Oscar sat across from one another in the glare of an open fire, with pints of cider resting on the blackened, oak table between them.

"I hope you don't think my hesitance in contacting you was a mark against my character," said Oscar. "I've been reliving the events of that night over and over in my head and I was in no rush to clarify things to a stranger. Had it not been for Rowan poking about in the case I don't think I would ever have replied to your emails."

"It's understandable. I think it's fair to say that Rowan's the reason I'm here too. I'd certainly not be prying into your life if it wasn't for her."

Oscar Kaplan took a beer mat in his huge hands and began weaving it distractedly between his fingers. "I'd been playing dominoes that night at the community centre. I've been playing since I was a kid, my father taught me. It's still popular throughout the West Indies and there are leagues in St Pauls. I've never been great at it but playing makes me feel like I'm paying homage to the past, keeping my dad alive in a way. He would've wanted to know that something in my blood was still part of his homeland. It was the most ordinary of nights. Nothing would've been remarkable about it had nothing happened afterwards. I probably stayed for less than two hours and won only a couple of games. I was due in to work the next morning so I wanted an early night. It seems so strange now to think that I could've had no idea, that there was no omen or warning telling me that something was wrong and my daughter was in danger. That my only worry would be not getting enough sleep and feeling tired at work the next day. You can't imagine how much I'd love for those days to be back again."

Franklin took a swig of his pint. "People vouched for when you left the community centre?"

"They did. It was probably just after ten. I actually walked straight past the pub Ruby was rehearsing in on the way home, if you can believe it. The same CCTV that showed her leaving also caught me at about quarter past. I wasn't quite ready to turn in yet, in fact, I had other plans I didn't want to be late for."

"On Dundry?"

Oscar's eyes met his. "What d'you know about Dundry Hill?"

"It doesn't matter what I know, I want to hear from you why you were there."

"OK. I'd only had a pint so I knew I'd be good to drive. I went home just to pick up my car, I didn't even pop in to see Rolinda. Stuff doesn't start happening until later on in the night but I was prepared to wait. I'm a very proud man, but I'm not proud of my sexual proclivities."

"I know you must feel ashamed, but shame has to be better than being a suspect?"

Oscar nodded. "I never joined in with any of it. I'd never want to either. For me, it was always just about the watching, just the huge taboo of seeing things happen right in front of you, as if it's perfectly normal. Sex in cars, sex *on* cars, women making out and putting on a show, guys steaming up the windows with their breath as they watch what's going on inside. It's like a drug, Franklin - and I'm a pharmacist, I don't say that lightly. It's intoxicating and addictive."

"How many times did you go?"

"Dozens," he shrugged. "At first I hated it. It was smutty jokes about how I should join in because of what they'd heard about black men, but I kept on going back for reasons I've never been able to explain. Yes, it was sexy, but I could've just watched porn at home, it was something else, it was wrong and *dangerous*. My life is... was, a very ordinary one. I had a healthy, happy family, a secure job with a good future. Day to day life was so safe and normal that it was the danger that had me going back over and over. It was just like dominoes, the safe moves usually guarantee a win if you play conservatively, but I would lose because I liked the thrill of the risk, casting down the tiles almost at random just to see what would happen, even if victory had been assured."

"You were risking your marriage. Your family if you got caught."

"Exactly. That was the thrill, and that's why I've never told anyone about it before."

"Even when the police were questioning you about where you'd been that night?"

Oscar nodded. "It probably sounds like madness, or arrogance, that I'd try to protect my reputation in the middle of my daughter's murder investigation, but shame has driven proud men to kill themselves and I would've rather died than have people know what I'd been up to. Not just Rolinda and Rowan, but neighbours, co-workers, just the everyday strangers you meet all the time, everyone knowing about the sordid things I'd been up to. Maybe I would've kept quiet about it forever, maybe I would even have gone to prison rather than let that secret out."

Franklin couldn't understand the man who sat across the table from him, but he didn't doubt him. For the first time ever he abandoned his pint, before bidding Oscar goodnight and heading home through the snow.

32.

It had been years since Rowan had last seen real snow. Occasionally it had dusted Bristol for an hour or two, or it could be seen in drifts upon high hills around there city, but it had rarely outstayed its welcome in her lifetime.

The sight of it was beautiful. Standing in the open doorway of her apartment building with her coat wrapped over her pyjamas, she gazed at it with wide, childlike eyes. It was pristine, untouched by foot or the churn of wheels. Still it fell, fluttering in the glow of streetlights, rendering familiar streets into unknown wonderlands, turning parked cars and trees into indiscernible white blobs of mashed potato.

Disappointedly Rowan had watched the news as winter after winter the rest of the country had found itself beneath a blanket of snow, yet her city had remained steadfastly barren. The last bands of the Gulf Stream driving up the Bristol Channel had brought with it tepid rain rather than this kind of magic. It was just as she felt joy bubbling inside her that the cruel voice in her head reminded her that "Ruby never lived to see a white Christmas." That was how it always happened for Rowan. The slightest trace of happiness would wake that voice to extinguish all joy. She stepped back inside and let the door swing shut behind her.

It had been a morose evening already. The brief respite the snow had brought was only a distraction to the task in hand. Just as the virgin white that carpeted the city would be turned to grey slush with the morning's traffic, so must her evening descend into horror. She cast aside the Edinburgh University syllabus and fell into the sole armchair in her flat.

She had put off reading the autopsy report for as long as she'd had it. It'd been among the first of the evidence Edison had managed to photocopy from the police files and had been smuggled out of the station at her request. How dare it be that the most private details of her sister's murder could be locked away, seen only by the eyes of people who had never known Ruby in life? That they could scour over the details of her broken body, yet the details be forbidden to her family.

"The only way to access the files would be a freedom of information request," Edison had grimly informed her. "And you can't just release the parts you want. If the request was granted, and I doubt it would be, as even if the case is cold, it's still open, but you wouldn't just be releasing the bits you wanted, everything, crime scene photos, private correspondences, graphic details of how she died, even stuff about the last thing she ate, that all becomes public record, and once it's out there, people can do with it what they want."

She had not found the autopsy report graphic at first. There had been nothing lurid about it, but its matter-of-factness had disturbed her. It had begun with a detailed list of her clothing, everything had been labelled, catalogued and described in meticulous detail, from the scuffs on the heel of her shoe to an untangled thread in a bra cup. There had been no use of her name, except in the header of each page, instead she was referred to as "*the body*" throughout. It was the kind of dehumanising language Rowan had found herself resorting to when she first began dealing with corpses at Gallow & Sons. The subject was not human, it had not lived a life or had unfulfilled dreams. Without a name, a body was simply a bag of chemicals and organs, unloved by anyone, and incapable of loving. This was why her sister had been robbed of her identity.

In the chair, by the window she sat, pausing to watch the snow piling up on the sash window when the horrors of the page became too overwhelming, but like an explorer, willing herself to delve deeper into uncharted caves, she urged herself on through the darkness. The final sheets of the report documented Ruby's wounds. It was only here that the writer had used a flourish of language, but the words he'd used were "*frenzied*" and "*savage*" as the details of the attack were described. One of the nineteen wounds had been made to her stomach, eight had landed on her chest. Her neck and shoulders had taken nine more, and a final wound had been more like a slash than a stab, tearing through her dress and across her abdomen. She had been dead throughout the onslaught with the knife.

Quivering hands replaced the papers in the folder and Rowan sat in silence for a while, forcing herself not to shy from the nightmarish images her mind had conjured. She'd not been able to fight her assailant because she may not even have seen him come at her. She had been strangled to death in a cold, damp, deserted warehouse with no explanation for why she was even there. She had been stabbed and slashed and abandoned on the concrete floor, where she was found by the police in the early morning. It was a brutal, pointless end to a young woman's life, but at least it had been quick.

Something struck Rowan. Like a tremor in her mind, a flash of something wrong with the report, something amiss and out of order which she could not quite place. She opened the folder and pulled out the first page again and read through the forensic list of everything she had worn that night. Her antique watch, an inheritance from her grandmother, was listed, and still working as her autopsy was held, the St. Christopher's Cross she wore round her neck had survived the onslaught, but there, glaring in its absence, was the thing that had rattled her unconscious mind. Where was Ruby's red plastic ring?

33.

"A paedophile?"

Hearing Franklin say the word made her recoil at the heft of it. "That's right."

Sunday mornings usually found Franklin and Rowan inside a coffee shop on the harbour, but the snow had turned the whole city into a wintry mystery and the pair could not resist a stroll along the docks, warming drinks in hand, and bundled beneath scarves, hats and coats buttoned all the way up to the neck. The snow had only relented at dawn, by which time it had covered the city, burying streets and gardens, painting roofs in white icing and floating through the harbour atop jagged sheets of ice.

"Isn't he a little young to be a nonce?" Franklin asked, as the pair wandered between the legs of one of the colossal iron cranes.

"The dirty old man thing is a bit of a stereotype," she said. "And don't say nonce."

Franklin raised an eyebrow. "Should I be using a politically correct term for kiddie-fiddlers?"

"Probably. And he isn't a kiddie-fiddler, he said he's never touched a child."

"And d'you believe him?"

Rowan nodded. "I don't know what else I can do. Honestly, you should have seen him open up on Friday night. I couldn't help but feel a bit sorry for him - the way he is isn't his fault."

"Jesus, Rowan. What a thing to deal with. I know things weren't working out for the pair of you but nobody could've been prepared for that. You should've told me before."

"In the strangest way it actually felt like a relief," Rowan looked at Franklin. "So much about him had been a mystery that finding it out, it suddenly made sense. I saw the whole picture and it was a grim one, but I understood it at least. The way he just dropped into my life out of the blue... I was even starting to think it was *him*." Rowan didn't need to elaborate on who the *him* was.

"But it can't be him, can it?"

"I don't think so. He wasn't even in the city when Ruby was murdered, but that's not the point. It's the same paranoia that makes me fill in the gaps about everyone I know. Was it him, or her? It's one of the madnesses that comes from not having answers, everyone becomes a suspect."

"Even me?" Franklin asked.

Rowan offered him a smile. "Even you. It might be unforgivable but as soon as I started working here, I went back over the records to see what you were up to that night."

"What was I up to?"

"You were on a night shift. At the time Ruby was murdered you were picking up a body from an old people's home in Clevedon."

"It's good to know I've been eliminated from your inquiries."

"If you're trying to make me feel bad, it's not gonna work. It was a year and a half ago and I barely knew you. If there were records letting me know what every person in the city was doing on that night in July, I would go through all half-a-million of them. You had a record of that night, I wanted to see what you'd been up to."

Franklin shrugged. "Fair enough. I'm sure I'd have done the same if I were in your position and Edison had been killed."

"How is Edison?"

"Your guess is as good as mine. I don't think there's ever going to be a time where he's fixed, just extended periods where he's doing better. Life isn't going to be easy for him and there'll be times when it's really, really hard, but there will be times when it's really, really good. He's on a rollercoaster and I'm in the queue, watching him go around."

"Life isn't going to be easy for any of us though, is it? For years I've been thinking about how it'll feel when we catch the killer, when he's finally put away. When that jury says "guilty" and I can look him in the eye and see remorse - or just fear. But what happens after that? Ruby won't be back and we'll all still be in grief. Her killer won't be free but neither will the rest of us. Everyone who knew her has to just pick up the pieces and move on, pretending that nothing's changed and that we're happy."

"Has someone slipped downers into your coffee this morning?" Franklin asked with a smile.

"It's just Christmas. Every year feels harder than the last. It's unbearable seeing all the adverts of happy families on TV and hearing about people reuniting after a year apart. I wish they'd all just shut up and keep their happiness to themselves, it's just rude."

"If it helps, I plan to have a truly dull Christmas in front of the TV with the Gallow clan. Dad makes a bigger deal out of Thanksgiving anyway, so it's hardly a big family event."

"Christmas used to be wonderful at our house," said Rowan. "We'd have a giant meal, even I'd be allowed a glass of wine, and afterwards we'd turn on the music and all dance around the kitchen in our pyjamas and slippers to whatever Christmas tripe was on the radio. That's what our family was, it was *joy* that we had stolen from us."

They paused to watch a man knocking icicles with a broom from the eave which overhung the M Shed Museum, shattering them like glass on the ground below. "Haven't seen a snowfall like this since '62," he cheerfully informed them. "Started snowing on Boxing Day and was still on the ground at Easter. Went sledging down Park Street all winter long, we did!"

"Merry Christmas," Franklin doffed his woollen hat to the man before he and Rowan moved on.

"The snow won't hang around for as long as that, will it?"

"I think global warming's put an end to those kind of winters, but I hope it sticks around for a little while longer. It does make everything look a bit enchanted, doesn't it?"

"There was something else," said Rowan, yanking the conversation to where she wanted it. "Something I found out last night when I was looking over the autopsy reports."

"You shouldn't do that alone, Rowan. I'll do it for you."

Rowan shook her head. "I'm glad I did, there's no way you would've noticed it."

"Go on."

"Ruby had this ring, a big, plastic ring that she got in a Christmas cracker one year and never took off. It was kind of a joke on her name, and kind of like one day she would get herself a real ruby that size - it was one of those oddball things that she was always doing."

"I remember it," said Franklin. "I saw a picture of you and her at a bar somewhere and she had this... ridiculous ring on and I thought she looked really fun."

"I loved that ring. She must've had it for years and she only ever took it off in bed. But here's the thing, it wasn't on her when she died - it was nowhere at the crime scene either."

"What?"

"The report listed everything that was found with her but that was missing. Because they didn't know she had a ring they didn't think it strange that it was gone. I had a look at the CCTV pictures again to see if I could spot it on her as she left the pub, but it was too grainy to see properly. Maybe if we could get the original footage we might be able to spot something?"

"I doubt it, but it's definitely strange. D'you think maybe they just missed it from the report?"

Rowan shook her head, incredulously. "Not a chance, did you see the size of that thing? The report went into everything that was found at the scene but the ring was missing. Why d'you think that could be?"

"Buggered if I know, but it is weird. It can't have been worth anything."

"Or maybe it was worth a lot, to the killer," Rowan sighed. "Like a trophy."

"But why? Getting caught with a murder victim's ring is pretty much guaranteed to get you arrested."

"Why kill her at all, Franklin? The whole thing was for some sick thrill. Whoever did it knew the risks involved but killed my sister anyway. This isn't someone who thinks rationally, this is someone killing for fun. Of course they'll want to take some kind of souvenir."

"You can't think like this, Rowan. It's not healthy, you'll end up in a really terrible place."

"I'm there already!" Rowan blurted. "I've been there for three and a half years and this is the first time I feel as I've stumbled on something that could unravel it all. Wherever that ring is, we'll find the killer."

"They probably dumped it years ago."

"Then I'll scour through the rubbish dumps until I find it, and then…" Rowan rubbed her face in her hands. "What's happening to me? D'you hear me? This is going to drive me insane, just when I think I'm making sense of something, or getting somewhere, it all amounts to a pile of piss."

"It is something though. At least, it's not nothing."

"Can you do me a favour tonight?" Rowan asked.

"It depends what it is, but go on."

"The Murder Club, that podcast you went on to talk about Blackbeard, they're doing a Christmas special episode tonight. They're recording it live in the Camel Toe… It's about Ruby."

Franklin's mouth fell open. "They're recording a podcast about Ruby, in the place she was last seen alive?"

"I know, it's in terrible taste, but that's not the point. I want to go there, I want you to come with me."

"That's a really bad idea."

"Is it? Would you rather I sit at home all night wrapping presents and decorating the Christmas tree? I'm going because I need to go, but I'd much prefer it if I had a friend to go with, and seeing as none of my friends want to go, I thought you'd do instead."

Franklin shook his head at her good-natured insult. "I don't approve of it, but I know what it's like trying to stop you from doing something. What time does it start?"

"Seven o'clock. Can you meet me outside? I want to slip in with the crowd so hopefully they won't recognise you. Try and dress a bit incognito. I've got the tickets already, I printed them off last night."

"Are you sure about this?"

"I'm not," Rowan sad, curtly. "But I don't know what else I can do. Maybe Cassie and Tariq have been doing their own investigating, maybe they've come up with something. If nothing else, I just want to hear what other people are saying about her, and my family."

Franklin's phone buzzed as a text message dropped. "If it gets too much we're leaving, though, even if I have to drag you out, kicking and screaming." Franklin read the screen of his phone. "Right, how would you like to meet Cal Colchester?"

"Who?"

"He's the videographer who was filming Morning Shiver that night. He says he has something to show us."

Rowan halted and turned to Franklin. "You tracked him down?"

"Trust me," he said. "You're not the only one who's had an eventful couple of nights."

34.

Cal Colchester had been tricky to track down. Franklin had not been deterred by the man's lack of a Facebook profile - the first place he had searched - and had instead scoured online reviews of wedding photographers until he landed on one which mentioned him by name.

The website was disconcertingly sparse, as if robbers had broken in and stolen all the goods from the screen, but Franklin had enough experience in tracking down people to know a website's current appearance was not the only record of it on the internet. A cached version of the site from early 2012 was not difficult to find, the robotics of the archived site had thrown up idiosyncrasies such as empty lines of text or little red crosses where once a photo had been displayed, but within the jumble of text and broken links he found what he had been looking for - an email address.

Cal had returned his message within an hour on Saturday night, and the pair had exchanged phone numbers by the following morning. *"Hardly anyone has tried to contact me over the years,"* he had written. *"Not even the police were interested in what I had to say."*

The snow had deluged Bristol but little else around it. Driving from the city, patches of grass began revealing themselves along the roadway until the snow became little more than a dense frost with patches of white in shadows the sun had not yet reached. Franklin and Rowan were at Bradford on Avon within the hour, where they parked the car and tracked the canal to where Cal's narrow boat sat low in the water, encased in ice.

The boat was named *The Kingfisher* and was moored along the towpath near a lock at the edge of the ancient town. It was green with red edging and bore signs of an attempted garden on its bow, with an array of terracotta pots containing ice-scalded plants which had succumbed to the bitter winter. A little chimney in its roof puffed smoke and the inviting smell of burning wood.

"Should we knock?" Rowan asked.

"No need," came a voice from inside, as a little wooden door in the stern of the boat creaked open and a white man with blonde dreadlocks poked his head out. "I saw you on the security camera. Welcome aboard, friends!"

The man vanished inside and Franklin and Rowan looked at one another. Franklin led the way and stepped down from the towpath and through the open door. Rowan followed him. Inside, the space was disconcertingly small, with a single, long room stretching out before them. The cramped space was devoid of decoration, the only furnishings being a table with benches bolted into the hull and a bed on a raised platform above it. An area towards the front of the boat had been delegated the kitchen, with a sink, washing machine and stove pushed against the far wall.

"Welcome to minimalist living," Cal declared, shaking Franklin's hand before reaching for Rowan's. "You must be Miss Kaplan. It's an absolute honour to finally meet you, I never thought this day would come."

Rowan smiled at his words but recoiled uncomfortably after the handshake had dropped.

"Thank you for taking the time to meet us. We really appreciate it." Franklin said.

"Not at all. I jumped at the chance as soon as I got your email."

"Your place is lovely," said Franklin. "Really cosy."

"Cosy's one way to put it, I prefer tiny. You should see the bathroom. I can sit on the toilet while I shower!" The man laughed and flashed at them a tongue stud as he did. Rowan estimated him to be older than Franklin, but not by much. He was draped in an oversized, knitted poncho and had used an elastic band to confine his tangle of dreadlocks to the back of his head.

"Well, it's nice and warm. That counts for a lot in winter," said Franklin.

"Heat, shelter, running water and a bit of food are all a man needs to survive, everything else is just clutter. You should've seen the place I used to live in, absolutely packed with just like... *stuff* that nobody needs, stuff we think we need because we see it on TV and think it matters. That's why I got out of the wedding business, all the flowers and dresses, all the things people are told they need, all the money pissed away on a day that's meant to be perfect just to impress people who aren't even enjoying themselves. D'you know what you need for the perfect wedding? Some friends and an open bar. Done." Cal laughed at himself before retreating to the kitchen area to make cups of mint tea which neither Franklin nor Rowan had asked for.

"So," Rowan began, "You said that the police aren't interested in what you have to say. What does that mean?"

"They think I'm a nuisance to be honest with you, and have almost gone as far as to tell me so in the past, but they wouldn't dare, in case I spill *their* secrets."

Rowan caught Franklin's concerned glance in her direction. "What d'you remember about that night? I read your statement to the police and you said you left soon after Ruby had sung "Downtown"."

"Sit," Cal demanded, and the pair obeyed, sliding into benches at either side of a formica table upon which he placed two mismatched mugs of steaming mint tea. "That's true, but that's not the end of my involvement at all. Can you believe that the police didn't even bother looking over all of my footage from that night? I told them how much I had but they weren't interested."

"You have more footage?" Rowan asked.

"Loads," he sat next to Franklin and scooted across until her friend was pressed against the wall. From underneath the table he produced a surprisingly up to date MacBook which he opened before them. "If you've got a memory card I can send it all to you."

To Rowan's astonishment, Franklin produced a USB stick from his suit jacket pocket which he handed to Cal. Somehow Franklin always knew what would be needed.

"You said in your statement that my sister got in a row with a couple of band members. Can you remember what it was about?"

"Music stuff. You know what creative types can be like, as soon as a group of artistic people come together, with slightly different visions of what a project should look like, the first thing they'll do is turn on each other. That's why I always chose to work alone with my videos."

"So this gig was something different for you then?" Franklin asked.

"Very much so, but it was the sort of thing I was looking into at the time. I didn't want to be a wedding photographer for the rest of my life and wanted to break into making short films. Back in 2012 we didn't really understand how online content could be marketed, but nowadays I'm sure I could make a fortune with some of the stuff I film, if that's what I was interested in. Really avant-garde pieces that are way out there. I think it was Douglas who got in contact with me. Did you hear what happened to him?"

Both Franklin and Rowan nodded.

"Poor chap, that's what secrets will do for you. They were all talented in an amateur way but Ruby was the standout, she was…"

"…Excuse me? Douglas had secrets?" said Rowan.

"Of course he did, they all did. That's what it was all about, that's what they were there for. That's even what I was there for. Look, this should explain." Cal stood up and reached into an overhead storage unit from which he produced a stuffed ring-binder which he slapped on the table with a thud. "That's three and a half years research there. It's as precious as gold dust and the stuff inside is explosive enough to take down corrupt police forces across Britain, probably a few governments too." Cal grinned smugly as he sat back down on the bench. Rowan felt her heart kick in her chest.

"You see, that night changed everyone who was in the pub. The knock on effects were much bigger than anyone could've imagined. Before I was a struggling artist with a wife and a house in the suburbs, but after, I vowed I would stop at nothing to find out what *really* happened to Ruby Kaplan. It affected me, I couldn't sleep, knowing that a beautiful, talented young woman had been savagely murdered just hours after I'd met her. It felt like I was meant to be there, like I had to tell her story and let the world know what happened."

Rowan leaned back against the bench. "And what exactly is that?"

"Your sister wasn't murdered, she was assassinated."

Franklin could see where this was heading. "I think we have all we need, thank you very much Mr Colchester... for your time."

"What d'you mean?' Rowan ventured.

"She was beginning to find out who she really was, the power she had. Who her parents really were."

"We need to get back to work. Come on Rowan,"

"Who were her parents?" Rowan's eyes fixed on Cal, a demented rage seemed to be barely contained behind them.

Cal simply flipped through the binder on the table until the pages stopped on an unmistakable image. Smiling from the confines of a glossy photograph was Diana, the tragic princess who had died the year after Rowan was born. She was wearing a pink blouse with a beige skirt and holding a bouquet of flowers in front of her stomach, the bouquet had been encircled with a black marker.

"Why do you think she's covering her stomach like that?" Cal asked. "That's Ruby in there. The black, illegitimate half-sibling to William and Harry."

"Fuck!" Rowan beat her fist on the table. "How many more time wasters are there going to be? If it's not witches it's conspiracy nuts. This is real life, Ruby was my sister!"

"I know it may come as a shock to you to hear that the Windsors played a role in Ruby's death but you have to believe me! The monarchy could not stand for a mixed-race relative, the press would've had a field day, so they murdered Diana and then came after Ruby once they tracked her down!"

Rowan yanked the USB stick from Cal's computer before rising to her feet. "Never contact me again, you... freak!" She barged past Franklin and through the door. On the towpath she grabbed a mound of frozen ice and hurled it at the edge of the narrowboat, Franklin flinched as the clod exploded into a shower of ice.

She collapsed into his arms as he hauled himself from the stern and wept into his chest.

"I'm sorry, Rowan. I had no idea he was a nutcase, I should never have contacted him."

189

"I can't take this anymore," Rowan wailed, tears streaming down her cheeks. "It's too much, I've waited for too long. I'm sick of having to be patient, and rational. I'm sick of everyone telling me that the police will deal with it and catch her killer, and bastards like him trying to tell the world that Ruby didn't even belong to us ,and I can't stand it! I'm gonna catch her murderer - and I'm gonna kill him!"

35.

At the precise moment that her sister was being murdered, Rowan was dancing. Lucy Welch's invitation to her house party had proven too tempting on that Saturday night. From her arrival it was clear that the evening was already in full swing as the terrace house in St. Andrews was trembling against the bass of loud music while coloured lights darted across the drawn curtains.

She hadn't known many people there. Some were half-remembered faces of people she had gone to school with, while others she recognised only through her friend Lucy. Some were complete strangers, creepily adult men partying with teenagers, but they had brought alcohol, so their presence was tolerated.

An area in the living room had been cleared of furniture as the designated dance floor with a kitschy disco ball hanging over it, and though the house was jammed with young people, the space was empty, as timid teens steered clear of it for fear of breaking ranks or losing their cool disengagement. After a few Smirnoff Ices and half a cigarette she shared with Lucy in the garden, Rowan was the first to accept the challenge. The sensation of music driving her to move was a familiar one and she'd never tried to fight it. It was as if the rhythm had somehow entered her blood and was pumping through her veins, finding the extremities of her body and twitching them into life. She slipped through the crowds to the abandoned dance floor and let the music move her. She was vaguely aware of the bemused looks and eye rolls she was receiving but was too lost in sound to care. It would be the last time in her life she would experience unbridled joy.

Having broken the invisible seal upon the dance floor, Rowan was joined by writhing bodies as the music ensnared more teens. Soon she was looking out across a sea of flailing arms and whipping hair as Lucy jostled through the throng to find her.

"Is your ringtone Downtown?" Lucy shouted above the music.

The weird question broke the spell the music had cast over Rowan and she at once stopped dancing. "Yeah. Why?"

"It just keeps ringing. Can you answer it?"

Confused and alarmed by this information, Rowan had a suspicion that it was bad news but could have had no idea that this was the first sign of the end of her world, and the death of everything she'd known her own life to be.

Her jacket had been cast onto the bed in Lucy's parents' room and was now buried beneath a pile of others. Shoving them out of the way she pulled her denim jacket from the tumbled mess and her phone from its pocket. The moment she flipped it open she knew something was terribly wrong and her gut heaved in panic. Twenty-five missed calls, sixteen text messages, three voicemails.

The text messages were all from her mother, and at first, read like apologetic inquiries. *"Hope UR having a good night. Have U heard from Ruby?"* and *"Getting a bit worried here, Ruby said she'd be home by eleven"*. But as the night had gone on, her attempts at level-headed questioning became more frantic. *"Why won't you answer your phone, Ruby's missing"*, *"Please get home. We're worried sick."*

In her hand the phone suddenly whirred into life, playing a tinny version of Downtown Rowan had downloaded from the internet. The display said her mum was calling, but when she answered the call, it was her father's voice she heard.

"Oh thank god," were Oscar's first words. "You need to get home, your mum's hysterical. We can't find Ruby and all her friends have gone home without her."

In the background she could hear her mother sobbing. Ordinarily, she would've protested the request that she must leave the party, but like her mother, Rowan knew that something was wrong. Ruby never let her parents worry about her, if there was a change to her scheduled plans, she would always call to let them know. It had been almost two hours without a word from her.

Rowan made no excuses to Lisa as she slipped away into the balmy, summer night. A bus had brought her here, but she didn't want to wait for another, erratically scheduled, late-night one, so instead began running. The mile and a half back to her home was a battle against her mind, and as she ran, it was as if she was fleeing from the assailing thoughts that had burrowed their way into her head. Visions of death, of murder, of never seeing her sister again. Terrible, unthinkable thoughts, too horrible to be true, yet throughout the night, one by one they'd all be realised.

Rowan let herself in, her heart beating in her chest with panic and exhaustion. At the table sat her mother, wrapped in a threadbare dressing gown with a freshly topped up glass of red wine in her trembling hand.

"Mum, what's happening?"

Rolinda Kaplan simply shook her head, seemingly unaware of anything that was going on.

"Ruby?" Rowan's father exclaimed as he darted into the kitchen. "Oh, Rowan. It's you."

"Have you heard anything?"

"We've called the police. They're coming round in a bit, but they say they can't do anything tonight as it's only been a few hours. She might've just gone clubbing."

"Ruby wouldn't do that. Not without telling me," Rolinda garbled.

There was a sudden rap on the door. Through the fogged glass Rowan could make out the silhouette of two police officers. She bit her lip and opened the door.

The two men in the frame had calm faces, one seemed middle-aged, the other not much older than her. Rowan felt immediately relaxed by their demeanour.

"Good evening," the older of the two began. "We've heard that there's a bit of concern about your daughter? We thought we'd drop by and take some notes, nothing to worry about though. My name's Constable Edison Gallow."

36.

"I'm so sorry," were Franklin's first words to Rowan on their drive home from Bradford on Avon. "I'm just so, so sorry. I wish I'd known he was such a lunatic. We should never have gone there."

"We needed to see him," was Rowan's stoic response. "He was with Ruby on the night she died, we had to hear what he had to say."

"At least we got the footage from him, maybe that'll be something. You don't have to look through it though, I'll do that, I know it'd be hard seeing Ruby in her last hours."

Rowan shook her head. "You won't see the things I'll see. It'll be like the red ring again, something the police missed because they didn't know she even had it. Or it'd be like that night... so much wasted time because nobody took us seriously."

Franklin didn't know how to respond to this. He and Rowan had known for years that Edison and his partner had been the first officers to visit the Kaplan house and had done so simply because there had been a window in their Saturday night shift which had allowed it, otherwise it would've been unlikely that anyone looked into her disappearance until the following morning.

"Three and a half years of your life wasted on some bullshit conspiracy theory. I'm sure he's been having fun, tying up a load of crap together, thinking he's cracking the case," said Rowan.

"He's mad, and sad... but I don't think he's bad. If we just met the killer it's a strange defence to mount, blaming it all on the monarchy."

"Honestly, I could laugh if it didn't make me sick. Then again, he wouldn't be the first person to plead insanity to get out of a crime, look at that Barnabus kid from the summer."

"And it didn't work for him either," said Franklin. "Getting an insanity plea taken seriously is extremely rare. Cal Colchester threw his old life away after Ruby was murdered, left his wife and his job, moved onto a boat and began formulating an insane theory. If he's pretending to be crazy, that's a long, long con he's pulling."

After parking his car in the driveway of Gallow & Sons, Franklin tried his key in the lock to the reception and was surprised to discover the door was already unlocked. Inside, Peterman was sitting on the faux-leather sofa with a box of his belongings next to him.

"What are you doing here?" asked Franklin.

"What's *she* doing here? It's Sunday, she's supposed to have the day off."

"Not that it's any of your business, but we've been working on a project."

"Right," Peterman sneered. "Another mystery for Sherlock and Holmes. I remember when you used to be a funeral director."

"First of all, it's Holmes and Watson, and secondly, I was under the impression that you no longer work here. I thought last night was a pretty definite resignation."

"Don't worry, I'm going. I just came here to collect a few things from my office. I'm just waiting for my niece to pick me up, she doesn't want me driving in the snow."

Franklin peered into the box beside Peterman. In it was a jumble of goods from his meagre life, a framed photograph of who Franklin assumed was his ex-wife, and another photograph of Peterman among the Brotherhood of Bigstowe Jury. A Newton's Cradle and a rainbow coloured slinky fought for space next to a savage looking cactus. Franklin felt his resolve melt. "Peterman, I'm sorry."

Peterman shrugged. "It can't be helped. We've all got to go some day."

"You don't know it's the end," said Rowan, her voice was genuinely sympathetic. "My grandfather survived two bouts of cancer. It was a stroke that got him in the end."

"Well, that's something to look forward to if the chemo works then."

The jet-black humour from Peterman was so unexpected and out of character that Rowan couldn't help but laugh. "That's not what I meant."

The crunch of tyres on gravel, followed by the beep of a horn signalled the arrival of Peterman's niece. "They treat me

195

like I'm an infant," he grumbled. "I can drive myself, I'm not losing my marbles yet."

As Peterman stood, Franklin blocked his path to the door with an extended hand. The man looked at it suspiciously, as if it was somehow a trick, before shaking it.

"We might not have got on together, but I never faulted you for your work. You were a fine funeral director and should be proud of yourself for what you did here."

"I know," was his gruff reply before he barged past Rowan and through the door.

Rowan rolled her eyes at Franklin before following Peterman out onto the drive. "Hey!" She held her hand out to him. "Don't forget me."

"I fully plan to forget you, Miss Kaplan," he said, but shook her hand anyway.

"You're a terrible, terrible person Peterman, but I don't want you to die. Good luck with everything."

Peterman seemed to flinch at her words, and for a flicker of a moment his face almost cracked, revealing the faintest trace of affection for the foe he'd never really understood why he detested so much. "I must get going. Good bye."

With that, Peterman hurled his box onto the back seat of the car before climbing in after it. The car pulled away and Rowan sighed as Franklin reached out to pat her shoulder. "He never did say thank you to us for saving his life this summer," said Franklin.

"To be fair, it seems we didn't save that much of it."

"Poor guy. He was a miserable old bastard but I might end up actually missing him being here. I hope the treatment works, I think he's earned a quiet retirement."

"Me too. Isn't that weird."

"Well, the offer still stands if you want to start training for his post. I could get you on a course in the New Year if you're up for it. It's not a legal requirement to be certified but it's good for the business if we can say we are. You could very well find yourself as the youngest, female funeral director of colour in the country."

Rowan shrugged. "I'll think about it."

Franklin didn't like that reply and hadn't anticipated her reticence. The position meant slightly more responsibility but nothing beyond what she'd experienced as an assistant. He was certain the pay increase would be welcome too. "I mean, you're virtually qualified already. It's just a certificate, and you'll have your own office."

"I said I'll think about it. I don't know what my future's likely to be, or even where I'm going to be. I can't hang around Bristol forever."

"You can't?" Franklin gulped hard. "Why not?"

"I've lived here all my life, and I like it… but I can't spend my whole life in the same place, can I?"

"So you mean like a gap year? Maybe go travelling somewhere, expand your horizons and then come back home."

"I don't know what I want. Perhaps I just need a change."

Rowan crunched her way through the snow back to the reception and Franklin watched her walk away from him. An unexpected rage passed through him like a static shock, blasting itself out as soon as it had arrived. Why couldn't she *understand* that the choice wasn't all hers? She had other people to think of, didn't she understand that her family needed her? That the business needed her? That without her, he would be lost, lonely and friendless. Why couldn't she think of *him*?

When his teeth began to chatter, Franklin wandered in from the cold and followed the sound of what seemed to be the tuning of instruments. Rowan was seated in front of his computer with the video footage Cal had taken on that fateful night.

"You don't need to do that now," he said. "You've had enough horrors for one day. Give it a rest."

Rowan shook her head. "I just want to get it over with. I don't want it hanging over me all Christmas. Besides, we're supposed to be going to this pub tonight, we might as well get used to the place."

On the screen all four members of Morning Shiver were getting into position. All of them were bathed in a soft, blue spotlight except for Ruby, who stood before a microphone stand with a scarlet beam illuminating her face and down to her chest, the rest of her body lost in darkness. As she brushed a coil of dark curls behind one ear the light caught the red ring on her finger.

"I *told* you she was wearing it that night. There's no way she'd take it off."

"But where could it've gone?" Franklin asked.

"Beats me but it's not as if it was worth anything."

Just then, the camera in Cal Colchester's hand zoomed into Ruby's face before lasciviously panning down to her cleavage where the image was held for an uncomfortably long time.

"Pervert," Rowan commented.

"Alright," said Ruby, adjusting the microphone stand. "Now let's get this right for a change. Lily, you're going too fast *again* and Doug, you shouldn't be trying to keep up with her because I'm keeping time with you and it makes the whole thing sound like shit. Kevin, just give it bit *more,* you know? You're playing like a girl."

The camera passed over the unfamiliar face of Kevin Casey, a young man with a dusting of a beard and a pair of blue-tinted John Lennon glasses balanced low on his nose. The comment had clearly stung him.

"That's just her being a perfectionist," Rowan was quick to say. "When a man acts like that he's just being forthright."

"I didn't say anything," Franklin replied.

"Good, well don't."

Ruby continued. "This is so important for me, so can we please get it right? I know we're the band but I'm the front woman, I'm the one who'll have all eyes on her and I don't want to spoil it because you guys are a bunch of amateurs."

"Perhaps you could try being less of a bitch," Lily spat from behind her. "This band isn't just about you!"

"See?" Rowan declared. "What's the first thing people call an ambitious woman? A bitch."

"Maybe if you knew how to play a song at the right tempo I wouldn't have to be a bitch."

In the background, Doug theatrically let his drumsticks fall to the floor. "That's it, I can see where this is heading, I'm going out back for a fag. Anyone want to join me?"

Wordlessly, Ruby and Lily followed him off the stage. An argument broke out off screen, muffled as the trio headed outside.

The camera came to rest on Kevin who sat alone on the stage "How're you doing dude?" Cal's disembodied voice asked.

"Oh, this is just swell," was Kevin's response. "I only joined this group for some fun and this happens every single time." Casting aside the bass guitar, Kevin dropped down from the stage and wove between a forest of small, circular tables. Retrieving his bag from where it had been discarded on the floor, he brought out a book and proceeded to read it whilst seated at the bar. The camera panned away from him and it was then that Franklin yelped as if stung by an insect.

"Go back!" He exclaimed.

"I didn't see anything."

"Go back slowly."

Rowan did as he suggested, peeling back the video footage one frame at a time until she saw what had caught her friend's eye. A window in the background of the shot had caught the blurred image of something that shouldn't have been there. She zoomed in and the image became a tapestry of pixels on the screen. Unmistakably, it was the image of a blonde woman, gazing into the bar.

37.

Unblinking, Rowan stared at the pale face on the screen. One frame in either direction, and the woman's features were lost in digital static, but for that instant she'd been captured and preserved for all time.

"Is that her?" Rowan gasped.

"You recognise the face?"

"I've no idea, but I just realised that I might be looking at my sister's killer."

Franklin squinted, hoping that it might somehow render more detail in the face. "She looks young, and blonde. Did Ruby know anyone who looked like that?"

"Ruby knew everyone."

"It could just be a passerby. Stopping to see if the pub's open, or just being nosey."

Rowan reached for her phone and sent a text message to Kay before returning her gaze to the computer. "Perhaps, but there's just something about it that seems... off. Kind of creepy, you know?"

"No doubt about that. Where d'you think that window is?"

"Doug said they were going out the back to smoke, I think the window's at the front of the street. I've been past the pub a few times but I try not to look at it too much."

Rowan's phone buzzed as Kay's reply arrived. "Kay's on her way to Bristol. She wants to meet us at the Camel Toe in an hour."

Franklin looked at his watch. "It's half eleven. Rowan, you missed church. Sorry."

Rowan batted away his words like a nuisance bug. "I knew I wasn't going to make it today and I wouldn't have been able to keep focused if I had."

"Won't you get in trouble with the other Quakers?"

She offered him a stern look. "It's not like that, nobody's keeping score of how often you go to meetings. It isn't even really church, it's a meeting house."

Rowan was used to being misunderstood when it came to her new found conversion to the Society of Friends. Most people saw her involvement as little more than a passing fad, something to distract the mind of a grieving woman, otherwise they thought she'd joined a cult and offered her sympathetic, but concerned, glances, if she ever brought it up.

In truth, her spiritual awakening had been both profound and accidental. In the dog days of summer she'd been shopping in Cabot Circus, following an unsuccessful attempt to find synthetic silk for a funeral service. The epiphany came once she'd left and decided to shave time off her journey home by weaving a way across St Pauls, via an unfamiliar and somewhat barren concrete square, when the front tyre of her Brompton elected to burst, sending her wobbling to a frustrated halt.

Inspecting the damage, Rowan became aware of a shadow beside her. "Can I help you, love?" The tiny, old man standing next to her wore a faded grey suit and a hat with a feather in it. He stood barely taller than her chest and spoke with a disarmingly gentle tone. "Are you here for the meeting?"

"Excuse me?"

The man pointed to a turgid, grey block of a building with a hand-stencilled sign which read *"Bristol Society of Friends Meeting House."*

"Oh, I'm not here for that. I'm kind of here by mistake."

"You look like you belong here," the man smiled.

Rowan sighed. "I don't want to sound rude, but I'm not really interested in getting converted today. I'm sure the Society of Friends are a lovely lot, but it's not really my kind of thing."

"We don't try to convert anyone," the man declared. "It would make us an insufferable bunch if we did. God finds his own way to bring Friends to our society. I truly did only ask if you wanted help with that nasty looking puncture."

Rowan looked at the fatal split which had ripped the tyre asunder, before her eyes caught the steady stream of people entering the Meeting House across the square. As a child she'd only ever attended one religious service, a confusing and boring affair which had been sprung on her after a sleepover at a friend's house. She had always remembered the miserable faces of those in the congregation, nobody, not even the vicar, enjoyed this weekly ritual in the draughty old church and attended simply out of habit or to curry favour with their wrathful Lord. The convocation of people arriving at the Society of Friends were a ragtag lot, mismatched in ages and dress styles, from the very formal to the lazily casual and coloured throughout in a pleasing array of skin tones.

"You don't think my puncture was meant to happen here do you?"

"Beats me," said the man. "Though I'd think it rather an unfair stunt to cause such expensive damage to win over another convert. Perhaps some things just happen as a happy coincidence."

"I've been on something of a spiritual journey, looking for something for a while. My sister died a few years ago - she was murdered." What was happening to her? These secrets were not meant for the ears of a stranger, but something inside her felt as if it was awakening, that something had unlocked and a small, but vital part of her, that had been shut away, was stirring into life.

"I'm very sorry to hear that, dear. It can be a detestable world sometimes, but there are still good people in it. I hope you have enough of them in your life to carry you through."

The earnest tone of the man's rich, quiet voice was intoxicating and Rowan was about to respond when the bark of a dog cut across the square. Looking up she saw a three-legged labrador cross wagging its tail at her. "Wait a minute, I know him!"

"Rowan!" Gordon Hooper called out to her as he approached. "What the blazes are you doing here?"

"I think I'm in the middle of an epiphany," she said to the former councillor.

"Should we be scared? Should we take a step back?" Gordon replied.

"It's good to see you, Mr Hooper. How're you doing?"

"Clean and sober and absolutely no fun at all anymore. Are you coming inside? I just need to run Rodney to the kennels behind the meeting house, but you're welcome to join us."

"Yes I am," Rowan declared, before folding her bike up and following the train of people inside, where they would sit and think, in blissful silence.

On the drive to the Camel Toe, Rowan sat beside Franklin and looked at the frozen image she'd saved on her iPad. Expanded, almost beyond recognition as a face, she tilted it from side to side, trying to observe it from an angle which might reveal some detail she had so far missed. It yielded nothing.

"Damn snow," Franklin huffed. "They still haven't cleared the roads. I've never known traffic to be this slow."

By the time they arrived at the pub, Kay had somehow got there before them and was bundled in a patchwork coat with a snood around her neck. She stood up to her ankles in a drift of snow. "Morning, well, afternoon," she said wistfully.

Rowan gave the woman an appreciative nod and then shivered, not from the cold but from the shadow of the foreboding building. It was an innocuous looking place, a dark cuboid of pollution-stained brick in a single storey and with a flat roof, piled high with snow. A couple of steps led down to a partially subterranean entrance, over which a garish, green and pink sign swung bearing the image of a camel over the name of the pub.

"Wow," said Franklin. "This place really is an old-fashioned dive."

"It's not always been like this. They refurbished it after Ruby died and tried making it look like a seedy hangout. It's all artificial." Rowan said.

Franklin seemed puzzled as to why anywhere would intentionally make itself seem down-market and dangerous, he'd known Bristol back in the days when there really were bars where you were as likely to get a punch in the face as you were a pint of cider, but he'd long given up trying to understand the strange fads the city would revive in the name of fashion.

"I think this is the window," Rowan pointed to a slightly tinted frame of glass, behind which neon lettering spelt out *"Cheap Beer"* in pink.

203

"I think you're right."

"What window? What's this about?" Kay asked.

Rowan peered inside, through to the darkness beyond, before turning to Kay. "There was someone else here on the night Ruby was killed. A woman."

"I know. Lily."

"Someone else. We saw her looking through the window. We got a video from Cal Colchester, the videographer who was here that night."

Kay threw a gloved hand to her mouth and gasped. "Someone was watching us?"

"D'you remember them going out for a smoke that night?"

Kay nodded. "There's a place around the back where the wheelie bins go, that's where they went for cigarettes."

At the edge of the pub, a narrow alleyway sliced a path between the low building and a terrace of much taller residences. Snow had piled high within the tight breach and had remained untouched. Without a word, Rowan scrambled her way over it, squeezing down the narrow path with both shoulders brushing along the walls as she went, until it opened out onto a small, nearly unused, road. Black bins lined the snow covered trail which passed behind a row of gardens. Overhead a web of power lines zigzagged messily. It was like stepping backstage of a city, to the secret roads the ordinary people were not meant to see.

Franklin was next out of the alley, looking frazzled by the tightness of the passage as he brushed snow from his shoulders. Behind him was Kay.

"This is where they came to smoke. That door leads back into the pub. They propped it open with Lily's handbag." Kay pointed to a metal fire door where a handful of cigarette butts had been scattered across the snow.

"There's no way anyone looking through the window could've seen them here," said Franklin. "Maybe she was just checking that they'd gone out."

"We could check it out tonight," Rowan said. "See if whoever was looking through the window could see them leave."

"What? You're coming here tonight?" Kay asked.

"Yes. The podcast recording, it's about Ruby."

Kay's head dropped guiltily. "We didn't want you to know."

"I know it's pretty tasteless, but I don't know how else we can find more information. She was my sister and if people are going to be talking about her I'd like to know what they're saying."

Kay sighed. "Lily and I have tickets."

"What? Why?"

"We've had them for a while, before Doug died. It's really sick and we both know that, we just wanted to come along for the same reason. We were changed by that night and it's haunted us all. We just need some answers, anything really. We thought we could hide in the back - nobody will recognise either of us, especially me."

"I get it. Don't worry, I'm not mad. We'll even sit with you, it's just that I know what those two are like. It's all a big game for them. A mystery to solve, but it's my life, and I want to look after Ruby - even if she's just a memory now."

Kay's lips trembled and for a moment it appeared that she might cry, she blinked back her tears. "So where's this video then. I want to see this face at the window."

Rowan reached into her rucksack and retrieved the iPad which was still frozen on the image. She handed it to Kay, and to her astonishment, the woman shrieked at the sight of it.

"You wouldn't know because you never saw her like that, when she was blonde and…normal. It's Orlagh!" She exclaimed.

"The witch," gasped Rowan.

38.

Kay stared, gobsmacked by what she saw on the screen, the mosaic of pale pixels representing a face stared back at her. "It's definitely her. What's going on?"

"Whatever's going on, it's creepy as hell," said Franklin as he peered over Rowan's shoulder.

"And you didn't see her that night? She didn't drop by at any time?" Rowan asked Kay.

"Nothing, I'd have remembered as we were all a little scared of running into her again. She took Ruby replacing her in the band really badly, like it was an honour thing or something or we'd besmirched her character. She was good, really good in fact, but when it comes down to Ruby and anyone else on the mic… Ruby's gonna win."

Rowan nodded. There was no denying that. "Have you seen her since that night?"

"Never. Not that that's a surprise, everything to do with Morning Shiver fell apart after that. We lost everything, including our past. It took ages before the three of us could spend time together, and even then it was never the same. About six months after the funeral Orlagh got in touch with Lily. She sent an email saying maybe we could get the old band back together. I don't think Lily even responded - there was no way that was happening, not a chance. None of us wanted to play music anymore, not together anyway. Ruby's ghost would've been everywhere."

"So Orlagh was pretty unhinged, right?" Rowan asked as she took her iPad back from Kay. "Was she vindictive, or violent?"

Kay shrugged. "She had a temper, but I've found that most creative people do. Not me, I suppose that's why I dropped out of the whole music scene. Orlagh wasn't so much vindictive, just sharp in her cruelty. She'd explode in a fit of rage and say the kind of stuff that would just cut you down in front of your friends. She said things to me in the past that made me want to cry, they were just so *mean*. And she'd stand there afterwards, smiling at you like she was so proud of herself. That's how she was, it all came out with her, there was nothing beneath the surface, she'd explode and let it all out, scorch the earth and damn the consequences."

"The witch stuff, was she doing that back then?"

"Always. I'd thought of it like an affectation, and to be honest, it seemed to give us a bit of an edge as a band at first. Don't get me wrong, we were artists first, but we wanted to make money too, at least enough to get by, and having a witch on vocals is quite an appealing gimmick. She was never too extreme with it, she just adopted a bit of a Stevie Nicks vibe in her outfits and would have a pentacle around her neck or a few candles on the stage, it was nice. I've always kind of liked that stuff, you know, aesthetically."

Rowan nodded in agreement. Like many girls, in her teen years she'd flirted with the concept of witchcraft and old religions, attempting to mix potions in her bedroom on full-moon nights, elixirs she had found within the plethora of books aimed at the brief teen-witch fad of the era. The results had been a disappointment and the paraphernalia quietly boxed away and stored in the attic. "She seemed to have gone harder into it after she got kicked out of the band."

"I think so. I only saw pictures of her online but she definitely jumped on the bandwagon as far as looks go. Dark hair and lipstick, black everything really. At its heart I think that's what witchcraft is about, claiming back power in society, so if the spells don't work there's always the uniform. Having people be frightened of how you look is kind of a power on its own." Kay shivered in the cold and pulled her coat around her. "Not that I'm about to judge anyone for changing their appearance, of course. Whatever works, right?"

Rowan nodded with a cautious smile. "Did you know Orlagh confessed to killing Ruby?"

Kay's eyes widened at the revelation. "What?"

" She thinks it's all her fault that Ruby was murdered. She put a curse on her, a death spell. She thinks it worked and has been dealing with the guilt ever since; a little self medication it seems."

"She was always into a bit of experimentation. Nothing too serious, I think she even dealt a little weed back then, which I just turned a blind eye to. None of that scene's for me but whatever other people want to do is none of my business."

"You know the curse could be a double-bluff," said Franklin. Both women turned to face him.

"How do you mean?" asked Ruby.

"However weird her method of doing it, in the strictest sense she did confess to the murder. If she'd actually been more involved, and had really been living with the guilt, admitting to some oddball curse might give her the sense that she's actually confessed. Edison says killers often own up to all kinds of smaller crimes they didn't actually do, it's like they don't want to spend their lives in prison but there's that part of them that feels they should be punished for something just to absolve themselves from the guilt."

"Maybe," Rowan couldn't hide her scepticism. "Why confess something that isn't even a crime then?"

"She was there that evening," Kay added. "That's pretty weird. Do either of you know how to get in contact with her?"

"I do," said Rowan. "I've been to her place."

"There's no time like the present," said Franklin. "What d'you think, Kay?"

"See Orlagh? I don't know, I'm really not into confrontation."

"It's not a confrontation, it's just a question of why she was there," said Rowan. "You remember that night, we need someone who can verify her account."

Kay's eyes dropped to the floor and she stamped her boots to clear the snow which had piled up on top of them. "Alright," she replied. "For Ruby."

The three of them squeezed back through the narrow alleyway, this time with Franklin leading the way, until they had lined up on the street outside the Camel Toe, staring at the tiny car which was waiting for them there.

"My Smart's not going to do the job. Anyone fancy a walk?"

The journey from Stoke's Croft to Park Row was not a long one, but the climb was steep and the pavement treacherous, with snow piled over ice for much of the route.

The trio made their way upwards from the foot of the hill in a slow convoy, while the few cars which had ventured out that day slushed through the grey and sodden road beside them.

At the block of flats, Rowan gazed up at the concrete edifice as fresh snowflakes began to drift from the purple sky, alighting in the orange glow of the streetlamps which were flickering awake in the afternoon gloom.

"Do we just ring the bell?" asked Kay.

"I don't know which flat is hers. She led me there last time," Rowan replied, studying the tower of buzzers built into the wall beside the entrance to the drab and anonymous building. Only about half the residents had provided names alongside the buttons that would allow them entry. "What would I even say to her?"

"The snow's coming down pretty hard," Franklin warned. "I hope my car doesn't get stuck."

Rowan watched the snow flutter down around their feet, filling the many footprints the residents had left as they'd come and gone throughout the day. Except for a strip on the topmost step, a band which stretched the length of the concrete and had left a trench through the snow a couple of inches wide. Rowan saw that Franklin had spotted it too, and recognised his expression, he was pondering the possibilities, just as she was.

It was then that a light beyond the door shimmered into life and the lobby beyond was illuminated in stark whiteness through the two circular windows. A figure clomped down the stairs and into view, a black silhouette, rendered a blur in the frosted glass.

"Is that her?" Kay remarked. Franklin and Rowan responded at once, neither had wanted a public encounter with Orlagh in the doorway of her own home, so they scurried down the steps and ducked behind a low wall at the edge of the pavement. Kay turned, quite indignant at their disappearance, just as the door to the block of flats swung open.

The young woman who stood beside Kay on the concrete slab of a doorstep offered her a curious glance. She was unmistakably Orlagh, swamped in a dark military coat with black lipstick smeared about her mouth.

"Hi!" Kay gasped, attempting to mask her panic.

Orlagh narrowed her smoky eyes. "Do I know you? You look familiar."

"Aah…. Sure, I live in the building. I think I'm in the flat above you?"

"3C?" Orlagh pulled a cigarette from a partially crushed packet in her pocket. "Did you forget the passcode?"

"Sure… I'm always forgetting it," Kay exhaled.

"Mr Rhodes is always changing it. You want in?"

"Oh yes, of course… thanks." Kay took the door by the handle from her.

"Keep the bloody noise down in the future. I have to put up with your shitty music all day, I shouldn't have to do it at night too."

"Sorry, yeah. I won't let it happen again."

"You'd better not. I'll call the landlord next time."

Kay nodded enthusiastically, but seemed to freeze momentarily as Orlagh lit her wonky cigarette. Rowan eyed her cautiously from her spot in the shadows.

"Are you off anywhere nice tonight? Christmas Eve and all…"

Orlagh eyed Kay as if she were a simpleton. "I don't celebrate Christmas, but I mark the solstice."

"How do you do that?"

Orlagh shrugged. "Getting trashed in some dead end bar if it's anything like last year." With that, she pulled the enormous hood of her coat over her head and stomped her way down the snow covered steps, leaving fresh prints as she went.

Kay let herself inside the building and let the door close behind her, only opening it again when she spied Rowan and Franklin making their way up to it.

"My heart's racing," she gasped as the pair entered the empty lobby. "I've never been good at lying."

"You did a marvellous job," Franklin complimented.

"What was that even about?" asked Kay. "I thought you wanted to come here and see her?"

"Not like that, though. Were we here for some snooping, not a nasty confrontation on the street. Last time I was here I left in quite a rage," said Rowan, sheepishly.

"She didn't recognise me," Kay seemed suddenly delighted. "Last time she saw me I was... Kevin. She didn't know, she didn't even guess."

"Well, it's quite a transformation," Rowan said. "You've changed a lot since then."

"Things have changed, but not everything has." Kay reached into her coat pocket and retrieved a set of keys which glimmered in the light like a treasure.

"Is that what I think they are?" Rowan gasped.

"If you think they're the keys to Orlagh's flat, then you're right. Orlagh may cast spells, but I still remember my days as an aspiring magician - that sleight of hand stuff never leaves you, and pick-pocketing was always my favourite trick."

"Kay, you're a legend!" Rowan squealed, snatching the keys from her hand.

"Are you sure your talents aren't being wasted on that farm?" asked Franklin, astonished.

Kay beamed proudly and took a theatrical curtsey. "It's all about deft hands and distraction."

"When she was lighting her cigarette?" asked Rowan.

"Perhaps," Kay shrugged. "I couldn't possibly divulge my secrets."

Rowan studied the set of keys in her trembling hand. Hanging from a keyring, shaped like a witch's pointed hat, were three keys in different colours. She marched up the staircase with Franklin and Kay behind her, almost sprinting as she reached the second floor landing. To her astonishment, it was the first of the three keys she tried which unlocked the door to 2C.

The smell of stale alcohol assaulted her as she felt about for the light switch, just as Franklin and Kay arrived in the doorway. The room flickered into light and revealed a scene of chaos.

When Rowan first came here the bedsit had been grim and bare, but in the matter of a few days it had become a squalid den, with upturned and broken vodka bottles scattered about the floor alongside plates of half eaten, abandoned food. On the bed, strewn with clothes as if they had erupted from the closet in an explosion, was a single, sinister and empty hypodermic needle and on a patch of carpet beside the bed was a puddle of dried, encrusted vomit.

"I think it's safe to say she won't be seeing any of her deposit on this flat," Rowan commented.

"Oh Christ," Franklin gasped. "We shouldn't be here. This is wrong, this girl needs help."

But Rowan wasn't listening. Seized by the opportunity, she went about throwing open drawers and rooting about beneath the bed, hauling out whatever she could find until her hands grasped a tan, leather briefcase, she slid it out and undid the latches on either side. The handsome case seemed as alien as a diamond in horse manure when presented in that depraved environment. Its presence rendered it eerie and foreboding.

"Stop this Rowan, please. Let's get out of here." Franklin begged.

Rowan shook her head and began rifling through a stack of hand written pages of what seemed to be poetry or song lyrics, until her fingers brushed against something buried at the bottom of the briefcase. Before she even saw it, she knew what it was.

"Ruby!" she sobbed as she felt it slide onto her finger. She held her hand up to Franklin who took a step away from her in disbelief. It was Ruby's plastic ring.

Even Kay knew what it was and a stunned silence fell briefly on the room. It was broken by a ferocious voice from the doorway.

"What the *fuck* are you doing in my room?"

39.

"How do lions know it's Christmas time?" Ruby asked her family as she read from the slip of paper which had fallen from her cracker.

"By the sound of jungle bells," said her father.

"Dad, you ruined the punchline!" Ruby smiled, slipping a gold, paper crown onto her forehead.

"Lions live on the savanna," Rowan informed the table. "Not the jungle."

"And zoos," Ruby added.

Rowan took a sip from her glass. She didn't know anything about red wine, but this was rich and delicious, more like a liquid Christmas pudding than the vinegary mouthwash she'd tried before. They were seated at the kitchen table, which had been draped with a festive cloth and decorated with candles and sprigs of holly. Plates heaved under the weight of food as Oscar Kaplan began carving the corpse of the steaming turkey that took pride of place on the table. Her family were dressed in kitschy Christmas jumpers and paper crowns, yuletide songs sang merrily from the radio.

"What shall we do after lunch?" asked Rolinda, as she drenched her plate in gravy.

"Same as we always do," Oscar declared. "Go out for a walk, back in time for Lizzie's speech, a board game and then we all get trashed and dance about like loons."

"Not Monopoly. That game goes on forever," Rowan whined.

"Not Scrabble, Mum always wins," said Ruby.

"OK, charades it is then." Oscar took his seat to the sound of groans from his family.

"And Rowan's not getting trashed," said Rolinda. "In fact, none of us are. That's a very bad example to set your children." Her sly smile suggested to Rowan that this rule was likely to be broken.

"What did you get?" Rowan asked her sister. "I got a jumping frog."

"Well aren't you *lucky*," Ruby smiled as she search through the shredded debris of her Christmas cracker. When she saw the ring she squealed with delight. "Oh my god, *don't you love it?* Look at it!"

Rowan just laughed. Her sister's reaction seemed completely earnest.

"I'm never taking it off. Ever. Look! It fits perfectly, it's like it was meant for me!"

The ring was made of transparent red plastic with a bulbous nugget of a fake gem, the size of a brussels sprout. Upon her elegant index finger, the cheap piece of tat was transformed into something edgy, cool and utterly Ruby.

"No offence Mum and Dad, I love the perfume, but this is the best thing I've got this Christmas. It's the best thing anyone's ever got."

The ring didn't leave Ruby's finger until the night she was murdered. She never received another Christmas gift that could match it, but then nobody could've known that she had only two Christmases left, and then there would be no more.

40.

For a moment the room was frozen. Orlagh with her hands on either side of the doorframe, Franklin and Kay looking on in horror, and Rowan holding her finger outstretched with the plastic ring encircling it.

"You said you were out for the evening," Kay was the first to speak.

"I came back for my keys, I didn't know you'd nicked them. Wait. You're not that bitch from upstairs. Who the hell are you? And who's this old man?"

"Look…" Franklin fumbled for words. "I can explain."

"I know who *you* are," she pointed a finger at Rowan. "Why are you going through my stuff?"

Of the four people in the room, Rowan was the only one to look not in the least disturbed by the interruption. She rose to her feet and wiped her lips on the back of her hand, and like a wild predator, pounced forward at Orlagh and struck her in the jaw with her closed fist. The woman fell backwards onto the scratchy, grey carpet of the hallway and in an instant Rowan had her by the feet and was dragging her back into the flat. She kicked the door shut.

Kay looked at Franklin in horror and he looked back at her. The sudden frenzy of the moment had disarmed them both.

Orlagh tried to scream, but Rowan pre-empted it by putting her ring-bearing hand over her mouth and sitting on her chest, pinning her to the ground. With her other hand she reached to the bed and grabbed the hypodermic needle.

"If you try to scream, I'll pump this needle full of air into a vein in your neck and you'll die. Do you understand?"

To Rowan's astonishment, Orlagh appeared to chuckle beneath her hand.

"What're you laughing at?"

She felt Franklin touch her shoulder gently. "Let her speak, Rowan. You need to hear what she has to say. She's not going anywhere, there's three of us and only one of her."

"Leave me out of this," said Kay, fearfully. "This wasn't part of the plan."

Rowan slid her hand from Orlagh's mouth and the young woman gasped a chilly laugh. An angry bruise was already blossoming across her cheek. "You stupid bitch, that only works in films. D'you know how much air you need to inject into someone's blood to cause an embolism? You'd need a bicycle pump not a needle. Cretin!"

Rowan slapped Orlagh hard across the face.

"That's *enough!*" Franklin roared.

Orlagh's face melted into a strangely placid expression. "You break into my home, trash the place, and then beat me up. Don't I at least get an explanation before you kill me?"

"No one's getting killed," Franklin said firmly.

"We didn't break in," Kay offered. "We used a key... Rowan did."

Franklin gave Kay a shake of his head. This was no time to shift blame or test Rowan's fury. He had never known her to be like this.

"I'm going to speak very slowly and very quietly," Rowan said to Orlagh, in a disquietingly calm voice. "Did you murder my sister?"

Orlagh held her gaze. "I told you I did. I put the destruction curse on her."

Rowan screamed as she grabbed the woman by the fringe of her hair and then smashed her head into the floor. "Did you stab my sister to death?"

"Franklin, do something!" Kay yelled.

"I didn't touch your sister," Orlagh's voice came out like a hiss.

"Then why d'you have her ring?"

"What ring?"

"This ring!" Rowan waved the plastic toy on her finger in front of Orlagh's face.

Orlagh's eyes darted back and forth in motion with the ring. "That thing? That was Ruby's?"

"Yes, it was Ruby's and you know it was. She wore it all the time."

Orlagh laughed a hollow laugh from beneath Rowan. "And I was supposed to remember that your sister used to wear some tacky bit of plastic years ago. She was always doing stuff like that for attention. Crazy bitch." Rowan slapped her again, but Orlagh barely winced. "Oh please, mistress, may I have another? Is this turning you on as much as me?" she released an ear-splitting cackle.

"I think she's on something," said Kay to Franklin.

"Where did you get this ring if it wasn't from Ruby?"

"I'm not telling you anything until you get off me."

Rowan turned to Franklin who said simply, "Let her go. Let her speak." She rose to her feet and stumbled sideways onto the bed, landing on her back on top of a pile of Orlagh's clothes.

Orlagh heaved herself upwards and reached into her pocket where she kept a metal hip flask from which she gulped deeply. To Rowan's surprise she held the bottle out to her.

"Here, you've earned it. You're a scrapper, I like that."

Rowan snatched the flask away and took a swig from it. She shuddered as the neat whisky burnt its way down her throat. "Don't ever say that stuff about my sister again."

"She was crazy alright, but she had nothing on you."

Orlagh sat on the bed next to Rowan and raised her legs onto the limp duvet. The two women lay panting beside each other. Once again, Franklin and Kay exchanged glances, bewildered as to how they should respond.

"I didn't know the ring belonged to Ruby, if I had I would've gone to the police. You won't believe me, but it's the truth."

"I don't believe you."

Orlagh took a gulp of whisky which she drank as if it was water. "That's the thing about the truth though, it is what it is. It doesn't matter whether you believe it or not, it's still the truth."

"So, you just happened to find it on the pavement? Fell off the back of a lorry? Quite a coincidence, don't you think?"

"Not a coincidence at all, it was something far more sinister. Somebody sent it to me."

"What?"

"Like, a week ago. I think it showed up in my pigeonhole a day or so after Douglas killed himself. I didn't know it had anything to do with Ruby. Why would I?"

"Because it was her *thing*. She always wore it."

"Just because you were obsessed with your sister it doesn't mean the rest of us were. We weren't all paying attention to every little thing she ever said or did, because everything always had to be about her."

"Don't think I'm past giving you another punch in the mouth," said Rowan.

Orlagh shook her head. "No, that's not going to happen. I can see in your eyes that the fire's gone. You're even starting to wonder if maybe I'm telling the truth."

"Well go on then, how did you end up getting Ruby's ring in the post?"

Orlagh snapped her fingers at Franklin. "Oy, Ginger. Pick up those sheets of paper Rowan was tossing about, the ones in my briefcase."

Franklin sneered petulantly at the woman but did as he was told. He handed her a jumble of pages.

"I *do* wish you'd come round more often, Rowan," she said sarcastically. "You always leave my place looking so tidy."

"It was a shithole before we turned up," Rowan spat.

"Here it is." Orlagh handed Rowan a crumpled note.

Rowan read it aloud. "*Dear Orlagh. My daughter is about to start secondary school and is very nervous about it. Please can you cast a spell to help calm her anxiety. I have included a ring she used to wear as a lucky charm. I hope it will aid you focusing your energies on her.*" Rowan read it again to herself. It was written in black marker in a featureless hand. "What the hell does that mean?"

"Orlagh the Oracle. That's me," she replied. "Hey, a girl's gotta eat, I have to make money somehow. As you can see, there's a standard of luxury to which I've become accustomed."

"So people send you letters? And... stuff?"

"They send me a PayPal payment first of all. It's all done online except for this stage. They send me a request and some kind of trinket and I create a spell just for that person." Orlagh looked about the wreckage of her squalid room. "Business hasn't been that great of late."

"Franklin, what does this mean?" asked Rowan.

"It means someone wanted to get rid of evidence tying them to Ruby." Franklin sighed deeply. "And they probably wanted to frame Orlagh, if her story's true."

"Gnarly," was Orlagh's response. "No wonder they didn't include a return address."

"But why would they want to take Ruby's ring in the first place? It'd only incriminate them," asked Rowan.

"I can field this one," Orlagh smiled. "It's called a trophy. Lots of killers take one from the scene of the crime, it's a way of remembering the murder, reliving it. Keeping it real in their mind." Orlagh felt questioning eyes fall on her again. "What? They were talking about it on Murder Club a couple of weeks ago."

"That bloody podcast," Franklin huffed.

"Now, if we're going to be playing the drawing room scene from an Agatha Christie book, might I bring your attention to the one person in this room who was *actually* there that evening?" With a thin, cold smile Orlagh fixed her eyes on Kay. "Don't think I haven't clocked who you are, Kevin. Or who you were…"

"It's Kay," she said, firmly. "And we both know I wasn't the only one there that night. We *all* do."

Orlagh flinched at Kay's words. "No I wasn't."

"Someone was filming the rehearsal," said Rowan. "The video shows you looking through the window."

"It's definitely you," added Kay.

Orlagh took a deep breath. "Alright then. I was there… for a little bit. Are you happy now?"

"Not really," Rowan replied. "Why were you there?"

She rubbed her swollen cheek tenderly. "Because I knew I'd made a mistake… with the curse. I was trying to undo it, or at least put some protection on Ruby. I didn't like the girl but I didn't want her to die, not really. Not just for her, but for me. D'you know what happens when you place a bad luck curse on somebody? It comes back even stronger on you. I didn't know how to undo the damage, so I tried to block the evil spirits. It might sound daft but you're meant to use…"

"…salt," Rowan interrupted.

"How the hell did you know that?" asked Orlagh.

"How *did* you know that?" Franklin echoed.

219

"Kay, when you left the bar that night, what did you say you saw on the doorstep?"

"It was this white powder, no, not powder, crystals, like salt."

"You saw the step outside this place," Rowan said to Franklin. "That band through the snow where she'd poured a line of salt. I guess that one was to protect her from the curse rebounding."

"Protection from malicious spirits," Orlagh confirmed. "They can't cross a line of salt, or of flowing water, so I thought if I put some across the doors and windows, she'd be safe and I would too. I've been doing it for years outside here and it's kept me safe."

"But I've read the police report," said Franklin. "They searched every inch of the building, inside and out, and didn't mention lines of salt anywhere that night."

"Because it rained," Orlagh's head fell to her chest as if in shame. "If only it hadn't rained then no evil would've got to her."

Rowan took the flask of whisky from Orlagh's hands and went to take a swig, only to discover it was empty. "Damn," she whispered to herself.

Orlagh's eyes began to flutter and her head lolled to one side. Softly she began to snore.

"She's pissed out of her head," Rowan confirmed.

"D'you want to call the police?" Franklin asked.

"No. I believe her and I don't want Ruby's murder ending up in their hands again. We're gonna solve this and we're going to do it tonight."

Before leaving, Rowan scrawled a note across a piece of paper and placed it on Orlagh's chest. "*I forgive you,*" it read.

"*You didn't kill Ruby. Somewhere inside you there's still a good person. Please get help for yourself. P.S. Your keys are in your coat pocket. I'm taking Ruby's ring with me. Xx*"

41.

After bidding them farewell and pledging to meet them both later that evening, Kay departed and Franklin waited until she was out of sight before he spoke to Rowan.

"What was going on there, Rowan? You were like an animal."

"I am an animal," she said, distractedly. "We all are."

"You know what I mean. I've seen you angry before but I've never seen you lose control like that."

They were standing outside Orlagh's block of flats on Park Row. The snow was falling in cotton wool clumps and the night was drawing in fast.

"I hadn't lost control, I was doing exactly what I needed to do."

"I don't like violence."

"D'you think I do?" Rowan scoffed. "I never invited violence into my life, it found me. I didn't ask for any of this to happen."

"Well, you're lucky that Orlagh's a flipping basket-case otherwise she would've fought back."

Rowan shrugged her shoulders. "I don't care anymore, I don't care about anything other than finding out who killed Ruby. If you don't like my methods, or you think I'm turning into an animal, you're welcome to go home. I can do this by myself."

"You know I can't do that. It's when we split up that the worst stuff happens." Franklin patted his chest where the scar left by an arrow piercing his skin was buried beneath layers of clothes.

"Well, you can't have it both ways. Either tag along and keep your mouth shut or go home and judge me in private. This is my story and it's going to end how I want it to end."

"D'you really think you will catch the killer tonight? It's a tall order."

Rowan nodded. "I'm sure of it. Things have been fermenting in my head. You know that feeling where all the threads are weaving together and you've been so focused on the minute details, it's only when you take a step back you see the whole tapestry. I think that's where I'm at."

"D'you care to elaborate?"

"Not yet. You don't mind do you?"

"Not at all, sounds like we're going to have quite a long night though."

"There's nowhere in the world more exciting than the city at night," said Rowan as she buckled up her coat. "Ruby told me that on the night she died. It's kind of poetic, don't you think?"

Franklin nodded. "There's certainly something special about night time in a city, there's a magic in the air. Especially on nights like this."

"Did you know we had an argument that night?" Rowan said softly.

"You never said. What happened?"

"Just a stupid fight that we would probably never have even remembered an hour later if she'd lived. She'd decided she wasn't going to go to university that autumn and I pretty much said she was ruining her life. God, it all sounds so pathetic now. None of it mattered one bit, but that was the last time we ever spoke."

"Oh Rowan, I'm so sorry. But you're right, it *doesn't* matter. All Ruby would've known at the end is that you loved her. Who cares about a stupid quarrel? She was loved."

"So much crap from that night resurfaces all the time, endless memories churning around, throwing stuff up. All the things that I could've done differently that might've changed things."

"I'm going to hug you now… If you want."

Rowan nodded and stepped into Franklin's open arms. "Thank you," she said.

"Nothing that happened was your fault," Franklin spoke into her ear. "It was nobody's fault except for the bastard who murdered her."

Rowan patted Franklin on the back, the universal signal that an embrace had run its course, and the two friends broke away from one another. "We'd better get the car. I could do with a bite to eat before we head to the Camel Toe."

"I'm not getting used to the name of that pub," Franklin smiled.

The journey down the hill to Stokes Croft was much easier than the one they'd had on the way up. The fresh snow lay untouched, it crunched welcomely under foot as the pair trudged onwards through a near blizzard of white. Between twinkling lights in pub windows, Franklin and Rowan saw Christmas Eve revellers singing carols and clinking glasses of mulled wine. In one, a TV was screening *It's A Wonderful Life*, another was screening *Die Hard*.

As Franklin had feared, the snow had ravaged his tiny car and by the time they reached it, it looked like a blob of vanilla ice-cream in a sea of white. "That's just what we need," he sighed.

"Should we try digging it out?" Rowan asked.

"I think it's pretty much stuck for the night. Look, the roads are abandoned, I don't think anyone's driving in this weather."

The length of the snaking road through Stokes Croft was surreally quiet and carpeted in snow. Only the occasional mound, which had once been a car or a post box, broke the pristine sea of white.

"Dinner at yours?" Franklin suggested.

"I'd rather not. Jude's at home and I don't really want to bump into him. I'm supposed to be young, free and single not hanging out with my boss on Christmas Eve."

Franklin laughed. "Agreed. How about some soup? I'm buying?"

"Sounds delicious," Rowan concurred.

They found a vegetarian restaurant within sight of the Camel Toe and were seated in a faux-leather booth in the window. Franklin offered to switch seats when he noticed Rowan was distractedly staring across the road at the ominous bar, but she declined.

The restaurant was dark, with a hearty, cottagey smell that welcomed their arrival. When the farmhouse vegetable soups were delivered to their table, along with a basket of warm bread, the pair set upon them like starved orphans.

"I'd no idea how hungry I was," said Franklin, between spoonfuls of soup.

"You made the right choice," Rowan found her eyes gazing back across the street as the neon sign in the window of the Camel Toe flickered on. "Just an hour until showtime. Look, they're arriving."

Two familiar figures were tramping down the middle of the snow-covered road. One was Tariq, a tall and handsome Asian man somewhere in his mid-twenties, who had taken to walking with a cane, seemingly as pure affectation, and the other was Cassie, a squat white woman of a similar age, whose ever-changing hair colour had settled on pink for the evening. They were the hosts of the Murder Club podcast.

"Christ, I forgot about those two," said Franklin.

Through the window, they watched as a couple of excitable teenage girls skidded awkwardly across the road to meet the hosts, giggling to each other before shouting in unison "We're all just one bad day away from becoming a victim or a murderer!" It was the sign off catchphrase Tariq and Cassie ended every show with, a motto that Franklin had become alarmed to see plastered across tee-shirts, mugs and reusable bags over previous months. The girls stopped to take selfies with the hosts before waddling away through the snow.

"Stupid girls," Rowan hissed. "Complete morons."

"I'm sure they're happier than either of us."

"Idiots are always happy. They're happy for the same reason that they're idiots - because they're not paying attention."

"It's an interesting catchphrase. One bad day away from becoming a victim or a murderer." Franklin wiped the bottom of his bowl with a crust of bread.

"It's not true though. I've never been a victim, even when my life was on the line I fought back. There's no way that's happening to me."

"But a murderer?" he asked.

Rowan locked eyes with Franklin. "I know what you're thinking."

"Well?"

"You want to know if I'm going to kill Ruby's murderer," she said.

"And are you?"

"Honestly, I have no idea. I want to, and don't think I wouldn't do it, but when it came down to it, who knows?"

"But you don't believe in capital punishment," Franklin pressed.

"I don't believe in state sanctioned murder, but there's something about civilian justice that I find very appealing. Kind of like homemade capital punishment."

Franklin wiped his mouth on a napkin. "I don't want you to."

Rowan shrugged. "It's not really your choice. You wouldn't be able to stop me if I went for it."

"It would change you, probably in ways you could never even realise. People say that when you take a life their face haunts you for the rest of your days. I wouldn't want that for anyone, least of all you."

"Would it change how you think of me?" Rowan asked.

"It would, yes."

Rowan nodded slowly. "Well. I might not be around for that much longer, so you wouldn't have to deal with it."

"What do you mean?" Franklin proceeded with caution.

"I've been looking at options...for like, my life. If I resit my science A level I'd have enough credits to get a late enrolment at Edinburgh University."

"Edinburgh?" Franklin blurted. "But that's in Scotland!"

"Oh is it really, Franklin? I had no idea."

"But it's so far away, it's... a different country!"

"It's less than an hour from Bristol airport."

"Well, how soon could you enrol?"

"I need an A in biology. I should've got it the first time around but I screwed up. Late enrolment is in mid-January."

Franklin's mouth dropped open. "January? But what are you even going to study?"

"Forensic psychology. I thought I could at least put my history to good use."

"But... but," Franklin's struggle for words made him feel like a child. "What about me?"

225

"You've got Alf, and Verity. But even if you didn't... what about me? I need a change in my life, I need to feel what it's like to be somewhere else for a change."

"It's expensive, and you'll hate it."

"Maybe I will hate it. Maybe I'll love it. I've got money saved up and my parents will help me."

Franklin leaned back in his chair and stared out the window. For a horrible moment Rowan feared that he was about to cry. "I'll *miss* you."

Rowan reached across the table and held his hands in hers. "I'll miss you too. You're my best friend."

Franklin smiled but shook his head. "Is there nothing I can do to change your mind?"

"I don't think so. I'm pretty set in my head, to be honest. Ruby never made it to uni, but I can. I can live the life she never had, or just... live the one I want."

"I thought you were happy."

"You said it yourself, neither of us are happy. We deal with dead people every day, death hangs over us like a dark cloud, it seeps into our thoughts and won't leave us alone. I just need a change."

Franklin nodded. "I know what you mean." He squeezed her hand tighter. "If this is what you need to do, then I'm with you and I'm happy for you."

"Thank you," she mouthed silently at him.

Both of them watched as across the road a queue began to form outside the bar. It was less than half an hour until the Murder Club would take to the stage.

42.

"Good luck, sweetheart. We're thinking of you." The text message from Rowan's parents reached her phone just as she and Franklin joined the queue which snaked its way around the grey, single storey block of the Camel Toe.

Franklin felt immediately ancient as he cast his gaze around the assembled throng, bundled in layers of fashionably mismatched clothing and stamping vintage boots into the snow to fight the cold, he was evidently the only person present beyond his twenties, and in his suit and black overcoat he knew he had never looked more like a funeral director.

The doors to the pub opened and a young man with an ostentatiously huge beard and a camel-hair coat addressed the queue. "All right, you sickos!" A cheer went up from the guests. "My name's Jeremy and I'm the landlord of the Camel Toe and for some reason I've let you nutcases come to my bar and talk about murder. Now, we've sold out tonight - because people are terrible, so it's standing room only and if you don't get a seat, tough. Now we've some ground rules. No heckling, in fact, keep your mouth shut while the hosts are talking, they're recording a podcast and don't need you messing it up. No vaporisers or e-cigs or whatever you call them nowadays, that stuff smells gross and messes with the projector beam, and finally, have a bit of common sense guys. I know true crime is your thing, but a girl died here a few years back, so try to show a bit of respect. Alright? Now we're gonna start letting you in, so please have your tickets ready."

The queue began inching forwards and Franklin leaned into Rowan. "Maybe it's not going to be as bad as you think?"

"I wouldn't count on it," Rowan replied.

Franklin felt a tap on his shoulder and turned to face a man and woman. She was draped around his neck like a scarf. "Excuse me mate," said the man. "Are you that undertaker who caught Blackbeard?"

"No," Franklin turned back to Rowan.

"Yes, you are. Man, I heard your episode. That was some freaky crap."

Rowan shrugged at Franklin's expression. "There's gonna be a lot of that tonight."

"You're really going to abandon me to this city of lunatics?"

"We're at lunatic central tonight," she replied. "Don't blame all of Bristol."

Rowan showed the tickets she had printed that morning and one of the bouncers on the door scanned the codes with his phone. After peering into Rowan's shoulder bag he nodded them through and they took the two steps down to the entrance and ducked through the doorway.

"You look nervous," Franklin said to her.

"It's nothing. Just have some stuff in my bag I didn't want the bouncer seeing."

"That sounds ominous."

"It'll all be revealed in time. I've come prepared," she said.

The Camel Toe had undergone a complete refurbishment since the night Ruby had been murdered. Rowan had known it only from photographs and the video they had copied from Cal's hard drive. The austere coolness of the previous interior - exposed brickwork walls and pipes across the ceiling, had been replaced with sickly, vibrant graffiti scrawls and neon signs, and the tables, which had been pushed to the edges of the room, bore a lava lamp. In the centre of the bar stood a sea of plastic chairs, the kind she'd occasionally been tasked with stacking after school assemblies, they faced the only fixture Rowan recognised from Cal's video - the wooden stage where Ruby had once sung her mesmerising song. Upon it now sat a pair of empty armchairs over a faded rug. Two microphones were poised expectantly.

"Very retro," Rowan commented.

"Sort of." said Franklin. "Grab a table while we still can, I don't want to be recognized.

Most of the audience had taken to the rows of chairs, but Franklin and Rowan slipped beside them and sat at a table in the far corner from the stage. It felt suitably hidden and lit only by the soft glow of a purple lava lamp.

"What can I get you?"

228

"Spirits," Rowan said without a pause. "Gin and tonic. Ice and a slice. Make it a double, please."

Franklin had never known Rowan to drink gin in a pub, but if any night called for hard spirits it would be tonight. He returned to the table with a large measure for her and the standard pint of cider for himself.

"How're you feeling?"

"Pretty anxious, to be honest," Rowan replied.

"I don't think anyone's going to spot us back here, they'll all be looking towards the stage."

"It's not that. I'm nervous about what they'll say - how people will react."

"They don't seem like a bloodthirsty crowd to me," said Franklin, watching as hordes of young people took to the seats. "They're just kids who don't really understand death."

Rowan winced at the strength of her gin, but took another sip regardless. "I don't care how young they are, it's pretty twisted to come and get drunk and hear a talk on the murder of a woman."

"I'm not saying I agree with it, just that I understand it. People need to figure out their relationship with death and it can be complicated."

"No," Rowan said flatly. "I've heard the Murder Club before. It's about turning atrocities into entertainment, listening to all the gory details of some poor person's violent end, like they have any right to."

"Death comes to all of us, don't judge anyone too hard for being preoccupied with it. You wouldn't be working with me if you didn't want to understand what it means."

Rowan gave a soft nod. "Perhaps, but don't try and get me to like these freaks."

Franklin caught Kay's eye as she and Lily entered the bar, and waved them both over.

Lily immediately gave Rowan another of her huge, but strangely insincere, hugs before pulling up a pair of chairs.

"Kay told me about earlier," said Lily to Rowan. "Orlagh's gone loop the loop, clearly."

Rowan raised her eyebrows in silent agreement as she sipped from her glass. "It was pretty intense."

"Talking of intense," said Lily as she gazed around the room. "This is a bit much isn't it?"

"You could say that. Have you been back here since that night?"

Lily shook her head. "I took me a long while just to walk past the building. It feels so strange coming in here again. It's all changed but it feels just the same in a way, almost like no time has passed."

"Me neither," said Rowan. "I'm not even sure why I'm here tonight, or what I'm expecting to find out."

"Stay strong, honey." Lily placed her hand on Rowan's. "Do it for Ruby."

Kay returned to the table with two glasses of red wine and handed one to Lily. "Well, this is a pretty messed up evening," she declared as she took her seat.

The assembled crowd hushed as Jeremy the landlord took to the stage. "Right then," he began. "We all know why we're here but we're going to run through the details before I bring our hosts for the evening to the stage."

A smattering of applause rippled across the audience.

"In the spring of 2012, nineteen year old Ruby Kaplan was found murdered in the deserted warehouse a couple of streets away. Earlier that evening she'd been rehearsing with her band *at this very bar*. Her killer has never been caught and no arrests have been made, but this evening the hosts of the *Murder Club Podcast* are hoping to get to the bottom of this mystery. This live recording will include graphic discussions of murder and violence and is not suitable for those of a sensitive disposition. Without further ado, please welcome to the stage Cassie and Tariq of the Murder Club."

As Jeremy left the stage the audience erupted into applause as the two hosts appeared from behind a red curtain. Both Cassie and Tariq were dressed in knitted Christmas jumpers with Father Christmas hats on their heads. Tariq held up a sprig of mistletoe and Cassie demurely kissed him on the cheek.

"Are you ready to do this?" she asked him.

"Let's do this," he replied, and the pair sank into the armchairs as the theme tune to *The Murder Club Podcast* played and a remotely controlled projection screen electronically unfurled behind them.

The atmosphere in the pub was tense with expectation. They were all cheering and clapping as the theme music concluded, except for those around Rowan's table, hidden in the shadows.

"They'll calm down in a bit," Lily told Rowan, warmly and with a smile.

"Merry Christmas everyone!" Cassie beamed from the stage. "We thought we'd dress appropriately for the evening!"

More applause. Rowan found herself grinding her teeth.

Jeremy briefly returned to the stage with a pair of champagne flutes, which he placed on the low table between the hosts. He whispered something to Tariq, who immediately announced to the crowd, "OK, we're recording. Let's get this party started!"

The cheers were interrupted by a projection on the screen which read *"Quiet Please."*

"Welcome to the Murder Club. You guys! I can't believe how many of you made it here. Thank you *so much!*" said Cassie.

Tariq took his cue. "This is one messed up story we have for you tonight. Who here has ever heard of Ruby Kaplan before?"

More applause and some cheers. Rowan bit her lip hard enough to break the skin. Ruby was meant to be famous, but not like this.

"This is such a tragic story, and it feels so weird telling it here!" Cassie laughed.

A man's voice from the audience shouted, "The dad did it!" and the room broke into laughter.

"Hold your horses, dude," Tariq said. "We haven't even started yet!"

"Although the dad *definitely* did it," said Cassie. More laughter.

Lily squeezed Rowan's shoulder. Rowan shrugged her away.

"We don't have to stay," Franklin whispered to her.

"I need to do this," she replied.

"Let me paint a picture for you," Cassie spoke into the microphone in front of her. "It's May, 2012. The Spice Girls have reformed for a hot minute, Carly Rae Jepsen is riding at the top of the charts with "Call Me Maybe" and London's getting geared up for the Olympics. In Bristol, a young woman with dreams of stardom took to this very stage and sang."

The lights in the bar dimmed and on the screen an image of Ruby emerged from the darkness. It was the recording of her singing "Downtown" that Cal had uploaded to YouTube. The projection matched where she would have stood on that night. Her voice, both clear and controlled, yet achingly fragile, echoed from the speakers. The audience gasped. The video played for no more than thirty seconds before the lights were brought back up.

"That *voice* man!" said Tariq.

"She was pretty goddamn talented," Cassie added. "The evening was May 5th and just a few hours after that recording was made, Ruby Kaplan was stabbed to death in an old storage warehouse in Stokes Croft."

The audience sat in silent awe as the details of her brutal slaying were told in forensic detail. "Almost two dozen knife wounds to the throat and chest," Tariq explained. "Whoever killed her wasn't fucking around. Usually when a frenzied attack happens like that it's someone known to the victim, but despite a huge investigation, nobody has ever been caught for her murder."

Cassie continued the tale. "Now let's rewind to 1993. Ruby is the first child of Rolinda and Oscar Kaplan," the audience booed as if a pantomime villain had arrived onstage at the mention of Oscar's name. "They had another daughter a couple of years later called Rowan - man, they really liked women with names that begin with R's in that family. Anyway, Ruby was an average student at school, never really excelling at anything until she found her voice. Schoolfriends told us that pretty much the moment she discovered she could sing, she didn't stop."

"That sounds kinda annoying," Tariq added.

"Doesn't it? Anyway, Ruby gets to nineteen and decides to join a band, and not only does she find one, she manages to get the lead singer kicked out so she can replace her. The band was Morning Shiver." A brief wave of laughter passed across the audience. "Guys, it was 2012, it was a different world, don't judge their crappy band name."

"Let's get out of here," Franklin said to Rowan. "I can't stand any more of this."

"I'm not going anywhere," she responded.

"Now Ruby was also in a relationship with Douglas Bennett, the drummer for Morning Shiver," said Tariq.

"Which probably explains how she managed to get the lead singer kicked out of the band," Cassie added with a chuckle.

On the screen, Doug Bennett's face came into view. Tariq looked at the image. "He was totally punching above his weight, right?"

"They don't know he's dead," said Kay. "They wouldn't be this mean if they knew."

"For a long time, he was the police's prime suspect, because... boyfriend, duh," said Cassie. "But his story checked out, according to the police. CCTV shows him leaving with the other band members and this like... video guy who was recording them that night."

"Videographer," said Tariq.

"Videographer. Ruby's the last one to leave. She locked up after everyone else, we don't know why she didn't leave with the rest, or what she was doing at the bar by herself, because this pub was undergoing a refurb at the time, so there were no security cameras on as it wasn't even open. According to the boyfriend, she wanted to try out some stuff unaccompanied, cappella singing or whatever. We've got no reason to doubt Douglas, other than, you know, boyfriends are always suspicious. She leaves at close to eleven o'clock and here's the weird thing..."

"...There's a bunch of weird things that happened next. Like the dad."

"Oh yeah, where's dear old daddy while all of this is going on? Stargazing, apparently. You heard that right, despite never having shown any interest in astronomy before, Oscar Kaplan decides he wants to drive out of the city to look at the stars. Only the weather was like this:" A still image from that evening's BBC weather forecast showed an enormous rainstorm poised to break over Bristol at 11pm. "Probably not the best conditions to test out your new found interest in stargazing, but let's just presume he didn't know the forecast. He drives all the way across the city, with no equipment, no telescopes, no star map, nothing at all. Goes out into the middle of nowhere and just waits around for an hour or so until his wife gives him a call. Give me a break!"

"So the boyfriend's gone home, the dad's away stargazing and the videographer's gone back to his wife - incidentally, that camera guy has quite a nutso Facebook group that's worth checking out. Ruby locks up the bar and is meant to head straight home, but what does she do? Even though it's already starting to rain, she decides not to turn left when she leaves the pub, which is the actual way back to her house, she goes right. Why? As far as I can tell nobody has ever given a decent explanation for why she did so, or why she headed towards an abandoned warehouse."

The lights in the room dimmed again and on the screen a video began to play in a loop. It was CCTV footage taken from across the road. It was staticky and grainy, and the image juddered rather than running smoothly, but it was the first time Ruby had seen her sister's final moments in motion.

"Oh my God," Rowan whispered.

The video showed Ruby coming up the steps from the sunken entrance after locking the door. Briefly she appeared to check her phone before looking either way and then steadfastly marching in the direction of the warehouse.

"Pretty weird, don't you think?" asked Tariq as the lights went up.

To the horror of Rowan and Franklin, Lily clambered to her feet and raised a hand, "Excuse me?" she called.

All eyes in the room turned to her. "The question and answer section comes at the end of the show," Tariq seemed bemused.

Jovial laughter filled the room, but Lily seemed unperturbed. "Where did you get that footage from? I've never seen it before."

Cassie giggled. "We have to protect our sources, babe! Holy cow, is that Franklin! Oh my god it is. Franklin, Franklin Gallow! It's the guy who caught Blackbeard!"

A cheer went up around the bar as Franklin slid lower in his seat.

"We need to get out of here," Rowan breathed. "Right now, all of us."

"Franklin! Come up on the stage, say hi to your fans!"

Franklin rose to his feet, but, unnoticed by the crowd, Rowan, Kay and Lily did the same. The roar of appreciation quickly turned to stunned incredulity as Franklin hastily fled for the door with three young women in tow. In an instant they were outside, standing in the centre of the snow covered road.

"Rowan, what's going on?" he asked.

"You saw it too, didn't you?" Lily added.

"I know who killed Ruby," Rowan's voice began to break.

"It was them, wasn't it?" Lily held Rowan's hand. "Cassie and Tariq?"

Rowan looked at Franklin. "It was," she sobbed.

43.

"Rowan, what are you talking about?" Franklin was stunned.

"You heard me. It's them, Cassie and Tariq. *They* did it."

"How can you say that? What did you see in that video?"

"I can't tell you right now," Rowan replied. "But I know what I'm doing. Please trust me."

Franklin nodded firmly. "OK, I trust you. What do we do, call the police?"

"Not just yet, I need to do something first." Rowan turned to Kay and Lily. "I want to visit the warehouse where Ruby was murdered."

Lily pulled her coat around her and shuddered against a blast of icy wind that whipped along the snow covered road. "Oh my god, are you crazy?"

"Not yet, but I'm going to be if I don't do this. Are you in?"

"I'm in," said Franklin.

"Me too," Lily added, reluctantly.

The three of them turned to face Kay, who was already shaking her head.

"I'm sorry guys. *I can't!* I know what happened to Ruby that night but I can't keep going back. I sat there through the Murder Club talk thinking, *why am I doing this? Why can't I stop revisiting that night and my past?* I saw Ruby on the screen and heard her voice and all I wanted to do was run. You guys do what you need and good luck with it. But this isn't me, just as it wasn't *me* on that night. I want out, I'm done."

"That's pretty cowardly, Kay," Lily spat. "You just came here to eavesdrop on a tragedy? You were *there* with us that night, I don't care if you're not Kevin anymore, you were *there* and you can't turn your back on it now. None of us can."

"You don't have to come," Rowan said softly. "Nobody has to."

"You're not staying at mine tonight." said Lily. "That offer's expired, I suggest you get a hotel or find your way back to that turkey farm. Doug's dead, Ruby's dead and we're the only members of the band left and you're just going to *abandon* us?"

"Oh please, don't act like we were some tight group who were going to be around forever. You were already thinking of quitting the band because it was all about Ruby. Yeah, I remember."

"That's not true," Lily said to Kay, and then turned to Rowan. "It's not true."

"I don't care about Morning Shiver. None of that band crap is of interest to me. Kay, thanks for the help earlier today, we couldn't have done it without you. Do whatever you need to do… Merry Christmas."

Kay offered a weary smile to Rowan before wordlessly turning away from the trio and marching off through the snow, leaving thick, deep footprints as she went.

"Good riddance," Lily huffed.

"What the hell was that all about?" Franklin demanded of her.

"I can't stand disloyalty," Lily said, simply. "Why d'you think I kept on employing Doug all those years? Or followed Kay through her transition. Hell, I've even smiled at Orlagh in the street, which is probably more than she deserved. Anyway, I don't want to dwell on it any longer. Can we just get this over with and then go to the police?"

Franklin rubbed his hands together. " Rowan, d'you want to lead the way?"

Rowan nodded and pivoted on the spot to face the imposing edifice of the warehouse, which loomed over the street through the falling snow. In her pocket her hand closed around Ruby's ring and at once she felt her sister was somehow with her, willing her on, urging her to keep looking because she was so close to the answers she had been searching for.

Not even Franklin had seen snow like this before. As they passed the spot where he'd parked his car, all that remained was a huge, white cushion. The streets had been abandoned by all but the most foolhardy Christmas Eve drinkers, who made their way unsteadily through the unblemished snow. None of them were heading towards the warehouse, why would anybody?

Franklin had a foggy idea of the gigantic warehouse being used for paper manufacturing and storage sometime in his youth. There was a faint recollection of a fire putting an end to the business sometime in the late '70s, but in truth, he had never given the fortress much thought. Staring up at it, he thought how it might once have been beautiful, before the city air rendered the once colourful tapestry of brickwork grey and characterless. The Bristol Byzantine style of the mid-Victorian era favoured fancifully shaped windows, but they had all been shuttered behind huge wooden boards, and an old door bolted and padlocked.

"How are we supposed to get in?" asked Franklin.

"I know a way," said Rowan.

Of course she did. During last summer she and Jude had found an entrance and Rowan had for the first time visited the location where Ruby's body had been discovered, along with a gigantic graffiti scrawl which read "*Oscar Kaplan murdered Ruby*".

"The nails are loose on this one," Rowan began jimmying the corner of one of the boards, and sure enough the nails began emerging from the wooden window frame. She let it drop onto the snow covered pavement, revealing a dark hole in the building like a wound.

"You're not going in are you? Have you lost your minds?" the voice from behind caused them all to turn and face the woman who was standing in the middle of the road. It was Kay.

"What are you doing here?" Lily demanded. "Go home."

"No. It's cold and dark and I just want all this to be over. Rowan, I'm scared but I'm not a coward."

Rowan nodded. "I know. You don't have to come in, but can you keep watch for us?"

"Of course."

Lily narrowed her eyes at Kay with contempt before she turned back to the building. "Are you sure about this?"

"Not really, but I don't know what else to do."

"Should I lead the way?" Franklin offered.

"No. I've been inside before. Give me a bunk up."

Franklin dropped to one knee in the snow and proffered his hands to her, woven at the fingers. She stepped into them and he hoisted her up into the darkness of the empty window frame. She dropped down onto the other side and immediately activated the torch on her phone. Franklin then helped Lily to scramble through the hole and she and Rowan together heaved him into the abandoned warehouse while Kay pushed him from behind.

In the light of three torches the open plan ground floor of the building was illuminated in stark white. It was a stretch of bare concrete interrupted by steel support columns, and in the centre of the room was a red, metallic staircase constructed across a pair of girders. From a hole in the roof came drifting snow, piling up on the steps.

"It's upstairs," said Rowan as she shon her torchlight into the menacing darkness above them.

"This place is so creepy," Lily whispered. "Babe, can I hold your hand?"

Wordlessly, Ruby reached out through the darkness until her fingers found Lily's hand. She led the way up the snow covered staircase with Franklin behind them, casting their own shadows ahead in the beam of his torch.

"What the hell was she thinking?" asked Lily. "What made her come here?"

"Something must've scared her," said Franklin.

Suddenly, there came a squawk and the sound of batting wings. A trio of pigeons, that had roosted in the rafters, woke abruptly and fled for the hole in the roof. Lily screamed and broke her hold of Rowan's hand.

"I forgot about them," said Rowan. "Sorry."

Lily allowed a flutter of laughter at herself. "Jesus Christ. I hate pigeons."

The landing of the warehouse revealed a long corridor, part of which was obscured by a pile of roof tiles and rafters which had collapsed from above. It seemed even more derelict than the last time Rowan had been here and she briefly wondered why the building hadn't simply been torn down.

Emboldened by the rush of adrenalin the pigeons had released in her, Lily scrambled over the pile of twisted wood, iced like a cake in snow, before Rowan and Franklin squeezed their way around it.

"This building doesn't seem very safe," Franklin warned. "I don't think we should be here much longer. I don't think we should be here at all."

"We've been in worse situations," Rowan reminded him.

"Don't remind me," Franklin patted his chest.

"And the underground river,"

"Oh god, the river."

"Me with Martin Maybridge," Rowan continued.

"Who?"

"This psycho. It was a couple of years ago. He killed a bunch of people and then kidnapped me."

"Sweetheart, you need to take a holiday when this is all over. Go somewhere trouble won't find you! How come I've never heard of any of this?"

"Sometimes it's easier to try and forget things, 3am is around the time the memories come for you," she replied.

Lily's hand came to rest on a doorway, through which the door had fallen from its hinges and now lay face down on the dirty and warped wooden floor. "What was this room?" she gasped as she stepped into the darkness, her torchlight fell upon a cavernous space lined with long, rusted metal tables.

Rowan's phone suddenly buzzed in her hand and the shock of it almost caused her to drop it. A text message had arrived. She turned the phone over in her hand and read the screen. The name simply read *"Gavin"* and she wondered for a moment who that was. *"Hi Rowan. This is Gavin from the prison visit programme. Just thought I'd say howdy and check you were having a nice Christmas Eve? Got anything good planned?"*

Rowan sighed. Gavin, the handsome man who'd been so kind to her on the day she'd visited her would-be killer in prison. She imagined what a Christmas Eve for Gavin would look like. A roaring fire and glasses of mulled wine, merrily getting drunk in front of an old movie with his parents, and a big, stupid dog asleep on the sofa with tinsel tied around his collar. That was what a normal family did together, a family that didn't have a hideous, gaping wound at the heart of it.

"Who is it?" asked Franklin.

"Nothing... Nobody."

"So, you think Tariq and Cassie met Ruby here?" Lily shone her torch around the room. "Why? Did they even know her? Did they even have a podcast back then? Were there podcasts in 2012?"

"There have been podcasts since 2004," said Franklin.

"Well I never," Lily replied. "So how d'you think they managed to get the CCTV footage of Ruby leaving the bar?"

"YouTube, probably. Crimewatch did an episode on Ruby, Dad wouldn't let me watch it but I'd heard that the footage was there."

"I hate to ask," said Franklin. "But do you know where it happened?"

Rowan nodded. "It was right here."

Franklin took a step away from her and gasped. "Oh my God. In this room?"

"Last time I was here there was graffiti on the wall. I guess the police have cleared it up since then."

"Not quite," said Lily, whose torchlight fell upon the faded letters on the wall, their message *"Oscar Kaplan murdered Ruby"* was barely legible. The beam from Lily's phone alighted on a single red rose upon the floor.

"That's new," said Rowan. "I mean, there was one last time but this is newer. The last one must be dust by now."

"It looks pretty dried out and…oh!" Lily's face contorted in horror as her torch passed over pristine and recent graffiti.

"I'm sorry, Ruby", it read. *"I didn't want to do it."*

44.

The four sat in silence in the back of the taxi as it slowly wound its way through the snow covered streets of Bristol. Franklin, who had his back to the driver in a collapsible seat, discreetly sent a text to his friend.

Rowan had been watching the tiny TV screen on the glass partition between the driver and passengers, which had been surreally scrolling through a series of adverts for summer getaways on remote, golden beaches received the message. *"How're you doing? Have you got a plan?"*

Without looking up, Rowan replied. *"I do. I need a distraction to get Lily and Kay outside when we get to the boutique"*

"I'm on it." he sent back.

After leaving the warehouse, Franklin had been surprised at Rowan's quiet, stoic response. The fresh graffiti and the rose had not stirred in her the waves of grief or anger he had been expecting. Instead she had fallen silent, processing the information piece by piece, sifting through sand to find the minuscule nuggets of gold within it. It had been Lily who suggested they all retreat to her shop in Redland.

"I have tea," she informed them. "And vodka. Cassie and Tariq saw us so we might want to think about a change of clothes if we're heading back to this area."

The only vehicles about were taxis. With the toll of last order bells, they had arrived in a cavalcade, ferrying drunken merrymakers home, cautiously rolling through the drifts.

"We should call the police," Kay whispered to Rowan, who was sandwiched between her and Lily in the back of the cab.

"Not yet," said Rowan.

"Bloody hell," the driver chirped merrily from the front of the car in a thick, warm Bristolian accent. "Haven't known snow like this in years. Can't remember the last time we had a white Christmas."

The driver's interruption was met with an uncomfortable silence in the rear of the vehicle, which Franklin found duty-bound to break. "Not since '63, I reckon. Not just Brizzle either, it's pitchin' all the way out to Bath and Weston. Lasted 'til Easter back then."

Rowan couldn't help but smile at Franklin. His natural accent was usually buried beneath an affected, neutral tone he had schooled himself to use but in the presence of a fellow native he'd turned it up to full strength in retelling the tale they'd both heard that morning. Franklin's greatest gift as a funeral director was his ability to become whoever the person he was speaking to needed him to be. Whether it was a grieving widow in a Clifton mansion or a penniless workman in a Knowle West block of flats, his chameleon tone would change to put them at ease.

"Cheers, driver," said Franklin as the taxi pulled up outside Wandering Lily and he slid a ten pound note into the driver's hand. "Keep the change. Merry Christmas."

As the cab drew away, three of them waited while Lily unlocked the door to her boutique and disabled the burglar alarm.

"I'm just going to be a minute," Franklin declared. "I need to make a phone call."

"Sure honey," said Lily.

Franklin had never been keen on overly-familiar pet names, even from people who knew him well, so he struggled to smile in response to Lily's forced charm and turned away from her to face the street. Up the hill, which veered sharply away from his vantage point was Edison's home, just out of sight. He called him.

"Ed, are you at work?"

"Hello to you too," his brother replied. "No. I've got a few days off over Christmas. Don't know why really, usually the people without kids are…"

"…I need you to do me a favour. Are you home?'

"Yeah. *The Wrong Trousers* is on catchup."

"I need you to get into your uniform and head down the hill to Wandering Lily."

"Is that the junk shop with the naked mannequins in the window?"

"That's the one, and it's a vintage boutique, apparently."

"Bloody Millennials. They can repackage any old crap and sell it to gullible kids."

Franklin couldn't help but be buoyed by his brother's tone. This was the grumpy, prickly Edison he had missed for too long. "There's three young women in there, one of them's Rowan."

"Wait. This isn't like a hen-do thing is it? I'm not stripping just because I have the uniform…"

"…Ed, listen. I need you to get Lily out the shop for a while, and the other girl. Just for a few minutes."

"What's this about?"

"I'll tell you later, but it's important."

"Alright," he said. "Give me a minute."

The line went dead and Franklin dropped the phone into his overcoat pocket before letting himself through the door. A little bell dinged to herald his arrival. Behind the counter, Lily was filling a teapot with boiling water while Rowan and Kay were seated on a threadbare sofa which was urgently in need of re-stuffing. The price tag was a staggering £500. Franklin sat opposite them in an armchair.

"So here's my theory," said Lily, as she carried a tray containing an artfully mismatched bone china tea set, which she placed on an ancient looking traveller's chest she was using as a coffee table. "Cassie and Tariq have got a ton of fancy recording equipment, and if you've ever heard their podcast it's like… crystal clear. There's no way they don't have previous sound engineering experience. One of the reasons they're so successful at what they do is because the audio quality is so much better than other podcasts. I reckon they've probably been at the edge of the music industry for a while, maybe they'd even offered to record Ruby that night and that's where she was heading after the rehearsal. It makes sense right? All you had to do was put an ad online and you'll have young women turning up at your door - and it would explain why she didn't mention it to any of us, because she didn't want us to know she was going solo. God, it's so simple when you put it like that."

"Is it?" Franklin asked.

"We already know they're pretty twisted when it comes to murder. They're both obsessed with it. You should hear her talking about Brady and Hindley like they're Posh and Becks, it's not right." Lily began pouring tea from the pot around the makeshift table.

"It makes sense to me," said Rowan.

"Really?" The leaps of logic in reaching this conclusion did not sit well with Franklin. What was Rowan up to?

"Last summer we met Cassie and Tariq to discuss psychopaths," Rowan went on. "I couldn't put my finger on it at the time but I *knew* there was something wrong with them. They're like groupies for serial killers. It's the perfect crime in a way - hiding in plain sight, hosting a podcast episode about Ruby's murder, nobody would expect anyone to have that kind of gall. They're probably getting off on the fact they're being so brazen and nobody's ever suspected them. I wouldn't be surprised if the whole podcast idea was just a cover, or for some messed up kicks."

"I don't understand it," Kay offered. "I mean, you both seemed to react to the exact same moment - that security camera footage from across the road. Rowan, that's when you said we had to go and Lily, you were like…"

"…It was her expression," Rowan quickly interjected. "I just saw Cassie's smug face as she was sitting there and it hit me all at once. She was barely even trying to hide it."

Franklin blew on his cup of tea and was about to take a sip when a series of heavy thuds thundered at the door.

"Open up, it's the police!"

"What the hell?" Lily stood up and marched over to the door.

Rowan gave Franklin the briefest of glances and he in exchange offered her a barely imperceptible nod of his head.

Lily opened the door to reveal Edison Gallow standing in the snow. Only the closest of observers would have noticed that his uniform was wrinkled and had been hastily thrown around him, or that his glazed eyes and rosy cheeks implied he'd been drinking that evening. "Can I help you officer?"

"I'm going to need to ask you to step outside, Miss. There's been a number of break-ins along this street in the past few months and I saw the lights on as I went by. I need to check that you have a reason to be here."

Lily peered over Edison's shoulder. The man had no police car with him, nor did he seem to be working with a partner. Franklin held his breath, hoping that she would not find either of these details peculiar.

"This is my shop," she pointed up at the sign over the window. "I'm Lily."

"I don't doubt it, but you see, that's exactly what a burglar would say. I just need to make sure."

Lily sighed. "Very well." She reached for her coat and pulled it demurely over her shoulders so that the arms hung empty and stepped out into a pool of snow whitened streetlight."

"And the rest of you," Edison announced to Franklin, Kay and Rowan. As they filed towards the door, Rowan hoped that the confused jumble of the moment would allow her to go unnoticed. She allowed Franklin to slip in front of her and ducked out of sight behind the counter.

Outside she could hear Edison asking for ID from Lily and imagined her rummaging through her pockets in search of a driver's license. There was no time to spare. She reached up to the wall-mounted safe behind the counter and tapped in the only four-digit code it could be if her theory was right, *3-5-6-0*. To her immense relief, the little red light beside the display panel turned green and the metal door fell ajar. She reached inside for the key and then tore across the shop to the door at the far wall. Unlocking it she scrambled her hand up and down through the darkness until she found the hanging light switch. She turned it on and the cavernous expanse below was revealed.

Taking the steps two at a time she tumbled down the last of them and spilled out onto the concrete floor in a heap. There was no time to feel pain, that would have to wait. She heaved herself to her feet, and once she was certain she hadn't broken any bones, ran to the end of one of the aisles between the laden shelves until she reached what she was looking for. The only place it could be.

Stacked between unopened boxes of junk and piled upon a tower of abandoned sewing machines stood a handsome, immaculately polished steel and chrome typewriter. Rowan ran a shaking finger along the bottom row of art-deco keys, pressing each one as she went and watching as the letter-spindle was catapulted forward to the ribbon with a violent clack, until she found the *M*. Not only did the spindle not rise, the key could not even be pressed.

That was all she needed to know. After years of hopeless searching and the misplaced suspicion she had layered upon every person ever to enter Ruby's life, everything at once fell into place.

She dashed across the basement and up the stairs, swinging the door shut behind her just as she saw Franklin reentering the shop.

"It's all just a big misunderstanding," Franklin said to his brother. "Nice to know there're still bobbies on the beat looking out for us. Have a good Christmas!" Franklin looked at Rowan.

"I need a moment with Lily," she said as she pushed past him and Kay, who was coming through the doorway.

Edison was already making his way through the falling snow away from the boutique when Rowan stepped out into the street in front of Lily.

"Rowan!' she gasped. "You're pouring with sweat. Are you ok?"

Rowan wasted no time. She slapped one half of Jude's handcuffs onto Lily's right wrist, the other half she tightened onto her own left wrist, so the pair were locked together.

"What's happening?" Lily was certain to call out to Edison, who could easily still see the pair of them, so Rowan showed her the dagger she had in her pocket.

"If you make a sound, I will stick this in your heart," she hissed. "Are you ready for a walk with me, Lily?"

45.

"How long have you known?" Lily asked, calmly.

"You don't get to ask questions," Rowan replied, holding the dagger against Lily's chest. "You don't get a say in anything that happens from now on."

"Ok, that sounds fair."

Rowan didn't want Lily to be reasonable, she wanted her screaming and panicked, fighting for her life. She yanked the handcuffs sharply as she marched Lily away from her boutique as soon as Edison had faded out of sight through the snow. Their walk would take them over Whiteladies Road and through Clifton Village. She hoped the late hour and curtain of falling white would keep the streets empty, or at least veil the two women and Rowan's actions.

"This is a ceremonial dagger from the Brotherhood of Brigstowe. They're an ancient organisation who disbanded last summer. I kept this when Franklin borrowed his father's robes. It's never been used and is incredibly sharp." Rowan held the weapon aloft and let it glint in the light of a streetlamp in the hope it might frighten Lily.

"Are you going to stab me with that? That's pretty badass, babe."

"You don't get to ask questions," Rowan repeated with a hiss.

"Wow. You've got this all planned out haven't you? I knew that *Murder Club* recording was going to shake something loose. It was the security camera footage, wasn't it?"

"That's another question!" Rowan barked. "But yes."

The road from Redland led them to the broad back of Whiteladies Road, through which cars had driven deep tracks through the snow. As Rowan dragged Lily by the wrist past Clifton Down Railway station, she remarked, "You walk so slow. That's what gave you away. Ruby always strode with purpose wherever she went, because she had places to go and things to do. As soon as I saw that footage, the very first frame of it in motion I knew that wasn't my sister. It was you, dressed as her in a cheap wig."

"St. Nicholas Market, actually," Lily said casually. "Trust me, it wasn't cheap."

"So she was dead already when you left the bar?"

"Yeah. I needed to make sure the cameras saw her leaving though, otherwise the whole plan would go tits up."

The words came so easily to Lily that Rowan could scarcely believe it. Years of hiding her dark secret had come unravelled at the first sign of discovery. Perhaps, Rowan thought, this was how Lily had always imagined the end of her story would be, it was just a matter of time. "So you showed up tonight just for the thrill of it, right?"

"Maybe. It was kind of exciting being there, watching it all unfold in front of me. I have to give you credit, you didn't give the slightest indication that you suspected me."

"I've suspected you for a long time, Lily. When we went into the warehouse I was watching you, just to make sure, in case I'd made a mistake. I didn't tell you where in that place Ruby was murdered, but you led the way. You actually took us right there."

"Shit," Lily giggled. "I ballsed that one up, didn't I?"

"That was all I needed to know, just to be certain. When you stood up during the podcast recording, right when they were showing the footage I *knew* you were making a distraction, trying to get me not to look too closely at the video."

"I was thinking on my feet," Lily said breezily. "A girl's gotta improvise sometimes. I didn't know they actually had video of it. The police only ever showed me photographs."

"They say thrill killers return to the scene of the crime afterwards and that they take trophies. How many times did you go back to the warehouse?"

Lily just shrugged. "Half a dozen, maybe more. But you see Rowan, I didn't kill Ruby."

"I know," said Rowan.

Franklin checked his watch. He had been making small talk over tea with Kay for ten minutes and the conversation, mostly about turkey farming, was wearing thin. Rowan had been outside with Lily for an uncomfortable amount of time and he was starting to feel a sense of unease.

"I wonder what's keeping them?" said Kay, as if sensing Franklin's tension, or possibly also bored of talking turkey.

"I'll check." Franklin stood up and peered through the reflections on the window and into the snow-laden street beyond. He saw nothing. He opened the door and looked out. Through the dark he could just make out footprints in the drifts of white, gradually filling with snowflakes. A wave of panic struck him at once, but he knew Kay could not be made a part of whatever was to happen next. "Could you keep watch over the shop for a bit? We won't be long. Just... wait here."

"What's happening?"

"Nothing to worry about. I think they've just gone for a walk."

Kay looked perplexed yet seemed to realise that the less she knew was probably for the better. "Alright."

Franklin's first thought was to call his brother. He pulled Edison's name up on his phone but changed his mind when he imagined the consequences of the police being involved. Instead he found Rowan's number and pressed the call button. As the dial tone began to chirp, he started to run through the snow, following the path of the footprints.

Rowan saw Franklin's name appear on the screen of her phone. She declined the call.

"Was that your boss?" asked Lily.

"It's nothing to do with you."

"So what's the story with you two? I know he's old and ginger, but he's kind of got that sexy daddy thing going on."

Rowan yanked savagely on the handcuffs. "Shut the fuck up, you lunatic. Don't you understand the kind of trouble you're in? You're cuffed to me, I have a dagger and I'm taking you somewhere away from people. Why aren't you scared?"

"You sweetheart," Lily said in a babyish voice that made Rowan want to stab her then and there, in the middle of the street in a deserted Clifton Village. "I know you. I remember when you were a little girl and you wore a tutu to non-uniform day at primary school. You're a dancer, Rowan, not a murderer. I don't think for a moment that you're actually going to do it."

"A lot has changed since then. I am nothing like that little girl and if you think you can sweet talk me into showing mercy then you know *nothing* about me."

Lily just shrugged her shoulders. "I can't see it happening. Wait, where are we going? Are you taking me up to the Clifton Observatory?"

Rowan had veered left at the top of Clifton Village onto a snow covered park, illuminated by the soft glow of Victorian streetlamps.

"Doesn't it look like Narnia?"

"If you don't shut up, I'm gonna…"

"…Wait? You're planning on throwing me into the Avon Gorge, aren't you? How are you going to do that while we're attached at the wrist? The instant you take this handcuff off me I'm doing a runner."

"Who says I won't be going down with you?"

In that moment, Lily fell silent.

Franklin was not built for running. The initial burst of adrenaline which had spurred him on through the snow had been burnt up and was replaced by an acid burn inside his chest. His heart pounded in his ribcage like a fist beating on a door, and sweat, cold from the winter air, stung his skin as it ran down his face.

He chased the footprints over Whiteladies Road, past the train station and through a jagged maze of residential roads leading to Clifton Village. He was certain he knew where this trail was heading but he had to stay on it in case he was wrong. He tried ringing Rowan again but it was declined, he tried twice more and heard nothing.

A couple kissing in the doorway of a patisserie paused for one of them to call out "Merry Christmas, Mister Scrooge!"

He raised a hand and attempted a playful "Merry Christmas" but there was no air in his lungs to speak. He tried phoning her again, for he had no other idea what to do.

46.

"Are you going to answer that?" said Lily. "It's starting to bug me."

There was a tone in Lily's voice that Rowan had been hoping for. It wasn't quite the panic she had wanted, but there was suddenly an edge, something close to fear, or at least a sense of the danger she was in. Rowan didn't answer.

"Look. I told you I didn't kill her, let's just talk this through properly."

"If you don't shut your mouth, I'll stab you through the throat." It felt good to feel Lily afraid as the mortal peril she was in began to dawn on her.

Rowan was not heading towards the Clifton Observatory, she instead dragged her prisoner by the wrist along the familiar serpentine bends of the approach to the suspension bridge. The gigantic East Tower loomed overhead like a fortress, the mighty chains which swooped down to meet the centre of the bridge had been dressed in green and red lights for Christmas. Silently she passed beneath the Samaritans Helpline plaque.

"People will see us," Lily's voice trembled.

"Let them. You'll be dead before anyone's here to help you."

"You're frightening me."

Rowan laughed as she fought Lily's resistance with every step until she found the point she had been looking for. Just over half way, where the cameras were blind. She looked out over the city, down to a tapestry of lights stretching all the way to the horizon. Half a million people were down there and not one of them knew they were here. She stopped walking, and Lily, now standing as far away from Rowan as the handcuffs and her outstretched arm would allow, did the same.

In the pocket of her coat, Rowan slipped the index finger of her right hand into Ruby's plastic ring and without warning, swung her body around, launching her balled fist into Lily's face.

The woman screamed and covered her cheek with her free hand. The ring had cut deep and blood streamed between her fingers. She dropped to her knees and wept.

Rowan calmly but swiftly unlocked her half of the handcuffs and stepped over Lily's huddled body to fasten it against the railings of the bridge. Lily slumped backwards, her head clanging against the metal.

"Rowan... I'm sorry!"

Rowan didn't care. "This was Ruby's ring. The one you took from her, and I hope it hurt!"

The moment she saw the back of Lily's hand drop to the ground, she drove the dagger through the young woman's upturned palm, pinning it into the compacted snow beneath. Lily exploded into a scream of agony and rage, sobbing and wailing at the sight of her impaled hand. "Why did you do that?"

"It's less than you deserve," Rowan spat. "If I leave you here you'll bleed to death. The cold at least will help speed it up, which is more mercy than you gave Ruby. If you give me a reason, I'll finish you off myself, but if you do exactly what I say there's the tiniest chance you'll survive."

Lily nodded quickly. "What do I do?"

"You answer my questions. Understand?"

"I understand."

"How long have you been seeing Martin Maybridge?"

Lily's mouth fell open and her bottom lip trembled. "How did you know?"

"Because you're still wearing the matching loom band you made for him as an engagement present, you moron! You didn't know it was me he tried to kidnap did you? I saw your face when I mentioned his name."

"He never said anything about you, if I'd known..."

"Then what?"

Lily had no answer.

"How could you know that I visited him in prison a week ago? Or that I'd clocked his incarceration number, 3,5,6,0? If you weren't so romantic as to set the password for the safe with your jailbird fiancé's prison code, you might not be in this situation. So tell me Lily, what exactly attracts you to psychopaths?"

"I don't know," Lily softly replied.

Rowan slapped the woman across the face, hard.

"I don't know!" she shrieked. "There's something wrong with me!"

"That's for damn sure. How d'you even find someone like that?"

As sorrowful as her tears made her, Lily looked at Rowan with eyes full of venom. "If you want the truth, it's that there's something *exciting* about killers. It's dangerous and sexy. I didn't even think I'd be able to find a real one, but I got on this pen pal programme. I went through a few of them until I found what I was looking for. They vet the letters before they leave the prison but you can find out who they are online. Martin was everything I was looking for and we just started talking and I got visiting rights. We hit it off right away and one thing led to another."

"How romantic," said Rowan.

"I know how it sounds, but I can't help being who I am. No other men excited me, I needed that danger. Come on, Rowan, haven't you ever fallen for a bad boy?"

Rowan's mind briefly flickered on an image of Jude, who had used the same excuse that he couldn't help who he was just a couple of nights before. This was not the same. "Maybridge killed three people."

"I know!" there was laugh in Lily's voice that was something close to hysteria. "He was a *real* psycho. Three dead and he didn't even care. It's the truth and I know I should be ashamed but I enjoyed hearing about it."

Rowan's hands clenched into angry fists. "What about Douglas. He wasn't a psychopath, was he?"

Lily looked down at her hand. Blood was blossoming onto the snow beneath it. "You weren't lying when you said you knew everything."

"How did you talk him into it?"

"He knew I was into some dark stuff in bed, not that pathetic E.L. James shit, but the really nasty stuff - and he liked it too, as long as it was just fantasy. Poor boy had no idea what he was letting himself in for. People think he dumped me for Ruby but that never happened. The moment she turned up I chucked him out like a used condom, because I knew he'd do absolutely *anything* to get back with me. That's how you wrestle power from a man, Rowan. You make him think he has to do whatever you want to win you back, and it worked like a charm."

Rowan's phone rang again. This time she answered it, as she needed a break from this terrible woman who would soon be turning delirious from blood loss. "Franklin, where are you?"

"I can see you," he replied. "I'm on the bridge."

Through the haze of snow, Rowan could see the outline of Franklin at the far end of the bridge, crowned in a halo of Christmas lights. "Don't come any closer, or I'll kill her."

"Is someone there?" Lily gasped.

"Don't do this, Rowan," Franklin warned over the phone.

"Turn on the record function on your phone. I need people to hear her confess."

"I will. Rowan, I love you."

Rowan let the phone drop to her side. "So you chose Ruby, just because you wanted him to be a murderer?" she asked of Lily.

Lily nodded. "It's as simple as that. It could've been Kevin, it could've been Orlagh, it probably would've been a girl. To be honest, she could be kind of annoying at times but I think the reason why we settled on her was because… well, the cops don't investigate black girls murders like they do white girls'."

With a scream of rage Rowan punched Lily in the face and sent her skull smashing into the metal struts behind her with a sickening crack. Blood bubbled from her broken nose but Lily just sat, unblinking and staring at Rowan.

Rowan was stunned by Lily's resilience; the cold had numbed her. "How did it happen?'

"With planning," Lily said, with an eerie calmness. The woman had decided that if she was destined to die, there was no point in holding back. "Every detail had to be got right. We'd mapped out where all the security cameras were and what our route would be. The morning of the murder, I parked my car in the alley behind the bar and we just went about our day like any other. I bought a wig like Ruby's at the market, Doug got the knife from a supermarket. The papers made out like it was some gangster kind of thing but it was just a kitchen knife. Trust me when I say that on the night, Douglas had no qualms and was every bit as into it as I was.

"There's something so powerful about having a secret like that over someone. Something as real as life and death and your victim has no idea. She went through that whole rehearsal with no inkling that these were the last minutes of her life. We left on cue and just drove around the corner to where the cameras would lose us and worked our way back through the alleys. It was exciting, like being part of some huge prank on Ruby... we were laughing!"

"How did you get back in?" Rowan held the phone out before her in her quivering hand.

"A pebble. That's all it took to prop open the fire escape. We hadn't factored in that idiot videographer so we had to wait around for him to leave, then it was just a case of me sneaking back in as soon as I heard Ruby singing. I *knew she* wouldn't be able to resist another go at the microphone. She was like that, in love with her own voice. Anyway, I played my role. Said I came back to look for an earring or some shit and found the fire escape open. I told her I really wanted to hear *one last song* from her and that's exactly what she did."

"What did she sing?" tears ran down Rowan's face.

"*Go Now* by the Moody Blues. It was really good."

"It's by Bessie Banks," Rowan corrected. "It was Ruby's favourite song."

"Whatever it was, it was excellent. Anyway, she's singing away and Doug creeps up behind her and I just watched as he jumped on her and strangled her from behind. It was amazing, like an animal you see on those nature documentaries. Don't worry, it was quick... we're not total sickos. She was down in less than a minute I'd guess."

"And then what?"

"It was all easy after that. We stripped her down to her underwear, I put on her dress and the wig I bought, walked one loop of the building until I could head back on myself away from CCTV and then it was back down the alley to load Ruby into the car. We only chose the warehouse because it was in one of those camera black spots, but it was so simple getting her inside. It wasn't like it is now, all boarded up."

"It was you who stabbed her, wasn't it?"

Lily nodded with a faint smile. "I wanted to be the one. We dressed her up, laid her out and I went at her with a knife. We thought it'd look like some frenzied madman had done it."

"You certainly made it look like that." Rowan held her phone to her ear. "Did you get all that?"

"I did. Don't hurt her anymore, Rowan," Franklin replied.

Rowan turned to face Franklin. Silently he had drawn closer. "Stay where you are," she called to him. "I need to do this myself."

"If you're gonna kill me, just do it," said Lily. Her voice had an almost drunken slur to it.

"It all would've been fine for you if Doug hadn't shown remorse," Rowan told her.

Lily laughed icily. "It wasn't remorse, it was fear. The night of the murder he was as excited as me. He came to my place later that night and I've never known him so horny, but it was the morning after that he started getting scared. He was worried about DNA and giving his statement, that we were too close to the victim, all that shit. He forgot it was supposed to be fun and just let the worry take over completely. It was all he ever talked about. He wanted to throw the police off the scent because he was sure they were closing in on us. They weren't, they weren't even close, but he was that paranoid."

"That's why he wrote to me and to the police," said Rowan. "You didn't know? He used to send me notes saying my dad did it, and to the police too. He used that old typewriter in the basement of your shop. I guess the fear consumed him in the end and that's why he killed himself."

"He was a coward," Lily said, almost in a whisper. "Not like Martin."

Rowan reached down and yanked the dagger sharply from Lily's hand but the woman seemed to barely flinch. The snow had iced her hand from pain.

"Are you going to do it?"

Rowan held her phone to her ear. "If I kill her, will you stand by me?" she asked Franklin.

"I will," he said. He now stood less than ten metres from her but still spoke into his phone. "But you won't be the same person afterwards. She'll be dead, but you'll have to live with the consequences."

"How would we get away with it?"

Franklin cleared his throat. "We'd cover her body in snow. You and I would walk back to Bedminster and I'd get one of the vans from home. We'd pick her up and take her back to the funeral home. Douglas' funeral is in three days' time and the pallbearers are all day labourers so they'd have no idea how heavy he's meant to be. We could hide her body in the casket and the pair of them would be incinerated together. Nobody would ever know. She'd just be another missing person."

"You've clearly thought this through."

"I don't want you to go to prison."

"She deserves to die."

"Perhaps," Franklin inched towards her while using his most placid tone. "Maybe Maybridge does too, and Larry and Lois Roker and Barnabus Hawthorne, but we let those people live, even if they didn't deserve it. Because we're better than them. They're terrible, inhuman people but we're not. You will never recover from having taken a human life and you'll never be the same, but whatever happens, I'll be there."

Rowan looked at the pathetic, bloodied woman chained to the railings of the Clifton Suspension Bridge and melting gradually into unconsciousness. It would be so easy and nobody would ever know. She felt Franklin's hand rest on her shoulder and the shock of the touch jolted through her as if waking from a dream. The dagger fell from her hand and pierced the ground beside Lily, she found herself drooping into Franklin's arms and felt him catch her.

"It's ok, I've got you," he whispered into her ear. "It's all over now."

47.

Franklin and Rowan hid in the shadow of the East Tower until the ambulance arrived and watched as Lily was wearily stretchered into the back. It had been Franklin who made the call, while Rowan reluctantly unlocked the handcuff which had held the woman as her captor.

"She'll be alright," Franklin said to Rowan as the pair made their way from the bridge to Clifton Village.

"Please tell me there'll be a time when I'm glad to know that."

"There will. Probably not soon, but you did the right thing."

"Am I going to get into trouble?"

Franklin shook his head. "Even assault charges get leeway in exceptional circumstances and capturing your sister's killer will certainly qualify. But if you need me to testify that she tried to attack you first, I can."

Rowan shrugged. "I can't see Lily filing an assault charge. I think she knows she got away lightly."

Rowan had left Lily with an icy whisper of "Be thankful of my mercy" hissed into her ear but before she departed she had scrawled "*I MURDERED RUBY KAPLAN*" in foot-long letters in the snow in front of Lily's huddled body.

"There will be a trial though," said Franklin. "You might have to defer university until the autumn."

"I know." Rowan took Franklin's arm and held onto him. "But I'm still leaving."

"I thought you might. What are you going to do?"

"I don't know. I haven't seen much of the world, I've got some money saved up, maybe I could travel around for a bit, experience life for a change."

"That's a nice idea," Franklin smiled. "I'm gonna have to look for a replacement soon. How am I going to find someone to match you?"

"You won't," Rowan laughed. "But I think I know someone who might have some potential. How would you feel about a tearaway teen with zero future prospects?"

"Meredy's kid? Are you serious?"

"Trust me, Gallow & Sons does all sorts of things to your mind. Nothing will set that boy on the straight and narrow more than a dose of mortality. Plus, Meredy will be there if he gets out of hand."

Franklin thought for a moment. "I've never gone wrong when I've trusted your instincts before," he declared. "I'll ask him."

The snow had stopped falling but Park Street was still carpeted in it. A few of the more intrepid of the night's merrymakers had begun snowball fights or were rolling huge balls of it down the steep hill. They looked to Rowan like children.

"D' you think the police will come for us tomorrow?" Rowan asked.

"I hope not. I think you deserve a Christmas with your family. When will you tell them about Lily?"

"Tomorrow, I guess. I don't want to keep it from them."

"I'll call Edison later. I'll tell him everything and send him the recording I made. Hopefully he'll be able to hold them off until at least Boxing Day."

"What about Douglas Bennett?"

Franklin thought of the young man - a murderer, still locked away in the freezer unit at Gallow & Sons. "I know a few undertakers who'll take on his service. I don't want to be the one to memorialise that little bastard."

"Thank you."

"Crap!" Franklin suddenly stopped in the snow. "I forgot to tell Kay. She's still going to be waiting at Wandering Lily's. I'll give her a call - and sort out a cab to take her home."

"That's going to be expensive tonight."

"I just want all the loose ends tied up."

While Franklin spoke to Kay, Rowan found herself gazing across the road to the shuttered shopfront of Ghurt Lush. She took her own phone from her pocket and sent a message to Gavin. *"Hi. Was wondering if you still wanted to go for a drink. Maybe in the new year? Merry Christmas."*

Gavin wasted no time in replying. *"It's a deal. Merry Christmas. X"*

"Everything alright?" Rowan asked Franklin once he'd finished his calls.

"Sorted," he declared.

"I think I have a date," Rowan smiled.

"That was quick. That prison chap?"

"Do *not* call him that. But yes."

"Good for you. I think I'm going to give Verity another shot. It wasn't right how things ended."

Once they reached the edge of College Green the mighty, ancient bells of Bristol Cathedral began peeling for Midnight Mass.

"Rowan!" Franklin exclaimed. "It's Christmas Day!"

Rowan threw her arms around Franklin, and in their embrace, she began to sob. To his surprise, Franklin did too.

"I'm sorry we can't bring her back," he whispered to her.

"I know."

"It's not much, but no one can take those memories from you. She'll be with you forever, even if it's just in your heart."

"Thank you." Rowan wiped her eyes with her sleeve and broke off the hug. "There's plenty of time for crying in the future. Tonight, I feel like just forgetting about it all."

"It's been a long day, maybe we both need some rest."

"I'm not sure if I do," said Rowan. "Not yet anyway."

"I really fancy a pint," said Franklin.

"I feel like dancing. Is that weird?"

Franklin shook his head. "Not a bit. I'll dance with you."

"You dance?" Rowan laughed. "How've I never heard this?"

"I used to be quite a mover back in my day. We're close to the Shilling, they should be open for another couple of hours. I haven't been there for years."

"Franklin! The Queenshilling? I'm game if you are."

Franklin offered his friend his hand and the pair made their way down the snow covered steps to the nightclub. High above them the milky, dark clouds parted just enough to reveal a single, twinkling star. Forever out of reach, but never truly gone.

Printed in Great Britain
by Amazon